Thee, Lord, is a God of justice. I know this, but my eyes see the weak suffering at the hands of the mighty. I see scars on backs and in hearts, families shattered, hope overthrown by hopelessness. Lord, how long? Will Thee ever free the slaves, Thy children? Set the captives free, please, heavenly Father, and help me to serve Thee faithfully.

Prudence Willard
Marietta, Ohio
January 20, 1863

SECRETS OF WAYFARERS INN

At Face Value

OCIEANNA FLEISS

Guideposts

New York

CHAPTER ONE

Marietta, Ohio
January 20, 1863

Pastel rays filtered through gaps in the meager barn's aging slats like the new year breaking through ruins of the old. Prudence Willard, solitary in her morning chores, tossed feed to her goose, Patience. "Be glad thee is suited for the cold, miss!" Even beneath her knitted gloves, Prudence's hands were nearly numb. "'Tis my duty to rise with the sun and feed thee, God's creature, and I do not mind the task." She threw down another handful of corn. "I mind it less when freezing cold does not beset my feet when they touch the floor."

The white-feathered goose tilted her head questioningly, and guilt dusted Prudence's conscience. "Forgive me," she said with a simple bow. Patience recommenced eating, so Prudence believed she was forgiven.

Softly humming her favorite hymn as she worked, her mind wandered. What would this New Year hold?

Opportunities to help free more lost souls from the shackles of slavery? She hoped so, but her deepest desire echoed that of every abolitionist—an end to the despicable practice altogether. How hard she prayed, how forcefully abolitionists pressed President Lincoln and the Congress. Those efforts, as well as the profound influence of *Uncle Tom's Cabin,* did thankfully contribute to the commencement of this war to free the slaves. When the war began, she thought slavery's end would be forthcoming. It had been almost two years since the battle at Fort Sumter thrust brother against brother. Yet still the weak suffered. Still injustice reigned.

A bald eagle's call floated to her, jarring her from her thoughts. *Come now, enough of this pondering.* The goose nipped at her, seeming to be more eager for breakfast than normal. "Have patience, Patience." She shook out the last bit of corn.

Her goose's antics made her smile, and Prudence peered out the open door at the snow-blanketed fields, glowing a peachy gold as they reflected the Creator's magnificent sunrise. She let her gaze follow the gentle descent to the river—frozen solid. Maybe she and Jason would take Moses to play on the ice later. Laughter would do them good.

Charity, her horse, whinnied loudly.

"My!" Prudence responded. "Thee is pushy this morn—"

But something stopped her words, and she spotted what was spooking her animals. She gasped.

A woman lay motionless in the hay of Charity's stall. Scenarios hastened to Prudence's mind. Had this stranger heard this was an Underground Railroad stop? Or was she simply seeking shelter from the cold?

Prudence knelt next to her. The woman appeared frozen… gone. Was she?

Curled up in a ball in the corner, her head rested against the wall, and her knees faced inward. Her hair had frosted over, her eyebrows, too, making them white, like an old woman's.

Prudence laid a gentle hand on the woman's shoulder, covered only with a thin coat. The freezing traveler didn't move, so Prudence traced her arm down to her youthful hand. She was no old woman.

And then another shock.

A wedding ring. Obviously forged from a rough metal, likely pounded into shape with a hammer.

Someone loved this precious one. Prudence pictured her and her sweetheart jumping the broom in the back of their master's barn, rejoicing in love even in the midst of hate. Prudence twisted her head to glance outside. "Where is thy husband?"

Not seeing anyone, she focused back on the woman, who still hadn't moved.

Then she spied the stranger's middle. She gasped again. "Do not let this dear sister and her baby be gone," she pleaded.

As if in answer to her prayer, the woman moaned, then slightly opened fearful eyes.

"Child, thee is going to be all right. Thee and thy little one."

The woman managed to nod, and her ebony-eyed gaze searched Prudence's. A silent moment lingered, and Prudence's own past pregnancy invaded her thoughts—the first one. Her sweet Hope, whom she held for but moments before the breath of life slowly stopped, and the Shepherd took the little one in His arms. That couldn't happen to this dear soul. In a rush, she stood.

"Stay here. I'll be right back. The Lord is with thee."

But as Prudence raced to the house to fetch Jason for help, the unwelcome doubts snagged her. She banished them. Who was she to question God's ways?

Could this afternoon be any more glorious? Tess Wallace basked in the crisp winter air as her ice skate blades scraped across the frozen river. "Listen up, legs." She peeked at them, covered in faux fur–lined leggings. "You remember how to do this, right?" She inhaled, relishing the faint smokiness coming from her neighbors' fireplaces. "I need this distraction today," she whispered. "Here we go!" With a nervous chuckle, she pushed forward. There was no stopping now. Then she quickly twisted around, landed, and continued skating. "Backward skate! I knew I could still do it." Her feet transported her in reverse across the ice, one skate after the other. Feeling the smile shining on her face, she peered up at the sparkling blue sky.

To her surprise, cheers sounded from the dock. LuAnn Sherrill and Janice Eastman, who were not only her dearest friends but also business partners, carefully paced toward the edge of the dock, their ice skates draped over their shoulders. Above, up the incline from the riverbank, their inn seemed to smile down on them.

"There you are!" Tess hailed as she glided nearer, still skating backward. "I didn't know you were watching me." She swooshed to a stop, her blades spraying ice chips.

"You are amazing." Janice's eyes gleamed. "I'm impressed."

Tess shrugged. "I didn't know if I'd even be able to find my balance."

LuAnn pulled her hat down over her ears. "You're really making us do this?" A strand of silver hair fluttered into her eyes. She tucked it back into the hat, shaking her head in mock reproach.

"Aw, come on," Tess urged. "The Ohio River only freezes once in a blue moon—we have to try. Plus, your body will remember what to do. Muscle memory—that's what the experts call it. It's true. I read about it on the internet." She grinned mischievously. "It worked for me. Even backward."

"You really want me to do this?" With an exaggerated sigh, LuAnn plopped down on the edge of the dock, then yowled. "It's cold!"

Janice tightened her coat and perched next to LuAnn. "Whoo! That is cold."

"No time to fret over cold backsides," Tess said. "Hurry and get those skates laced up."

"Okay. I'll give it a try." LuAnn carefully hopped down onto the ice. "You coming, Janice?"

"I will . . . but I need to admit something first."

LuAnn pushed off to join Tess, and they studied Janice like moms waiting for a child's confession.

"Let's hear it," Tess said.

"I've never skated before!"

"What?" both Tess and LuAnn blurted.

"Don't judge!" Janice pleaded.

Tess shook her head. "How is that possible? Never mind, we'll help you." She gripped Janice's left arm while LuAnn clutched the other, then, with a little yelp, Janice hopped down from the dock.

Janice's broad smile warmed Tess's heart. She was grateful for a distraction today. Her friends refreshed her spirit.

"I always made an excuse to stay home when the kids went skating," Janice continued. "Cooked soup, made hot chocolate, cookies—for the skaters when they returned." She sighed. "But truth be told, I was just too flat-out scared to try and learn."

"Well, this is a brave new day for you, my friend," LuAnn exclaimed, "and this is one more fear we are here to help you conquer."

One step at a time, Tess and LuAnn taught their friend to glide over the ice.

"I should've known this was so much fun . . . and nothing to be afraid of. This time the treats will have to be provided by Winnie and her new kitchen help. Kylie's a welcome addition since Taylor's still gone and Constance moved to Canton."

Janice's blades etched steady lines in the ice. "She seems like a sweet girl."

Tess gently lifted Janice's arm from hers. "Do you want to try on your own?"

LuAnn tilted her head. "I bet you can."

In answer, Janice sailed across the ice as if she'd been skating for years. "I'm doing it!"

"I would say so!" Tess sped up to reach her.

LuAnn, still a little wobbly, grabbed Tess's arm. "I'm not so sure."

A frown shaded Janice's face. "You're not sure about what?"

"I mean about the new kitchen help."

"Oh."

"That girl...I don't mean to be unkind," LuAnn said. "But..."

Tess chuckled. "You are so nice, Lu. I know where you're going with this. She's not the, uh, sharpest tool in the shed, is she?"

"Well." LuAnn eased closer to Tess and Janice, and they fell in sync with each other as they made their way along the river. "Let's just say this morning I caught her putting sugar in the salt shakers."

"Oh no!" Tess came to a stop, chuckling.

Janice bumped into her. Almost losing her balance, she grabbed Tess's coat. "Sorry!" She nearly rolled over Tess's back, then managed to straighten. "I don't know how to stop yet."

They recovered, then skated forward.

After skating a few yards, Janice lowered her head and peered over her glasses at the two others. "Kylie will get there. She just needs some more time."

"Of course." Tess skated ahead, then returned. "I was imagining our guests salting their soup with sugar."

"Yeah, me too." LuAnn chuckled softly.

Janice spread her arms wide. "Skating is so fun. I never knew!"

"It really is." LuAnn slid the opposite direction. "We should advertise skating as one of the inn's excursions this year."

Tess leapt at the idea. "Yes! I'm sure we could rent skates from somewhere in town."

"And offer thermoses of hot chocolate!" Janice added.

"Let's do it!" Tess slid away from the others. "I do love skating." The thought triggered a pang, but she dismissed it and sped ahead. "Watch this!" She increased her speed. "Jeffrey taught me."

As Jeffrey's name slipped past her lips, memories flooded her thoughts, flashes of skating adventures with him. She couldn't halt them.

On their first date, forty years ago, he'd taught her how to skate. She'd fallen so many times, he held her hands like the Olympic couple skaters, just to steady her. Well, not only for that reason. Even from that first date, she'd felt comfortable with him, relished his touch. She basked in the comfort she'd felt with his arms around her, guiding her, like he always did.

Then another memory came. A year to the day after that first date, he took her skating again. As he skated to her, he faltered, lost his balance, and fell. She couldn't believe he'd fallen. But she soon realized it had been no accident. With those blue eyes drenched in love, he took a knee and produced a box. As he opened it, Tess gasped at the diamond's sparkles. "Yes." Of course she'd said yes.

These memories lasted for mere moments as Tess continued to skate.

"You're going too fast!" LuAnn called.

Tess had been setting up to show off a mini-jump, but the distraction of her memories threw her off. Her legs continued reaching for the jump, but her mind wasn't in it, and with an awkward, twisted tumble, she crashed down onto the ice.

"Tess!" Janice blurted as she and LuAnn skated to her and knelt down.

"Oh, girl." LuAnn held her hand. "Where does it hurt?"

Tess rubbed her hip. Already she knew a bruise would soon appear. What was she thinking, trying a jump? "I'm sorry." She ventured a chuckle. "I guess I'm not as agile as I used to be. I'm fine, though. Don't worry."

LuAnn and Janice stared at her. They weren't buying the cool front Tess was selling.

She exhaled and observed her visible breath until it disappeared, then shifted her gaze to the two still gaping at her. As embarrassed as she was, her friends' concern meant the world to her. Who else would she rather fall on her backside in the middle of a frozen river with? No one. Finally, she stretched her legs out in front of her.

"I was thinking about Jeffrey. It's the anniversary of our first date...and engagement. He asked me to marry him on the ice."

Janice's eyes crinkled with compassion. "I'm so sorry. Anniversaries can be hard. I knew yours was coming. I forgot."

Tess exchanged a glance with Janice. Janice's husband had also died, more recently than Tess's. Her friend really did understand how painful anniversaries could be. And it hadn't even been a year since LuAnn's mom's funeral. She'd experienced this type of pain too. Tess knew that she could rely on her friends to listen and offer support. It was because of them, she thought, that this year's anniversary seemed different—not as painful as years past. Maybe she was healing from Jeffrey's death. Maybe the inn had brought joy back into her life. Maybe she had a whole lot to be thankful for after all.

"It's okay, really. Anniversaries are hard, but wonderful too. I treasure my memories with Jeffrey. I loved being married to him." And maybe, someday, she'd be ready to move on. Could she? She wasn't too sure, but right now, she had other things on her mind. She pulled herself to a standing position.

"Your ankle is okay?" LuAnn asked. "You didn't reinjure where it was sprained, did you?"

"No, it's fine." Tess skated a few yards, none the worse for her fall. "All right, ladies." She returned to them. "We should get back to the inn. We can't leave Winnie without us for too long, even though she's got Kylie with her."

"Thorn's there too. I saw him come in this morning. He's working on fixing Winnie's radio. She loves that old relic."

"Yeah, ever since Marcus dug it out of storage for her, she's been singing those World War II songs her mother sang."

Winnie had become one of Tess's favorite people since coming to the inn. Not only had her cooking given the soup café the best reputation in town, she also served the clients with gracious hospitality and demanded the highest standards of herself and her cooking. Tess wondered how Kylie was handling Winnie's expectations. Standards were good for the young woman, and helping a young person learn responsibility could only be positive—at least she hoped so.

The three women exited the ice, changed out of their skates, and trekked toward the inn. Not wanting to tramp their snowy boots over the inn's hardwood floors, they clomped through deep snow toward the back entrance. After sloughing off her winter wear, Tess thought she heard a car out front. With a peek, she spotted a car pulling into the parking lot.

"That must be our new guest." LuAnn moved next to her. "I thought she was going to arrive earlier."

"Our new guest?" Janice joined them. "I'm glad she made it before dark. I'll double-check her room. You two want to check her in?"

Nodding in unison, Tess and LuAnn made their way across the parlor to the reception area. Janice hiked up the stairs, then, as the doorbell jingled, Tess and LuAnn took their places behind the desk.

A woman with chin-length, straight brown hair walked in, pulling a suitcase behind her. "Hello." Her tone was business-like but pleasant. Taking her satchel from her shoulder, she lifted her chin and reached out her hand. "Allow me to introduce myself. I'm Bonnie Bradshaw. I have a reservation."

"Welcome to Wayfarers Inn," Tess said as she shook Bonnie's hand. She couldn't remember the last time a guest greeted her so formally.

LuAnn checked the reservation book she had already opened, then pointed. "Yes. I have you right here."

Ms. Bradshaw smiled. "I'm glad to have made it." She offered her driver's license to LuAnn.

"We're glad you made it too." LuAnn wrote down the information from the license.

"It was a long, snowy drive from New York." She smiled again when LuAnn gave the card back. "I'm here to do a radio story about judges from the Civil War."

LuAnn's eyes sparkled like they always did when someone mentioned history. "What about them?"

"Civil War judges?" Tess asked. "How is that connected with Marietta?"

Bonnie leaned forward. "I'm actually pretty excited about this story. My great-great-great-great-grandfather was a judge in Pennsylvania—where our family still lives. It was a Free State, you know. But because of the Fugitive Slave Act—do you know what that is?"

LuAnn nodded. "It was an Act, upheld by the Supreme Court, that gave bounty hunters the right to enter Free States and recapture slaves to bring them back to their owners in the South."

"More like kidnap," Bonnie said. "But that's right." Her eyes shone approval of LuAnn's explanation.

"Show-off," Tess murmured with a grin.

"Anyway, Grampa Graves resided over the district court that either gave permission or denial to the bounty hunters. They had to have the correct documents, etc. I'm going to be researching that process as I work on the story."

"How interesting to have someone like that in your family history," Tess said.

"Yes. We've always been proud of our abolitionist history— apparently Grandma Graves was also an activist." She replaced the satchel over her shoulder. "Is my room...?" She pointed toward the stairs.

"Of course." LuAnn chuckled. "I was so captivated by your story. I'll show you."

In a moment, Thorn arrived, and Janice appeared at the same time, giving a thumbs-up about the room's readiness.

As Bonnie started to follow LuAnn toward the stairs, Tess realized their guest hadn't answered their question. "Uh, excuse me, Ms. Bradshaw."

"Call me Bonnie."

"Oh, thanks. What connection did your grandfather have with Marietta?"

"Right." She paused. "He stayed at this inn when it was called the, uh..."

"Riverfront House." Tess finished her sentence, her mind spinning. An abolitionist judge from the Civil War era stayed here? Did he know about the Underground Railroad stop? If he did, did he help with some of the "parcels"?

"Yes. And, well, he died on his return trip home, not far from here. They say it was from a heart attack, but there are rumors of foul play."

Tess met eyes with LuAnn and Janice. Many mysterious incidents had happened surrounding the inn since they'd bought the place, but nothing like this.

"Foul play?" Janice must have been thinking the same as Tess.

"I'm hoping to find some answers about that as well," Bonnie continued before following LuAnn toward the stairs.

"Let us know if there's anything we can do to help," Tess called after her.

LuAnn and Bonnie disappeared up the stairs.

"Something new to learn about the inn's history." Janice tucked her hair behind her ear.

"And so mysterious," Tess added.

"We should introduce her to Maybelline," Janice said. "I wonder if she knows anything about this judge."

Before Tess could respond, a bloodcurdling scream sounded from outside.

CHAPTER TWO

W hat's going on out there?" Tess scrambled from behind the desk, Janice right behind her. Tess got to the back door and flung it open. Outside, the new kitchen help, Kylie, giggled as a teenage boy leapt from behind her black Ford Focus to throw snowballs at her. She tried to dodge it, but his snowball hit her on her head, and she screamed—the same sound Tess had heard a moment before.

Tess and Janice shook their heads.

"The squeals of young love." Tess chuckled.

Janice's breathing slowed. "They're kind of cute. Don't you think?"

Kylie tromped to the boy, who flipped his shaggy bangs. She attempted to smash a snowball in his face, but he playfully grabbed her arm, and she missed.

"See." He wrapped his arms around her middle from behind. "Admit defeat. You'll never get me!"

Before Kylie could reach for another snowball, Winnie stepped outside. In seconds her voice cracked through the air. "Kylie, I told you not to be playing with Mason when you're supposed to be working. Tell him to get on, and you get to work."

Kylie lifted an innocent smile toward Winnie. "Really?" her voice sang. "I'm sorry. I didn't know it was against the rules."

Her lips formed a pretty pout, then she kissed her boyfriend on the cheek and moved to Winnie. No hint of amusement at her new helper's antics appeared in Winnie's deep brown eyes. "Get inside. I'll be right there."

Tess grinned at Janice. "Were we ever like that?"

"Of course," Janice said. "Ah, the freedom of youth!"

"Aw, you sound like that youth is long past. We'll always stay young!" Tess tossed a snowball at Janice, hitting her in the arm.

"You!" Janice grabbed a handful of snow and tossed it at Tess, who intercepted it with her hand, avoiding a direct hit.

"Okay you two," Winnie intervened. "You don't have to go to such extreme measures to prove your youthfulness, do you?"

"You're right," Tess said. "That's why we went skating this afternoon."

Brushing snow from her sleeve, Tess noticed a cell phone with a pink case lying in the snow. She picked it up, thinking it must be Kylie's. She slipped the phone in her pocket, then joined the others returning to the inn.

As Tess approached the back door, she spotted their dog in the open doorway. Somebody must have forgotten to latch the door. "Huck?" She pointed to the scruffy figure trotting back and forth as the ladies stepped closer. "What are you doing?"

Janice cast a glance at Tess. "He's growing on you. Admit it. Huh?"

"Maybe a little."

"I'll go get our sweet boy." Janice rushed ahead.

"He's got something in his mouth." Tess followed Janice. "Do you see that?"

"He didn't catch a . . ." Janice swallowed. "A varmint, did he?"

"It's not a varmint." Winnie chuckled. "It's too round, and look at the way it catches the sunlight."

Janice got to the back porch first, scooping up Huck, who whimpered in protest. The item fell from his mouth.

Tess picked it up. "It's a purse. It's old. Looks antique."

"Where'd that come from, Huck?" Janice asked.

"Wonder if it's one of the guest's," Tess said as Winnie and Janice passed through the doorway.

Tess latched the door shut behind them.

Frank Sinatra's crooning vocals floated from the kitchen, then Thorn's voice joined in. As he moved out of the kitchen, he spotted the ladies and smiled while finishing the line, "'You could be swingin' on a star.'"

"Nice singing!" Tess teased.

"Hey, ladies," Thorn answered, unfazed at being caught singing. "Fixed Winnie's radio. I love old radios. Took the part I needed from one I found in a thrift store last summer. And then I found this station that plays oldies but goodies."

Winnie beamed. "Thank you!" she said. "Thorn, you're a marvel."

"Sure. Let me know if you need anything else, okay? I'm going to go work on oiling the gears in the elevator."

"Okay."

"I'm fascinated by that purse!" Janice said.

"Let's take a look, see if we can figure out who it belongs to." Tess carried it toward the kitchen table, but before they could sit down, Janice's phone rang.

She eyed the screen. "I have to take this, it's Stacy. I'll be just a minute."

"That's okay," Tess said. "We should wait for LuAnn anyway." She moved away and joined Winnie and Kylie at the stove, where Winnie stirred her great-grandmother's hot chocolate recipe.

Tess placed the purse on a shelf in the mudroom, then fingered Kylie's cell phone in her pocket. She paced past Winnie and over to Kylie, who had moved to the counter.

"Kylie."

At her name, Kylie turned toward Tess. "I'm such a dork. I can't even..." Her face filled with a pleading smile, and she nodded toward the mangled parsley she was chopping. "I'm trying, but it keeps snagging on the knife." A tinge of guilt needled Tess at her earlier impatience toward the girl's slow learning curve.

Tess set the cell phone down. She washed her hands, put on a pair of kitchen gloves from the holder on the wall, took the knife from Kylie, and put it in the sink. Then she took the smooth chef's knife from the butcher block holder. "I'm not the home-ec teacher"—she tipped her head toward Janice, then rocked the knife over the tiny leaves, forming perfectly sized bits—"but I can handle chopping parsley."

"Thank you so much." Kylie wiped her hands on the green Wayfarers apron she wore. "Next time I'll use that knife. Duh." She seemed to relax.

"It's okay, hon. We all had to learn this at one time." Tess pushed the cut parsley into a container and grabbed another bunch. "By the way, I found your cell phone in the snow outside. It must have fallen out of your pocket when you and your boyfriend—"

"Mason? He's great." She placed a hand over her heart and sighed brightly.

"He seems like a nice young man."

"Yeah, he found me when I was going through stuff." She grabbed a dish towel and wiped the sink. "I've had rough times, but things are better now—thanks to him mostly." She folded the towel and placed it over the edge of the sink, then touched Tess's arm. "And this awesome job. I can't believe I get to work here. So nice of you guys to hire from the agency—even though I had no experience. It's so amazing!" She glanced toward Janice and LuAnn, who had planted themselves at the kitchen table to drink their cocoa and wait for Tess to examine the purse.

"It was really Winnie's idea, but we're glad to have you and happy to teach you."

After pushing the rest of the parsley into the container and sealing it, Tess fetched Kylie's cell phone from the counter and handed it to her. Kylie swiped open the lock screen, and a chess app popped up. She quickly closed it.

Chess? Kylie didn't seem like the kind to play chess. Tess pointed to Kylie's phone. "Was that an online chess game? I used to love playing chess with my dad."

Kylie shifted her feet. "Most of the games are Mason's, even the chess app. He's always losing his phone, so he downloads weird stuff on mine—mostly games." She put the phone in her pocket. "I never thought I'd date a gamer, but I am."

Tess's son, Jeff Jr., had gotten into gaming when he was a teen, but she'd never been tempted by the time waster—she had her own guilty pleasures. And she did like chess.

"You should try chess. It's actually really fun."

Kylie crinkled her nose. "Seems kinda hard, but maybe I'll ask Mason to teach me." She smiled. "Well, I have a lot more chopping to do. Carrots next. Thank you for helping me. It'll be easier now."

Tess returned the smile. "You're very welcome."

Janice stepped next to Tess and got herself a glass of water from the sink. "Stacy had asked if I could watch Larry today, but she's got it covered, so...let's look at that purse."

"Where is it?" LuAnn called.

Tess wiped her hands on a kitchen towel. She grabbed the purse from the shelf in the mudroom where she had set it, carried it to the table, and pulled up a chair.

She admired the faded green and white material. In the middle was an eight-pointed star, like the ones her grandmother used to sew onto quilts, but more delicate. Tiny pearls and gems were woven into the pattern along the points of the star.

"All those gems. It looks valuable," Janice commented.

"Let's take a look inside." Tess fingered the metal latch. "Maybe there's something in it with the owner's name." She gingerly opened the delicate fabric. "There is something in here."

Janice reached for the purse but hesitated. "What is it?"

Tess pulled a yellowed, folded fragile slip of paper from the purse. She set the purse down and very carefully unfolded the piece of paper.

LuAnn leaned closer. "Is that a recipe? And does that say, 'Five toadstools in this will kill him?'"

CHAPTER THREE

Tess held the paper close to her face, examining it. The page was thin, and very yellowed, with bold strokes of black. A few ink spots reminded her of the spots in Prudence's journal, but the handwriting was different—much bolder and more sweeping.

"Tess?" Janice tilted her head. "I would kind of like to know what it says."

"Sorry." Tess held the paper out for Janice and LuAnn to inspect. "Other than the 'kill' part, I can't see it very well. I don't have my reading glasses."

"I can't tell what it says either," Janice said. "I'll be right back." She disappeared and returned with two pairs of reading glasses—she was already wearing her own.

Tess put on her glasses, grateful for the clarity. At the top of the paper were the words *Riverfront House.*

"Wow, the Riverfront's stationery." LuAnn ran a finger over it. "Look at the drawing of the old hotel."

"And the fancy font."

Below the letterhead was a recipe for "Captain Pork and Navy Bean Soup." Then, there it was. "Five toadstools in this will kill him."

The friends eyed each other. Tess's mind flooded with possible scenarios to explain the recipe. Strange things seemed to surround Wayfarers Inn and its history—when it was called the Riverfront House—but a poison recipe was something new. Life at the inn sure helped Tess and her friends keep their vow to never be boring or bored.

LuAnn put the obvious question into words. "Why would a recipe to kill someone be written on the inn's letterhead?"

"It's hard to fathom," Janice said.

Tess looked at the purse. "We need to find out who this belongs to. I would assume chances are good it belongs to Bonnie, since she's delving into the history of the inn. Maybe she'll have some answers."

"That makes sense," LuAnn said.

Janice held up her hand. "But we need to follow our policy for a lost item. We need to let the person who lost it come to us and ask about it first. Whoever lost this will certainly ask about it. Then we won't need to worry that we gave it to the wrong person."

As they spoke, Winnie appeared from the lobby, holding a basketful of towels. Tess smiled at their friend. If anyone would get excited about a Civil War recipe, it was Winnie.

"Look at this." She called Winnie over to the table.

"What is it? A purse?"

Janice nodded. "It is. It's beautiful, but look what we found inside."

LuAnn handed the recipe to Winnie.

"Oh my!"

"The part about the toadstools. Isn't that strange?" Tess asked.

Winnie shook her head. "What? I'm talking about this recipe. My grandmother had a book written by Captain Sanderson. It was a cooking manual for soldiers in the Civil War." She chuckled. "Men back then left the cooking to the women, so when they went off to war, they knew nothing about making a meal—even pork and beans. I'd love to make this for the café."

"That's a great idea!" Janice clasped her hands together.

LuAnn stood. "Should we plan on serving it Monday for lunch?"

A clatter sounded, causing Tess to glance toward Kylie, who had paused cubing potatoes to drop her knife on the cutting board. "Oh, that's a wonderful idea! Please, Winnie, let's have that soup Monday."

Winnie handed the recipe to Tess, who carefully replaced it in the purse. "I think I have most of the ingredients already, just need the pork. I'll send an order to the store this afternoon."

Winnie's grandson Marcus had started delivering groceries to the inn the month before. Their common love for food and cooking made them a great team for the inn.

Tess held up the purse. "Then we have a plan? Two-pronged. First, concerning the purse, we'll put it in the safe and see if anyone approaches us about it. Second, I'll make a copy of the recipe for you, Winnie, and we'll have that soup for lunch on Monday."

"Sounds good," Winnie said. "I'll work on that order." She turned to her helper. "Kylie."

The girl turned at her name.

"I'd like you to put those potatoes in water and then start chopping onions. We need them for the breakfast casserole for the guests in the morning."

"Okay," Kylie said. She moved to follow Winnie's instructions.

Winnie slipped out of the kitchen. Tess and Janice started to stand up from the table, but LuAnn stopped them as she sat back down.

"I wonder if we could add another prong to the plan," she ventured. "I got a call this morning I'd like to talk to you about." Before she could continue, the back door creaked open. They heard rustling in the mudroom, and then Brad entered the kitchen.

His face brightened as his gaze landed on LuAnn, who blushed to see him, just a tinge.

"Hi, ladies." He rubbed his hands together. "Is that Winnie's hot cocoa on the stove?"

"Help yourself," Tess said. "Do you need to ask?"

After offering the ladies refills, he poured himself a mug, then joined them at the table. "What's that?" he asked, pointing to the purse. "It's beautiful."

"It is." LuAnn handed it to him. "I'll tell you about it later. You'll love it."

"Another urban artifact?" He grinned.

"Maybe," Janice said.

"I can't wait to hear." He shifted his gaze back to LuAnn. "Did you tell them?"

"I was just about to."

"He's in on whatever it is?" Janice leaned forward. "Now I'm curious."

"Me too." Tess cupped her hands around her mug.

"I got a text from a social worker I used to work with. She was wondering if we would be interested in helping get sponsors and publicity for a fund-raiser for foster kids. It's a skate-a-thon down at the river."

"Interesting," Tess said.

"And, well, they weren't planning on serving anything. I thought they might want to serve hot food to the skaters."

"You did?" Tess eyed her friend.

LuAnn nodded. "And they agreed. They were hoping we could help with that and publicity. Getting sponsors."

"When would it be?" Tess asked.

LuAnn looked at Brad, who answered, "Next Sunday. A week from tomorrow."

"Oh my."

"I know it's quick, but it really won't be that hard. We can serve soup—"

"Our specialty," Janice put in.

Ideas surged through Tess. "And Winnie's hot chocolate. We can ask the local businesses for sponsorships..." She eyed Brad. "Would you?"

He grinned and nodded.

"He's the one who called earlier," LuAnn added. "He's already a sponsor."

"LuAnn mentioned it and asked, so—"

"You already said yes, didn't you, LuAnn?" Tess interrupted.

LuAnn shook her head. "No. I said—well, yeah." Her lips curved into a grin. "But I did say I had to confirm it with you two."

"Anyway," Brad continued, "I wanted to let Lu know my business has been supporting Grace Youth Services for years. I'm already on board."

"Isn't that awesome?" LuAnn asked.

Tess nodded. "It really is."

"So you guys are in?" LuAnn's eyes sparkled knowingly.

"Of course we are." Janice propped her chin on her hands. "Now for the planning."

By ten thirty Monday morning, the magnificent aroma of pork, beans, and spices filled the inn. Tess could barely wait to taste the soup as she cleaned Maple and Mum after the guests checked out. The young couple who had spent the last four days there were new parents. Tess could tell by the state of the room that they'd been overwhelmed by the pressures of parenthood. Being a new parent was hard—she remembered her learning curve when Jeff Jr. was born. And some babies were more difficult than others.

Finishing up, Tess followed her nose to the kitchen, where Winnie tended the soup pot sitting on Big Red, the vintage stove that had been fully restored to her original glory and painted to match her name. "That smells good!"

Winnie looked up. "It's good soup. It really is." Her eyes danced. "Oh, and you got a message from that new farmer, Clint. He wants to come by to talk to you."

"Really? Why?"

"Didn't say."

"Howdy." A man's voice interrupted. "The woman at the front desk said you'd be back here."

A tall, well-built man with salt-and-pepper hair and worn cowboy boots stood before her. Tess removed the pen from her ear and gripped it in her hand.

He reached out his hand. "I'm Clint Lowery. I thought I would come by and introduce myself."

Tess heard a new owner had moved onto the farm at the edge of town. Why he wanted to talk to her, she had no idea. "I'm Tess Wallace." She shook his hand. "It's nice to meet you."

His gaze lingered on her a bit longer than seemed natural. Was that sadness hiding behind his eyes?

The moment passed, and Clint looked around. "Whatever's cooking smells amazing."

Tess chuckled. "Yes, we're very excited about it. It's a Civil War soup recipe."

"Fitting."

"You know about the Civil War history around Marietta?"

"Yes. It's one of the reasons I fell in love with the town. That, and the beautiful farm the Lord provided. I call it Butterfly Farm. Love the picture of transformation butterflies bring. I couldn't imagine a more perfect spot to spend my 'tender years.'" He chuckled. "Not that I'm ready to completely retire. I'll still be growing a few crops on a boutique-type farm. But the reason I'm here—"

"I was wondering."

"I'm going to be offering sleigh rides in the winter and carriage rides in the summer. I'd love to work some kind of reciprocal marketing with Wayfarers."

Tess welcomed any opportunity to market the inn. "I like the idea, but we offer several excursions already. I'd like to discuss it with my partners first. Maybe check out your services."

"I understand. If it would help, I could give you a complimentary sleigh ride."

"That sounds fun. My partners would like that."

"Uh, yes, of course, for all of you."

Had he meant a ride with just the two of them? She pushed the thought away. She probably read him wrong.

"Let's make it happen, soon." He scanned the room again, his gaze landing on the soup pot. "What time do you serve lunch?"

"Usually not until eleven. It's ten forty-five. Can you wait a few minutes?"

"*I* can't!" Kylie burst into the kitchen. "It smells so good, and I deserve a bowl."

Clint seemed to appreciate the girl's enthusiasm. "You helped make it?"

"I did. I chopped the vegetables."

"I'll pay special attention to those, then." Clint smiled at her and made his way to the café.

Mason strolled in, his hands in his pockets. "Hey, guys," he said with a crooked grin. "Soup done?"

Kylie moved to him. "Almost." She pointed to the kitchen table. "I'll serve you a bowl when it's ready."

His expectant grin seemed to lift her spirits.

Winnie faced Tess. "She can't keep letting him help."

"I know. The last thing we want is a problem with the health department."

As Tess pondered when and how to talk to Kylie, Bonnie tapped on the wall next to the kitchen door. "Excuse me. I'm sorry to interrupt. There was no one at the front desk. I'm wondering if you have a lost and found."

"Yes, we do." Tess stepped toward her. "We have a policy not to describe any missing items..."

"Has someone found an antique purse?"

Tess nodded. "That's right. It's yours then?"

"It is. I'm so relieved you found it. I must've dropped it somewhere."

"Well, I'm afraid our dog found it. But don't worry. There was no damage—at least not that we could find."

Bonnie's brow furrowed briefly but then relaxed. "I'm sure it's fine. The purse belonged to my grandma Graves. Did you look inside?"

"Yes, we did, to see if there was any ID inside."

"So, you saw the recipe. That's why we think Grandpa Graves's death may not have been an accident—that recipe in Grandma's purse. We have other letters from her, so we know it's not her writing..." She looked at her phone. "I'd love to tell you more about this, but I was wondering. I know it's a tad early, but could I eat lunch now? I have an appointment, and I'd love to taste whatever it is you have cooking at the moment."

Tess checked the clock. Five till eleven. "Of course. We'd be happy to get you some, especially since it's the recipe from the purse."

"It is?" Bonnie beamed. "That's so cool."

"We were excited to try it. Of course, we'd love to honor you with the first taste." Tess led the way to the dining room, where the tables were beginning to fill with other customers.

"You can have some too," she said over her shoulder to Clint, sitting at a corner table, reading the paper. "I'll be right with you, and then we'll see to our other customers." He tipped his head in response.

Tess seated Bonnie at a table with a view of the frozen river.

"Would you like a bowl or a cup?" Tess asked.

"A cup would be perfect."

"Let me know if you'd like anything else."

"Maybe some bread, and—"

Before Bonnie finished, Winnie arrived with a cup of soup and a freshly baked baguette.

"What wonderful service." Bonnie smelled the baguette. "You read my mind. Thank you."

Winnie crossed the room and put a bowl on Clint's table. He thanked her, then dug a spoon in the soup and lifted it, blew on it, then set the spoon back down. Tess thought it must be too hot for him.

Returning her attention to Bonnie, Tess grabbed her phone from her pocket. "Do you mind if I take your picture? We're trying to figure out this social media marketing thing." She chuckled.

"Of course I don't mind." Bonnie held up a spoonful of soup, thick with chunks of pork and potatoes, and smiled.

As Tess clicked her phone camera, LuAnn and Janice came into the café, tying on their aprons and getting their order pads out of the pockets.

Tess herded them behind Bonnie for a few more pictures. Kylie and Winnie came out of the kitchen, and Tess recruited them for several photo ops also. As the "models" dispersed to take orders or return to the kitchen, Tess turned to Bonnie. "Thank you so much."

"No problem, feel free to use them on your pages. I'm happy to support local businesses—and you all have been wonderful." She swallowed another bite, then exhaled a satisfied sigh. "Besides, this is so good. I've had the recipe for years but never thought to make it. I'm not much of a cook."

Tess smiled at Bonnie. "I don't think we've ever found a recipe in such an interesting way before."

"I bet." She chuckled.

Tess pointed to the office. "We put the purse in the safe. Would you like us to keep it there until you come back from your appointment?" She noticed Clint stirring his soup, but he didn't take a bite.

"Yes, that's perfect. Thank you. When I get back later." Bonnie took a breath and continued. "I'll tell you more about the purse then, if you'd like."

"Oh yes!" Tess said.

"One thing I'll say, Grandpa Graves died in January—just a couple of days after visiting the inn on the twenty-third. It's one of the reasons I wanted to do the story this month."

"That's today," Tess observed. "Imagine. Over one hundred fifty years ago, on this very day, your ancestor could have been eating this same soup."

Bonnie broke a piece of the bread and dunked it in the almost finished soup. "I'm looking forward to doing my piece about the Civil War–era judges. Grandpa Graves has been the pride of our family for generations—means a lot to all of us." She paused, wiping her brow. "I may want to record some segments here at the inn, if that's okay with…"

In the middle of her sentence, the color in her face drained, leaving it a pale green. Then her face contorted.

Tess inched closer. "Are you all right?"

"I'm fine," she said, but then her hand flew to her mouth and she gripped the table. "I need to lie down."

CHAPTER FOUR

Tess helped Bonnie, who was gripping her stomach and crying in pain, to the sofa.

LuAnn grabbed Tess's arm. "I'll call 911."

With a nod toward LuAnn, Tess knelt down next to Bonnie. "The paramedics are on their way, okay?" She rubbed the woman's back, but Bonnie flinched at the touch.

The folks gathered in the kitchen must have heard the commotion, because they raced out.

Clint came to Tess's side. "I'm certified in CPR. Can I help?"

"Just be available in case she needs it." Tess inspected Bonnie's pale face coiled in intense agony. "Please." She prayed it wouldn't get to that.

"Okay." Clint straightened. "Then for now I'll wait for the ambulance and let the paramedics know where to go."

Tess gave him a grateful smile. "Thank you."

As he left, Janice rushed to fill his place, pillow and blanket in her arms.

Tears spilled down Bonnie's cheeks as Janice gently placed the pillow under her head and tucked the blanket around her.

The doorbell jingled, grabbing Tess's attention momentarily. A large party arrived. Immediately drawn to the scene, they stood around watching, muttering, and then tapping on their phones.

Tess thrust away thoughts about the impact of the incident on the inn's business. What mattered now was this poor, ill woman. Surely it wasn't food poisoning. Their groceries came fresh, delivered by Marcus, Winnie's grandson. Winnie was careful to follow every health department guideline and more. Maybe Bonnie had suffered an allergic reaction to something.

After what seemed like an eternity, an ambulance arrived. Paramedics rushed in, assessed Bonnie's condition, put her on oxygen, and lifted her onto a gurney.

Tess huddled next to the woman. "Get better, okay?"

Bonnie moaned, too sick to speak.

The Inn Crowd followed the paramedics to the parking lot where Kylie and Mason already waited. They watched them load Bonnie into the ambulance. Ambulance scenes brought unhappy memories to Tess—to anyone, she figured. She prayed for the Lord's comfort and healing, for wisdom for the doctors, for safety on the icy roads...

"I feel so bad for her," she said as the ambulance drove away. Although Tess told herself the cause of Bonnie's collapse wasn't food poisoning and definitely wasn't intentional, the fact that they'd discovered the ominous recipe in that old purse worried her. Maybe it was a coincidence. But Tess doubted it.

They paced back to the inn.

"Did that really happen?" Janice asked.

"I was just taking pictures," Tess said, "enjoying the scrumptious soup fragrance..."

As they entered the café, they found Clint setting the tables back in place that had been disturbed in the chaos. All the other customers were gathering their belongings and leaving. "Boy, that was a shock." He touched her arm. "I'll be praying it wasn't food poisoning."

"Thank you," Tess said. "I appreciate it."

"You're welcome. Let me know if I can do anything to help." His eyes showed kindness. "And let me know when you'd like to talk about the idea I mentioned."

"I will," Tess said.

After Clint left, Tess heard a commotion from the check-in desk, where the earlier group still loitered. Winnie was attempting to help them, but a stout older man with a red face, who seemed to be the leader, swiped his finger on his phone. "I've gotten food poisoning at a restaurant before. The health department must be called."

"We don't know it was food poisoning, sir," Winnie answered calmly. "It could be anything."

The man ignored her and began to speak to the health department hotline. Winnie threw Tess and the others a defeated glance as the man hung up, glowered, then left. The inn suddenly seemed eerily quiet after the chaotic events. Tess looked at her friends and shrugged. "I suppose we should get back to work."

After about an hour of worrying and cleaning and hoping for the best, Huck's bark jolted Tess's attention. He galloped toward the door.

"Huck!" Tess called. Someone wearing a uniform always triggered him. The mail carrier had learned to bring dog treats to fend off Huck's fierce barking. Not that he would hurt anyone.

LuAnn and Janice, apparently also alerted by Huck's barking, converged on the front door. In a moment, a short-statured bald man entered, wearing a blue uniform with a badge on a lanyard. He held a clipboard.

"Good afternoon," he said. "I'm Inspector Hancock from the health department. I understand there has been a threat to public health. A victim has been hospitalized."

"Yes, a woman became ill," Tess answered.

Without further ado, she ushered him into the kitchen. The women watched as he observed Winnie drying her hands on a paper towel and donning plastic gloves. Kylie wiped tables in the café, her hair in a neat ponytail. Tess inhaled with satisfaction. She knew Winnie's kitchen would be up to snuff.

Inspector Hancock crossed the room to Big Red but seemed unimpressed by the stove's glory. He got a few instruments out of a small satchel he carried. After donning plastic gloves, he stuck a thermometer in the soup.

"Too cold." He wrote something on his clipboard.

"That's because we weren't going to serve it, so we turned off the heat," Janice explained.

"I would normally put it in the refrigerator," Winnie put in. "I would never leave it sitting out, but—"

"It was piping hot when we offered it to guests—well, just Bonnie and Clint, I suppose," Tess added.

After inspecting all the areas of the kitchen, he turned to the ladies who had assembled in a row, watching him. "I need to ask you some questions."

"Of course," Tess said.

"Is everyone here who had access to the soup?"

Tess looked around. "I think so. Other than Bonnie."

"I believe Mason, this girl's boyfriend"—Winnie pointed to Kylie—"was also here while the soup was being made. I didn't see him, though, until after the soup was done."

The inspector turned his attention to Kylie. A nervous chuckle escaped her lips as she inched forward. "Yeah, but just for a few minutes. He was helping."

"Anyone else?"

"Well," Tess started. Her stomach ached at the thought of putting suspicion on anyone, but she knew she had to tell the inspector. "The soup was just about done when Clint Lowery came by."

"I will need information for this Mason, and Mr. Lowery." He marked something off on his clipboard. "Who made the soup?"

Winnie stepped forward. "I did. We got the recipe from... from an old Civil War–era purse."

The inspector looked up from his clipboard.

"A guest brought the purse with the recipe," Tess explained. "It's from her family—an heirloom."

"I'll need to see that."

"I have it here." Winnie pulled the photocopy of the recipe from a magnetic clamp on the refrigerator and handed it to him.

Tess held her breath as she watched the inspector read the recipe. His brows tightened into stiff lines when he reached the bottom.

"We didn't put the toadstools in the soup," Janice said.

Inspector Hancock pursed his lips, but he said nothing.

"I'll need to ask you some questions now." He pointed to the long kitchen table.

"Of course." Tess awkwardly pulled out a chair, and they all settled around the table. Winnie sat directly across from him.

"Where did you purchase the pork?"

Winnie sat forward. "At the grocery store in town. They deliver."

"So the delivery person would have had contact with the ingredients." He seemed to be talking to himself.

Winnie frowned, surely thinking about Marcus.

"Did you put anything in the soup other than the items in the recipe?"

Winnie shook her head. "The first time I make a new dish, I follow the recipe to the letter. After that, I sometimes add this and that to make it better, but the first time I want to keep as a baseline."

The inspector nodded. "What is your procedure for food preparation?"

"We follow the USDA standards of clean, separate, cook, chill. Everyone is required to wash their hands as well as wear gloves."

"She's a real stickler on that one," Janice put in.

"We are careful not to cross-contaminate. Wash dishes in one sink. Have another sink for food prep. Use freshly cleaned cutting boards, so ready-to-eat food doesn't touch uncooked food."

He took notes as she described their food preparation procedure in great detail. When she finished, he looked satisfied, but Tess wasn't sure.

"And heating foods. Your procedure?"

"Again," Winnie said, "we go by the USDA standards for internal temperatures."

The inspector asked more questions, took more notes, and examined every nook and cranny of the kitchen. He finally seemed to reach the bottom of his list.

"I appreciate your cooperation. You obviously adhere to a strict regimen. I'm giving you a rating of 'excellent.'"

Tess and the others sighed in relief.

"Yes, that's good news. I will need to verify the ingredients were not contaminated anywhere along the supply line, but I'm confident no contamination happened here." He pulled a vial out of his satchel. "However, since someone has been sent to the hospital, we still need to do a toxicology report." He went to the stove, opened the vial, and spooned in a sample of the soup. "The preliminary results shouldn't take long to get back."

Relief washed over Tess. If nothing else, their reputation as a clean restaurant held. But then the inspector continued writing on his clipboard, longer than Tess could bear. Finally, lifting his chin, he spoke calmly and with a hint of compassion. "I'm sorry, but until we rule out any further food contamination, this café is to remain closed."

CHAPTER FIVE

Tess exhaled as she watched the inspector leave. "That wasn't very fun."

"Sure wasn't." Winnie sent a meaningful look at Kylie before retrieving a sponge and wiping down the counter. Kylie took the hint and grabbed the broom.

"At least he said they'd get the toxicology report back soon. It'd be torture to have to wait very long."

"That's true," Janice said. "Then we can get this all behind us."

"Yes," Tess agreed. "I'm thinking we should visit Bonnie at the hospital."

LuAnn nodded. "We should give her a couple of days to recover though."

"We can pray for her while we wait," Janice said.

"I'll put a request on our Facebook page," LuAnn offered, then turned her attention to her phone. After a moment, she sucked in a breath. "Oh, no."

"What's wrong?" Janice asked. "Something on Facebook?"

Tess frowned. "What bad news is on there now?"

"It *is* bad news," LuAnn answered. "But not like you think." She held her phone for Tess and Janice to see.

Tess looked at the inn's Facebook page. There was a post at the top that showed a dark, creepy picture of the inn, and the title of the post was "Wayfarers Inn Murderer." It had a picture of Winnie appearing mean and angry. She read the caption out loud. "'Follow this link to find out more. I have proof that Winnie Washington attempted to murder a customer of the popular inn.'"

Tess felt like she'd been punched. "Why on earth would someone post this?"

"People can post—"

"Anything." LuAnn finished Janice's sentence. "When I was a teacher, kids put all kinds of stuff on Facebook—rumors, slander, though nice things too sometimes. You never knew what was coming next." She tapped on the poster's avatar, and a generic Facebook page came up, with nothing to give them a clue about who would be doing this to them.

Winnie stepped next to them. "What? Me? They're saying I tried to murder that poor woman?"

At that moment, the back door opened and Marcus entered the kitchen. "Grandma!" He held up his phone. "Did you see this?"

"Marcus," Winnie greeted him.

He pulled away. "Maybe you didn't see." He displayed the same Facebook post LuAnn had.

Winnie frowned. "Oh, I saw it." She pointed to the screen. "It's going to reflect badly on the inn."

"Winnie." Janice touched her arm. "Don't worry about that. We're just sorry this is happening to you."

"It's not right, Grandma," Marcus said. "You would never do anything to hurt anyone."

Tess was getting a headache. "The fact is, it will have an effect on the inn's business. We've been promoting Winnie as the best chef in Marietta." She waved at Winnie, who frowned. "You are."

LuAnn's jaw tightened. "Our reputation is everything. First Bonnie going to the hospital. Now this."

"Do you think it will affect business?" Janice asked.

"It definitely could," Tess said. "That's why we can't waste any time getting to the bottom of both the Facebook page and what happened with Bonnie." Tess pondered the post, then deleted it. "I saw the customers with their phones after Bonnie collapsed. I guess word got out about Bonnie getting sick, and someone decided to use it to hurt us, or Winnie."

"Or both," LuAnn added.

"The question is why." Janice tapped her chin.

The group dispersed, and Tess headed up the stairs. First, she would do an immaculate job on Bonnie's room. She unlocked the door and stepped inside. The quiet coziness of Woodbine and Roses embraced her as she slipped into the rhythm of dusting, vacuuming, emptying the trash, removing the sheets. As she spread the clean and freshly pressed sheets onto the bed, she remembered her mother teaching her to make a bed when she was a child. She'd struggled to get it right—at least "right enough" for her mother's standards. Housekeeping was never Tess's strong point, and now here she was cleaning rooms and bathrooms, doing laundry for her living. And she loved it. Somehow, she'd found purpose, even peace, in lovingly performing these tasks.

She took a deep breath as she scanned the room, checking off the tasks from her mental "to-bless list" as she liked to think of it. She noticed the drawer in the nightstand was slightly open. She crossed the room to close it, but it was stuck, and she had to open it to get it back on the track. When she did, she saw a small cardboard folder covered with fabric. It was folded open, revealing an old sepia photograph. Studying it, Tess spotted a group of people standing in what looked like the inn's parlor. What she saw next made her gasp.

In moments, Tess practically leapt down the stairs. She zipped across the floor and landed in front of the check-in counter where LuAnn and Janice stood. "You're not going to believe what I found in Bonnie's room."

January 20, 1863

The below-zero temperatures froze the dirt in the tunnel leading to the secret rooms beneath the inn, and Prudence's boots clacked as she walked. What kind of prison had the desperate child she'd discovered in her barn, clearly no older than eighteen, endured?

"Good evening." Prudence entered the room, and the sight of the woman stretched out awkwardly on the shadowed cot pierced her. She viewed her thin yet muscular arms, the swollen belly, the sunken cheeks. She had seen the scars on her back when she'd given her a sponge bath the evening before, and she'd prayed for mercy. Even those words fell, unheard. At least it seemed no one heard.

Elizabeth, her helper in the inn, had tarried with the woman, whose name was Angelica, through the night. Elizabeth's tall, slim frame shifted when Prudence entered and quietly closed the door behind her. Angelica stared at the door behind Prudence, tears pooling in her eyes.

"Thee is not a prisoner here. I closed the door, so thee will not be found." Prudence stepped closer. "Thee is safe with us. We are friends."

The slight girl lowered her head and held her bulging belly.

"How is she doing?" Prudence asked Elizabeth.

"Her body seems to be gaining strength. Her breathing is much stronger, but…" She smoothed the sheet over the mattress where the girl lay. "It is dreary down here. I am afraid a depression grows with each moment."

Prudence picked up Elizabeth's knitting basket from next to the chair. "I thank thee for caring for her this night. Thee may go now. Rest." She offered her most compassionate smile. "It will take time for her to trust us," she whispered as Elizabeth stepped toward the door.

"I know. I will pray for her with all my heart."

Elizabeth opened the door, her presence replaced by the icy cold that swept in.

Prudence turned to her guest, who shivered. She pulled the wooden chair close to the bedside.

"How is thee feeling?"

"Some better," she answered. "But, if I die…" She rubbed her rounded belly. "If *we* die, I want you to know about what happened to me and my husband…Jermaine." Her eyes flickered like stoked embers, then faded again. "And about the judge who betrayed us."

"What did you find?" Janice's face beamed, reflecting Tess's excitement.

"Follow me."

Tess led her friends up to Bonnie's room. She'd left the drawer open and the picture exactly as she'd found it.

"It's an old photo?" Janice asked when Tess showed them.

"Is that—" LuAnn squinted through her reading glasses.

"It is, isn't it?" Tess's heart raced.

"It's the inn," Janice said. "I'd know that fireplace anywhere."

Tess leaned over the photo again. "And the wood floor."

LuAnn continued to study it. "That woman, with the frown, standing next to the tall man..." Her eyes lit up. "It's Prudence?"

Tess nodded. "It's her, wearing an apron—"

"Like we do!" LuAnn rubbed her hands together.

"But why would she pose for a picture with those distinguished people?" Tess couldn't understand it. "And what's with that strange look on her face?"

"I know people in photos back then always look stern because they had to hold their poses so long, but her face seems even more tense than the others'."

"Yeah, she seems, sort of, I hate to say it..." Janice shifted her gaze more directly toward Tess and LuAnn. "Angry."

"Not the kind of look I would have expected from her." LuAnn straightened. "Not from what we've read in her journal."

"Wait!" Still staring at the photo, Janice pointed to something in another woman's hand. "Is that the purse?"

Tess bent forward. "It is! I hadn't noticed that before. Good eye."

"Thanks," Janice said, then put her reading glasses on and leaned closer. "Did you guys see what it says on the bottom of the frame?" Before they answered, she read, *"Riverfront House, Marietta, Ohio, 1863."*

"That answers the question of where and when it was taken," LuAnn added. "I wonder why Bonnie didn't mention it earlier."

"Maybe that's what she was going to tell us. Remember she said she wanted to share more of the story about the purse."

"I'm dying to know who those people standing next to Prudence are."

"The man seems very important." LuAnn grazed the photo with a finger.

"You don't think that her grandpa and grandma Graves, do you?" Janice asked.

"That's a good guess, since Bonnie has it," Tess answered. "I wonder if there's anything in Prudence's journal about this." LuAnn weaved her fingers through her hair. "Maybe we could help Bonnie find some information about her relative. She seemed very proud of his work for the abolitionist cause. She'd probably love to find out more."

"I love that idea." Tess slid the drawer shut.

As they headed down the stairs, Tess's phone rang. It was a call for the inn, but when no one answered it, the call transferred to her phone since she was the on-call Inn Crowd girl for the day. Before answering it, she glanced at the screen. Her caller ID read: "Health Department."

She showed it to the others and then answered. "This is Tess Wallace."

"This is Inspector Hancock. I have the preliminary results of your toxicology report."

CHAPTER SIX

Tess hung up after speaking with the inspector, but before she could tell her friends the results, the bell over the front door jingled, and a family of eight arrived—parents, kids, and grandparents. The three women moved to the desk to help them.

"Mama, I drinky." One of the little boys tugged on his mom's coat.

"I'm hungry," a girl who looked slightly older added.

Soon, the rest of the group joined the chorus of hungry little ones. The mom's eyes pleaded with Tess. "Your café's open, right? Do you serve macaroni and cheese?" She exhaled. "Tell me you do."

Tess shot glances to LuAnn and Janice. "I'm so sorry. I'm afraid we've had a situation. We had to close."

The dad, who held a child in each arm, looked up. "Your café's closed?"

"Yes," Tess said. "Until further notice."

Janice knelt down in front of the little boy. "You like mac 'n' cheese?"

"I do!" the little girl interrupted.

Janice smiled. "I'd be happy to run out and get them some." She winked at the boy, stood up, then grabbed one of their suitcases and slung a backpack over her shoulder. "As soon as we get you to your rooms, okay?"

The boy smiled, and his mom heaved a sigh. "Thank you."

When Janice returned, she sidled up to Tess and LuAnn. "Closed until further notice? Does that mean...what does that mean? It was food poisoning after all?"

Tess shook her head. Her stomach ached to have to tell them. "They confirmed a foreign substance."

Janice covered her mouth with her hand.

"I don't understand why someone would do this," LuAnn said as she rubbed her neck.

"I don't know either, but we need to find out." Tess took in a breath. "As soon as possible."

"You can say that again," Janice added.

Tess had one more piece of information. "He also said someone from his office would be here in about fifteen minutes to gather evidence."

"I suppose he means the pot and the utensils, Bonnie's cup?" asked Janice.

"Yes, I would imagine he means those kinds of things. I'm sure they'll have a list of things they want." Tess's mind went into planning mode. "But that doesn't stop us from doing our own investigation. I think before anything else we should rule out the connection with the recipe, don't you?"

LuAnn nodded. "I agree. If it's a coincidence that Bonnie was poisoned in the same inn as her ancestor—it's a big one."

"Where would someone get toadstools this time of year?" Janice asked. "Burrow down under the snow?"

"Can you dry them? I've seen dried mushrooms in the health food section of the grocery store. Do you think they came from there?" LuAnn picked up a pen and tapped it on the desk.

"Wait a minute." Tess interrupted their onslaught of questions. "We don't know that it was toadstools. The health inspector said they didn't know yet what it was."

"But I think it's what we have to go on right now, considering the recipe," Janice said. "We don't want to waste time waiting on them to confirm something we could be right about. We need to get some answers soon to clear Winnie's good name."

LuAnn wrote something down. "I wonder if that place where Brad's niece is working part-time would know. It's called All Pro Nutrition."

"Should we call them?" Janice pulled her phone from her pocket.

Tess shook her head. "I think we should go there. That way we can ask them if they'd like to sponsor the skate-a-thon too."

"Now you're talking." LuAnn smiled. "I could ask Brad if he'd go with us since his niece works there, plus I'm pretty sure he knows the owner."

"It's always good to have someone along who has a personal connection," Tess acknowledged. "Give Brad a call."

"Why don't you two go," Janice said. "I'll stay back and watch the inn."

"Sounds good," Tess agreed. "I wonder if Brad would mind driving. The roads are still icy, and his new SUV is heavier than any of our cars."

"I'll ask," LuAnn answered. "Should we go tomorrow?"

Tess rubbed her hands together. "Absolutely. Ladies, the game's afoot!"

Climbing down the stairs after cleaning Lily and Lace the next morning, Tess couldn't help but ponder the repercussions of all the negative publicity the inn was receiving—a poisoning sending someone to the hospital and closing the café, and the post on their Facebook page. They had disabled their Facebook account right away, but how many people had already seen the damaging accusations? How would the inn get through this? Could businesses temporarily closed down by the health department bounce back? If only Jeffrey was there to comfort and advise her. What would his business sense tell her to do?

The people from the health department had come just as they'd said, and gathered not only the pots and pans and utensils used to prepare the soup, but also the dish towels, dishcloths, and aprons that they'd used yesterday. Every item had been handled with gloves and bagged in separate ziplock bags.

"Tess?" LuAnn's voice pried Tess from her pondering. Just as well, as there was nothing she could do about the situation other than try to find who poisoned the soup—exactly what she was ready to do.

Glancing up, she spotted Mason standing at the desk.

"Hey." He waved.

"Hello," Tess said, joining them.

"Well, anyway." Mason continued his conversation with LuAnn. "Kylie told me you were doing a skate-a-thon. Did you know I own the Ski and Skate Shack?"

"No, I didn't know that," LuAnn answered. "We're not running the skate-a-thon, just helping with a few things."

"Oh. Well, that's okay. Maybe you could put in a good word for the Shack. I could give the skaters a good price."

"My contact did ask me if I had any leads on skate supply," LuAnn commented.

"Helping kids is awesome. I could set up a booth near the dock. Rent skates from there."

"Sounds like a good idea," LuAnn said. "But I'll have to get final approval from my contact."

"That's cool. I'll even give a percentage to the foster care organization. The Ski and Skate Shack is stoked to help. How many people are you expecting?"

LuAnn shrugged. "I have no idea. We're helping with the publicity and food—it'd probably be good for us to know too. I'll ask my contact and get back to you."

"Let me know ASAP, okay?"

LuAnn nodded. "You got it. I'm hoping for a lot of people."

Tess nudged LuAnn's shoulder. "Praying."

"That's right."

Mason flipped his hair, then left.

"Is this going to work?" LuAnn folded up her notebook. "Are we crazy?"

"Yes! But it's also a nice distraction from all this poison stuff. And it's always a blessing to help."

LuAnn nodded. "That's the best part."

"Definitely, but"—Tess grinned mischievously—"it'll also be fun to skate again, even though Janice nearly outdid us."

A thought niggled at Tess's mind as she watched Mason cross the parlor. "He was here yesterday morning, wasn't he?"

LuAnn's forehead gathered. "He was."

"We need to find out more about him."

"Why would he poison anyone?"

"Maybe he's got something against Winnie or the inn that we don't know about. We really know nothing about him. We should go check out his Shack."

"Good idea."

As LuAnn spoke, the front door opened and Brad entered. Thirty minutes later, Tess, LuAnn, and Brad walked into the All Pro Nutrition health food store.

The first face Tess saw was Saffron's. She stood at the front counter arranging muffins in a glass display case.

"Uncle Brad." She looked up and smiled.

"Hey, Saffron. How's it going?"

"Good. What are you guys doing here?"

"Can't an uncle visit his niece?"

Saffron rolled her eyes. "Can't a niece get a straight answer from her uncle?"

Tess chuckled and stepped forward. "Hi, Saffron. We were wondering if you sell dried goods here, like dried mushrooms or—"

Saffron frowned. "Why?"

LuAnn tilted her head. "That does sound like a strange request, doesn't it?"

"No, actually. Dried mushrooms are very good for you. And we do carry them. I'll show you." She came out from behind the counter. "They contain B complex vitamins, vitamin A, vitamin C, vitamin D, calcium, magnesium, potassium, selenium..." Saffron crouched down to look at their shelf of dried roots, leaves, and mushrooms.

Tess was almost sorry to stop her. "That's interesting," she finally said, "but what we're really looking for is dried toadstools. Would anyone use those for health reasons? I know they're poisonous, but maybe in small doses they help with something?" Tess felt like she was stretching, but she needed an answer.

Saffron stood back up. "I don't think we would carry toadstools—Jack!" She called to a man walking by who looked like a bodybuilder.

He peered around the aisle. "Yeah."

"We don't carry dried toadstools, do we?"

He tilted his head. "No. Too poisonous." He started to leave, but Tess moved toward him.

"Excuse me. Do you know how someone could get her hands on some this time of year?"

He crossed his arms. "You want them for...?"

"No, no!" Tess, LuAnn, and Brad all rushed to say.

"They had an incident at their café," Brad explained.

Jack eyed Brad for a second. "Brad, right?" He shook Brad's hand. "You're Saffron's uncle?"

Brad nodded. "That's right. Good to see your store's doing so well."

"Thanks. We're growing slowly but surely."

"We understand that," Tess said.

"We were wondering where someone could find toadstools in the middle of winter." LuAnn redirected the conversation.

Jack shifted his stance. "The internet's always a possibility. Actually, now that I think of it, my other employee, Cheyenne. She was telling me that she dries them to use as rat poison. Much more natural than chemicals and not as painful as traps. I think she hates killing the 'poor rats,' but she rents out a few of her rooms, and her tenants were complaining."

Tess exchanged glances with the others. "Could we talk to her?"

"Cheyenne?" Saffron interjected. "She's gone to visit her boyfriend in Cincinnati. She left this morning. She'll be back in a couple of days, I think."

"Could you give her a call for us?" Tess asked.

Saffron removed her phone from her pocket, moved her thumbs rapidly over the tiny keys, and then looked up. "Texted her. I'll let you know when she gets back to me. She's not the best at answering texts, though."

"Okay," Tess said. "That's the best we can do for now, I guess. Thanks for your help."

"No problem," Saffron answered.

Tess shifted her gaze to Jack. "And thanks for your help too."

"Sure. Good to see you again, Brad." He nodded toward Tess and LuAnn. "Ladies," he said as he walked away.

"Oh, I forgot to ask him if he'd be willing to sponsor the skate-a-thon," LuAnn said as they reached the counter.

"That's so cool." Saffron perked up. "Uncle Brad told me about how the event is to sponsor the foster kids. I'll ask Jack. I'm sure he'd be happy to. He's pretty cool. He's really taught me the importance of eating right. There are so many natural alternatives not just to the stuff we eat, but our beauty products too. We recently got in a new line." She pinched her cheek. "I've been using the skin care products. They're amazing! And all organic."

LuAnn smiled. "You look lovely."

Saffron frowned, apparently not comfortable with compliments.

"Anyway," Tess said, "thanks for your help with the toadstools, the skate-a-thon, and the beauty tips."

As they were leaving, Tess noticed a community bulletin board on the wall. "Would it be okay if we put a flyer for the skate-a-thon up there?"

"Oh, sure. It's a worthy cause."

As Tess moved closer, she noticed a flyer with a photo of someone that looked familiar. She pointed, showing LuAnn and Brad. "Is that Winnie?"

They rushed to the board to find a half-sheet flyer, on a marbleized black and blue paper, with a picture similar to the one on the Facebook page—Winnie with a mean expression on her face. A caption in an angry black font read: *Cook at Wayfarers Inn attempts to poison customers. She didn't succeed this time. Will she try again?*

Instead of a Facebook address, it had a website in bold letters: www.winniethemurderer.com.

CHAPTER SEVEN

Tess's heart pounded. One thing after another was threatening the inn's reputation, not to mention her and her partners' livelihood, their employees' well-being, and an honorable, godly woman's character. She ripped the flyer from the board and walked back to the counter where Saffron was now pricing vitamin drinks. Brad and LuAnn followed.

"Do you know who put this up there?"

Saffron examined the flyer. "This is terrible. It was on our bulletin board?"

"It was," LuAnn said.

"I organized that this morning. It must have been put up recently, like, really recently."

"I can't believe this." LuAnn looked as concerned as Tess felt.

Brad put a hand on LuAnn's shoulder. "Let's take the flyer with us. See if anyone knows anything about it."

Tess nodded. "You're right. Panicking won't help."

LuAnn smoothed her hair behind her ear. "Should we start at Jeremiah's? Grab a coffee for strength?"

"Sounds good," Tess said as they waved goodbye to Saffron and headed out. "It's only a couple of minutes away. Let's walk."

In the promised time, Tess, LuAnn, and Brad entered their favorite coffee shop. Tess hadn't realized how stressed she had been that morning until the scent of Jeremiah's fresh-roasted coffee relaxed her tight shoulders. The warm shop was like a peaceful oasis from the storm.

Drinks in hand, they searched for a table and found one next to the brick wall.

Tess set her mug down, then studied the bulletin board. "I can't believe someone put that flyer up at All Pro."

"Me neither." LuAnn set her purse beneath her chair. "Do you think someone is specifically trying to hurt Winnie? Or is the inn the target?"

Tess rubbed her temples. "I don't know. That flyer and the Facebook post seem to be more about Winnie than the inn."

"But why would anyone want to hurt our amazing cook?" LuAnn asked. "I can't imagine she would have any enemies."

No answer came to Tess's mind. She wished she knew what evidence the mystery person allegedly had. Even so, nothing would make her doubt Winnie. She knew that for sure.

Brad wiped a crumb from the table. "I guess word about the poisoning has gotten out."

"Yeah," LuAnn said. "Facebook moves fast, but I didn't expect flyers to be up. What are they hoping to accomplish?"

The three sat in silence for a few moments. Before the poisoning, everything had been going well, at least pretty well. They'd had lots of bumps to navigate, but this seemed like the biggest bump they'd faced yet.

"One thing we know is that only the people who were there that morning could have put the poison in the soup."

"That rules out Marcus," LuAnn said.

Finally, good news. "You're right! He delivered the groceries Saturday night. Winnie will be so relieved."

"Rules me out too." Brad winked.

LuAnn gave him a teasing look. "Of course."

"We don't even know if it was toadstools for sure. Still so many questions." Tess sighed. "Anyway, let's go back to who was there."

"Mason and Kylie."

"We definitely need to talk to them," Tess agreed. "I like Kylie, and I'm glad we used the social services organization to find her."

"You did?" Brad asked.

LuAnn nodded. "After Constance left we were in a bind, so Winnie suggested we use this service that places low-income folks with local businesses."

"That's a great idea."

"It is, but we really know nothing about Kylie's background," LuAnn said.

"She sure seems like she wants to learn, but you're right. Maybe we should talk to her caseworker," Tess suggested.

LuAnn took a sip of her coffee. "We need to talk about that new farmer, Clint, since he was there too. But since we're in town, do you want to stop at Mason's Shack?"

"Sure."

As they gathered their things, a young woman's voice grabbed Tess's attention.

"Do you think Winnie knows?"

Then a male voice she also recognized caught her. "Doubt it."

"Kylie? Mason?" Tess nearly bumped into them as they moved toward the door. Kylie was carrying a large coffee cup.

"Hey!" Kylie twisted a strand of her hair. "What are you guys doing here?"

Tess ignored her question. She thought about the nasty flyer accusing Winnie in the pocket of her purse. "Kylie, shouldn't you be at the inn? What are you doing here at this time?"

"Oh." Kylie angled her head. "The café's closed, so Winnie told me to take the day off."

"Yeah," Mason said. "She seemed bummed, so we thought we'd bring her coffee—not the plain drip kind you have at the inn." He seemed oblivious to his passive insult.

"Poor Winnie," Kylie put in. "Have you seen that Facebook post? She deserves a yummy mocha with lots of whip. Don't you think?"

"That's nice of you," Tess said.

"Thanks. Winnie's been good to me. We even have a few things in common." She bit her lip and held up the cup she was carrying. "I should get this to her before it gets cold."

"And I need to get back to the Shack." Mason tilted his head toward Kylie.

Kylie pouted. "You do?"

"That's actually good," Tess interjected. "We were on our way to talk to you about yesterday morning."

"And check out the skates," LuAnn added.

"Cool. I'll meet you over there. Gotta make a quick stop at All Pro. We carry their energy drinks. Sell pretty good."

"We'll see you at the Shack in, say, twenty minutes, then?" Tess asked.

"Sweet." He kissed Kylie's cheek and left.

As Tess watched Kylie head toward the door carrying the "yummy mocha with lots of whip," she couldn't help but chuckle. "I can imagine Winnie's reaction. She's always bemoaning those 'fancy, expensive coffees.'"

"I was thinking the same thing." LuAnn smiled. "But it was nice of Kylie."

Tess agreed, though it did seem a little odd that Kylie seemed to feel so connected to Winnie. Winnie could be pretty hard on her help. Tess didn't have time to ponder, because before they reached the door, LuAnn paused. "There's Jessica. Perfect. I'll ask her if she'd be willing to sponsor the skate-a-thon." She waved at Jessica.

Jessica waved, but instead of a smile, her forehead tightened. As she walked toward them, her attention was on something over Tess's shoulder. "I was just going to remove it," she said.

Tess turned, following the line of her gaze, and what she saw sickened her. A copy of the same flyer that had been at the health food store.

Tess practically leapt to the board, pulled down the flyer, and stuck it in her purse. Swiveling back to LuAnn and Brad, she tightened her lips. "There!"

LuAnn followed and, using the same pushpin, tacked on the skate-a-thon flyer. She turned to the others. "And there!"

"Well, ladies." Brad buttoned up his coat as they stepped outside. "I have an appointment. Do you want me to pick you up and drive you back when I'm done?"

Tess looked at LuAnn, and they shook their heads.

"We can walk home," Tess said. "The cold air will be good for us."

He eyed LuAnn. "Text me if you change your mind, okay?"

"I will, thanks."

"Text me anyway?"

"Sure." LuAnn smiled.

He returned her smile, then walked in the direction of his car.

Tess and LuAnn reached the Ski and Skate Shack on Front Street nestled between the florist and an empty storefront. Tess squinted against the sunlight at the sign. Normally the roughly painted letters merely said *Ski Shack*, but a wood slate with *and Skate* painted on it had been tacked to the sign. Tess smiled. It was smart of Mason to key into the opportunity the frozen river presented them.

As they approached, Mason, who was dusting snow from the Shack's eaves, greeted them with a crooked smile.

"Hey, guys. Let's talk skates." He opened the door, and they entered the shop decorated with posters of skaters and skiers doing dangerous feats.

LuAnn stepped forward. "I'm not sure how many will come out for the event, but just in case, I want to make sure we have plenty of skates."

"You bet." He pointed through an open doorway. "See all those shelves? Full-on packed with skates. All sizes represented. Since we heard about the skate-a-thon, we've been calling around to skating rinks, rental places...getting as many as we can for ya."

LuAnn smiled. "Thank you, Mason. I'll talk to my contact at the foster care agency about your shop. I'm pretty confident they'll use you. They won't be able to do the skate-a-thon at all if they don't have skates."

"I'm excited to help the kids." He took on a somber tone. "I know some foster kids myself."

"Really?" Tess asked. "Where are you from, Mason? Did you grow up in Marietta?"

"Nah, I grew up over in Clarksburg."

"Clarksburg?" LuAnn leaned her elbows on the counter. "Where did you go to high school?"

"Robert C. Byrd."

"What? That's where I taught English and History. I guess you didn't take any of my classes."

Mason slipped his hands in his pockets. "Nope. I wasn't that into school. Mostly I skateboarded and snowboarded."

"And played video games?" Tess's hands had finally warmed enough to remove her gloves.

"Nah. Not really into games. I'd rather board or play my guitar or…" His thin lips loosened into a sheepish smile. "Hang out with my girlfriend."

"Not even chess?" Tess asked, glancing at LuAnn.

"Chess? Not me."

"Were you dating Kylie in high school?" LuAnn asked.

Mason jarred to attention. "Sorry. No, that was a different girlfriend." He chuckled awkwardly. "I've only known Kylie for like…like six months or so."

LuAnn removed her hat. "Do your parents still live in Clarksburg?"

"Um, yeah, they did. Not anymore. Got shafted by the system. You know what I mean, right?"

Tess really didn't. How were they "shafted"?

Her face must have expressed confusion because Mason explained.

"My dad was laid off from his job. Mom was a veterinary technician, but she got sick, so she had to quit. And they were stuck. Lived in our car for a few weeks."

"Mason, I did have another question. You were there yesterday morning when Bonnie got sick from the soup."

He nodded. "I was. Poor lady. That Civil War soup smelled so good. To take a bite and then—*bam!*"

"It wasn't exactly a *bam!*" Tess countered. "But I know what you mean."

"You didn't see anyone do anything to the soup, did you? Something odd? Anything out of the ordinary?" LuAnn asked him.

"I saw Winnie stirring it. Nothing weird."

The front door of the shack scraped open, and a young man with short bleached braids came in.

"We should be going." Tess smiled. "Thanks for your help."

"Sure."

As Tess and LuAnn started to leave, Tess paused. "You said you do business with All Pro Nutrition?"

Mason nodded.

"Do you know an employee named Cheyenne?"

"Yeah. Cheyenne's cool. Knows everything about health food." He nodded at his waiting customer. "Is there anything else I can do for you?"

LuAnn replaced her hat. "We'll stay in touch about the skates, okay?"

"Yup."

As they walked toward the door, Tess's heart dropped into her stomach for the third time today. Without a word, she walked over to the Shack's bulletin board and removed the same heinous flyer they'd seen before. She showed it to LuAnn, and they turned back, waiting for Mason to finish talking to his customer.

When he approached them, eyebrows raised in question, Tess showed him the flyer. "Do you know who put this up?"

Mason read it and frowned. "Oh, man. Wish I did. Who would disrespect Miss Winnie like that?"

"I don't know, but we need to find out," Tess responded.

Mason went back to work, and Tess inspected the flyer more closely. "I suppose these could have been printed anywhere, but the high-quality sheen on the paper makes me think of Marty's," she said. Wayfarers used Marty's Print Shop for any bulk printing they needed.

LuAnn rubbed the paper between her forefinger and thumb. "It does feel like quality paper. We should talk to Marty. Even if it wasn't printed there, he could tell us who in town would carry this kind of paper other than him, or at least what it's called."

"We've been gone a while." Tess peered outside. "It's already starting to get dark."

"Such short winter days," LuAnn said. "But we should really go talk to Marty. It won't take long."

"Do you think Janice is okay?" Tess asked.

LuAnn nodded. "Janice will be okay. She's got Winnie. And, don't forget, the café's closed. So they didn't have to clean up after lunch today."

"How could I forget that? Anyway"—Tess donned her gloves—"we'll go to the printers, then walk home."

"And I'll text Janice to let her know."

As they stepped outside, Tess saw a young man holding a handful of papers striding down the street toward them. When he reached them he stopped and smiled brightly. "Hello." He held one of the papers out to them. "Have you heard about the new bed-and-breakfast in town?"

Tess sent a silent inquiry to LuAnn. "No, we haven't heard."

Tess took the paper from him and felt her blood boil when she recognized the handsome face looking back at her in living color.

Chapter Eight

Tess wrapped her coat tighter around herself as she and LuAnn walked to Marty's. "He didn't say anything about opening a B&B. Acted like he wanted to work together on publicity. All the while, he was thinking of us as competition."

"We don't know that for sure," LuAnn said. "There's nothing wrong with someone opening a B&B."

"Of course not, but why didn't he mention it? Why did he talk about his boutique farm but not about the B&B?" She started walking in the direction of Marty's Print Shop.

"I don't know. We should talk to him."

Tess held up her phone. "Yep. He gave me his card, and I put his number in my phone." She scrolled down till she found him. It rang.

"This is Clint."

Tess's nerves suddenly fluttered. "Hello. This is Tess Wallace from Wayfarers Inn."

"Hey, Tess. Good to hear from you. I was wanting to talk to you."

"I had something to talk to you about too. I mean, my partners and I."

"Would it be okay if we met in person?" His voice sounded sincere. Was it real or fake sincerity? Tess wasn't sure.

"Meeting in person is probably best."

"I tell you what. There's a snowman competition along with a winter campfire at Muskingum Park going on right now. Do you want to meet me there? We can talk by the fire."

"Well." Tess tried to quickly estimate their time at the print shop. "We can do that. How about in twenty minutes?"

"Perfect. I'll see you then."

"Fine." Tess hung up. "He's going to meet us at the park in twenty minutes."

"Sounds good." LuAnn's voice reflected caution as they walked. "What do you think of him?"

"He seems like a nice-enough man. Something's been bothering me though. He was so nice to all of us after Bonnie got sick."

"He really was. Very gentlemanly."

"But he didn't eat any of his soup," Tess continued. "I watched him dip his spoon in, but then he got distracted, I thought, by the newspaper he was reading. He never took a bite."

"You think he knew not to eat it?"

"If he did, there's only one way he could've known."

"If he poisoned it himself." LuAnn's shoulders slumped. "I hope that's not what happened."

"Maybe to ruin the reputation of the competition?"

"How would he have known about the recipe, and Bonnie's history, and all that?"

"That's why we need to talk to him."

As Tess finished talking, they approached Marty's Print Shop and stepped inside. Two copy machines sat in the lobby, and Marty, an older gentleman with a baseball cap and white beard, stood working behind the counter. When they approached, he looked up.

"Hey there, wayfarers from Wayfarers." He chuckled. "What made you wander over here?"

Tess stepped closer. "Hello, Marty. It's good to see you."

"Do you have an order for me? I'm pretty slow after Christmas."

"Not this time," LuAnn answered. "Maybe next month for Valentine's Day."

"That's what everyone says." He straightened a stack of papers and placed them under the counter.

Tess leaned on the counter. "Marty, we have a question." She pulled the flyer out of her purse. "We found these at several locations around town. Do you know if it was printed here?"

Marty picked up the flyer. "What kind of person would accuse someone like this? I know Winnie…" He shook his head. His glasses slipped down his nose as he examined it closer. "Poor design job. See how it's not centered correctly? And the font makes it hard to read. What's the point of having a flyer if it's not easy to read? I can tell you, it wasn't designed here. Aside from the despicable message, I wouldn't design something so shoddy."

LuAnn nodded. "We figured."

"What about the paper?" Tess asked.

Marty felt it. "It is the kind we use in our copiers. Only the best."

"Have you noticed anyone copying flyers recently?"

"No, but someone could always come in here and use their own paper they got off the internet."

"Yes, but have you seen anyone in here doing that?" Tess asked.

Marty shook his head. "I'm sorry, I haven't. I was out running an errand for a short time this morning though. My nephew watched the shop for about an hour."

"Can we talk to him?"

"He's not here, but let's see . . . " He scratched his head. "I don't know what his mom has him up to now. He's homeschooled. They do all kinds of things. Probably visiting an alpaca farm." He chuckled. Sorry I can't be of more help. Come back when you need that Valentine's order, okay?"

"You got it."

Marty disappeared into the back, and the two women walked toward the door. Tess paused at the copy machine. "Just in case . . . " She eyed LuAnn, then lifted the cover. "Sometimes people forget their originals."

"I've done that a million times."

Tess moved to the next one and lifted it. There was something there. Tess picked it up. It was a menu from Nacho Average Taco on white paper. Tess smiled. "That's not very helpful."

"Not really," LuAnn agreed.

As she spoke, the door opened, and a woman with dishwater-blonde hair and wearing a raspberry scarf walked in. She moved toward the copier, seeming to notice the cover open. Then she looked at Tess and LuAnn and frowned.

"You have my paper," she said. She yanked it from Tess's hand, whirled, and stalked out the door.

Streetlights reflected on the snow as Tess and LuAnn started walking toward the park where they were going to meet Clint. They had only been there a couple of minutes when sleigh bells filled the air. Coming over the bridge, a white sleigh about the length of a Cadillac was pulled by four beautiful white horses. White lights lined the side of the sleigh, and their muted reflections shone on the icy river.

A few minutes later, the sleigh pulled up in the parking lot, met by a group of onlookers. Clint sat in the driver's seat, a broad smile on his face. As Tess stepped closer, she noticed a banner on the side of the sleigh that read, *Butterfly Farms and B&B*.

Seeing her, Clint hopped out of the sleigh. "I told you I'd meet you here." He shrugged apologetically. "I hope you don't mind."

Tess and LuAnn moved closer to talk to him.

"Of course, we don't mind." LuAnn smiled. "What a beautiful sleigh."

"Hello, Clint," Tess greeted. "Is there a place we can talk?"

He pointed to a gazebo next to the river. "There's a fireplace in there that they usually have lit. Will that work?"

Tess looked to LuAnn for approval. She nodded, so they headed that way.

They sat on the benches angling around the center fireplace, Tess and LuAnn on one bench, Clint on another, where he could keep his horses in sight.

"Isn't this nice?" he asked.

Tess warmed her hands at the fire. "It is." She looked at LuAnn, knowing her friend would read her thoughts that it would be fun to have something like it at the inn. "So, Clint, we have a few questions."

"Can I apologize first?" He tilted his head. "I should have told you about the B&B." He took a breath. "I didn't want you to worry that I was trying to tap into your market."

"There's plenty of business for both of us," Tess said.

"Of course there is. I...didn't want to worry you." His eyes shone with sincerity. He was either a really good liar or was telling the truth. But why would he care about worrying a perfect stranger?

"Really, you had no obligation to tell us. Maybe a professional courtesy, but no more than that. And even that could be debated." Tess smiled, then after a pause she continued, "It did seem a little odd that you would leave out that bit of information, though."

"I can imagine. I really got off on the wrong foot. I do want to do some co-marketing. I will be happy to support Wayfarers any way I can. Like you said, there's no reason for us to be in competition."

Tess immediately felt better. Her instincts were telling her he was sincere about this, but still something seemed hidden behind his eyes.

"I used to be a businessman," he said. "The last thing I want is to get entrenched in competition. That type of life-style is how I lost someone close to me." His gaze rose above the trees. "My wife. She divorced me because I was a worka-holic."

"I'm sorry," LuAnn said.

"She deserved much more love than I ever gave her. After the divorce, I was bitter for a long time. I turned against God and everyone, but then, the Lord..." He picked up a stick and tossed it into the fire. A moment passed before he contin-ued, and when he did, he looked at Tess directly. "He convicted me—used something tragic to do it, but I finally turned to Him."

"He's good about that," Tess said.

"So I gave up my business and bought the B&B and the farm. I hope to get it and the boutique opened soon. Settle in to my new life."

"It sounds like you've chosen a good path now," LuAnn commented.

A moment passed, and Tess shifted in her seat, then faced him. "I need to ask you...Why didn't you eat the soup yesterday? It was sitting right in front of you. You put your spoon in..."

Clint chuckled. "You were watching me. I don't really know, except maybe God's providence. I was waiting for it to cool off, and then a story in the paper caught my attention. Then all the commotion with Bonnie happened. I'm sorry I don't have a better answer." He grinned. "You think I did it?"

Tess shook her head. "We're trying to rule everything out. Our inn's reputation is at stake. Did you see anything strange or suspicious?"

"No. I don't think so. I'll let you know if I remember anything." Clint stood up. "Well, friends—I hope we can be friends. I know it's only, what, about four thirty? But it's getting dark out there. Would you like a ride home?"

Tess eyed LuAnn. "What do you think?"

"Sounds like fun." LuAnn winked at her.

They walked back to the sleigh, and Clint helped the two women into the back seat and then took the reins.

"I think you'll like this," he called to them. Then he clicked his tongue, rustled the reins, and the sleigh glided over the snow down the tree-lined lane. Tess pulled the thick Alpaca wool blanket that lay on the seat over her and LuAnn's legs.

"Beautiful," she said as they crossed the bridge over the river.

After a few minutes, they turned onto the street leading to the inn's front door. Suddenly a shadowy figure raced in front of the sleigh, causing the horses to whinny and seize up. Tess nearly screamed as Clint yanked back on the reins.

CHAPTER NINE

Tess's heart raced as the horses' whinnies echoed through the twilight air. The sleigh tipped to the side, spraying snow and almost flipping over, causing Tess to slide into LuAnn. "Oh my goodness!" She braced her arm against the side to avoid crushing her friend, but she couldn't hold herself up for much longer.

Clint worked to guide the horses that had veered halfway into the ditch. "Whoa!" Finally, they settled down, and Clint was able to get them to straighten out enough to right the sleigh.

"Sorry," Tess said as she pried herself off of poor, flattened LuAnn.

"No problem." LuAnn shifted. "I always wanted our friendship to grow closer." She chuckled as she brushed snow from her sleeve. "What was that?"

"Don't you mean *who*?" Tess asked. "Someone ran across the road in front of us."

Clint pulled the horses to a stop, then turned to face the ladies. "You okay?"

Tess gazed at LuAnn, who nodded. "Other than crushing LuAnn, I think we're fine. How about you?"

"I'm good. The horses are good." Clint straightened his cowboy hat. "Did you see that man race across the road? I think he was chasing a dog."

Tess hadn't seen a dog, but she wasn't surprised. She knew a dog who was prone to getting out.

"A little scruffy dog?" LuAnn asked what Tess was thinking.

"Sounds about right," Clint said.

Tess shook her head. "Naughty."

As they spoke, Marcus stepped out from the roadside, holding Huck in his arms. The light from the sleigh's lamp illuminated his face. "Hi. Uh, sorry."

"Marcus!" Tess waved him over. "What on earth?"

"I was making a late delivery, and Huck got out. I went after him." He waved at Clint. "Sorry. I didn't see you. You need some better lights on that thing."

Clint smiled. "You may be right. I apologize. Are you okay?"

Marcus held his chest, then chuckled. "Yeah, I'm fine. Scared me half to death though."

"Can we give you a ride back to the inn?"

A smile spread across Marcus's face. "Sure. If you don't mind."

The two women scooted over to let Marcus and Huck climb aboard.

As Clint covered the half mile left to the inn, Tess remembered that she hadn't paid for the last grocery order. "When we get back," she said to Marcus, "I'll look over the latest orders, okay? Would you tell your boss we'll make a payment soon?"

"Sure."

"After this little adventure, would you like to come inside for something warm to drink?" LuAnn offered.

Marcus shook his head. "I've got to get back home. Grandma's making that lasagna of hers. Can't keep her waiting."

Clint pulled the sleigh alongside the inn's driveway. "It'll be a little easier for me if I drop you off here. That okay?" he asked.

"Of course," Tess said.

Clint hopped out and stood waiting to help the passengers step off the sleigh.

Marcus climbed out first, followed by LuAnn.

"I'll talk to you soon, okay?" Clint asked, as he helped Tess.

"Sounds good," Tess answered. "And thanks for the ride. You were right. It was fun."

"Even after our near miss?" Clint's smile lines crinkled. "I'm glad."

Tess and LuAnn waved goodbye as he clucked to the horses and rode away.

"Here's Huck." Marcus unloaded the animal into LuAnn's arms. "You be good now. No more sneaking out." He scratched Huck's ears.

Tess shook her head apologetically. "Thank you so much for finding him."

"No problem," he said, then climbed in his car and drove off.

Tess and LuAnn headed to the inn. When they opened the door, the smell of something delicious reached them as well as a greeting from Janice.

"My! You two were gone all afternoon." She poked her head into the mudroom and spotted Huck. "And you. Marcus must have found you." She leaned toward Huck, who sat in LuAnn's arms, looking cute and comfy.

"I'm sorry we were gone so long. We have a lot to tell you. How'd it go here?" Tess asked as she walked into the kitchen.

"Good. I got a lot of prep and cleaning done."

LuAnn set Huck down outside the kitchen and followed Tess. "Can I help with dinner?"

"Sure. Chicken Alfredo's in the oven, but if you want to make a salad..."

LuAnn reached under the island for a bowl.

"I'm going to work on paying the bills unless you need me in here," Tess said.

"Of course."

Tess sat in the office while Janice and LuAnn finished getting dinner together. The inn was pretty quiet. Tess was grateful the rooms were mostly full.

She pulled up the grocery order for last Saturday scrolled through it. Potatoes, onions, pork loin, the usual staples. After the normal items, there was a place for special orders. What Tess saw there took her breath away.

Toadstools. Do you carry them? Tess read the words several times. Who could have added that note? Did they not realize others would see it? Was it a joke?

She poked her head out of the office. "LuAnn, Janice, can you come here?"

In a moment, her friends stood over her shoulder gaping at the words on the screen.

"That's so strange," Janice said. "Who placed the order?"

"I thought it was Winnie." LuAnn straightened.

"I did too. It usually says who placed the order up here." Tess scrolled to the top of the order. No name appeared where it normally would.

LuAnn shook her head. "That's weird."

"That's putting it mildly," Janice added.

"Either someone forgot to log off or purposely took his or her name off the order." Tess tapped her fingernails against the desk. "Winnie's the one who usually places the order, but I can't imagine she would order this 'ingredient.'" She glanced at the others. "None of us did, correct?"

LuAnn and Janice shook their heads.

"Who was here?" Tess asked.

"Kylie," Janice offered. "Possibly Mason."

"Guests?"

"Someone besides us must have gotten on the computer that day." Tess rested her hands in her lap.

"Yeah. They somehow got into the office—was it left unlocked?" LuAnn asked. "And got onto the computer."

"We need to find out," Tess said.

"I don't know if there's a way to find out, unless someone logged on."

"The web browser history might give us a clue who was on," Janice suggested. "I mean, if an unusual website came up, and the culprit didn't clear the history."

Tess and LuAnn gaped at each other, then at Janice.

"You never cease to amaze me," Tess said.

"I only know how to check for what sites the computer went to on that day though. It'll take someone more tech-savvy than I am to know what time someone went to those sites."

"Brad's coming by tomorrow." LuAnn took out her phone. "Should I ask him to bring his tech guy? Maybe he can figure out who was on at that time." Without waiting for an answer, she started texting.

"Goodness!" Janice perked up. "Our supper. I better go check it."

Tess put the computer to sleep, and the three stood. "We should eat, and hopefully Brad's guy can help us tomorrow."

Early the next morning, Tess lay awake in her bedroom. "I need coffee," she mumbled.

Sleep had kept its distance, her thoughts on high alert and hunting for answers. Yesterday's activities had delivered more questions. What did Cheyenne from the health food store and her dried toadstools have to do with the poisoning—if anything? Who put those flyers up? What secrets was Clint hiding behind his sincere eyes? And the most pressing question at the moment—who inquired about the toadstools on that grocery order? Tess and her friends had assumed it wasn't Winnie. Tess couldn't imagine any possible reason why she would order such things, but just in case, she'd ask her later. In the meantime, she'd try to figure out who else had used the computer that day.

Tess showered, dressed, and headed for the Inn Crowd's common room. As she reached it, her phone rang. Glancing at it she saw her daughter Lizzie's name. Tess had texted her about the skate-a-thon before she'd gone to bed the night before.

"Hi, Lizzie. You got my text?"

"Mimi, it's me. Not mommy." Tess heard her granddaughter Harper's voice.

"Oh, this isn't my sweet little Harper, is it?"

"It is! We coming to skate-a-thing. I like to skate."

Tess's heart nearly burst. "You know how to skate? I didn't know that."

"Yep."

"Sounds good, sweetie. Is your mommy there?"

Tess heard some shuffling and then Harper came back. "She's dwiving, but she loves you."

Tess chuckled. "Okay. Tell her I love her too. And Liam and Henry and you!"

"Bye." And the phone hung up.

Tess sighed as she headed downstairs. What a blessing her family was. She would never forget the joy the birth of her grand-triplets brought her soon after Jeffrey passed away. How he would have reveled in their non-stop chatter and antics.

Before reaching the kitchen, she heard LuAnn's and Brad's voices talking and laughing. She was so happy that her friend had found companionship with a good, honorable man like Brad. Would she ever be ready for love again? Maybe in time, but for now Brad was a good friend to her and the rest of the Inn Crowd.

When she entered the kitchen, she spotted them, plus a bearded man standing next to the island. LuAnn, Janice, and Kylie were also there, preparing breakfast for the guests.

"Good morning," LuAnn said as Tess made her way to the coffeepot and poured herself a cup.

"Good morning," Tess said after taking her first sip. "Winnie's not here?"

"No, she had an appointment for her knee."

"Has it been bothering her?" Janice asked.

"I think it has. She would never mention it, of course," LuAnn answered. "She set out everything for the guests' continental breakfast—even though we still can't serve to the public."

"I brought my tech guy." Brad indicated the bearded man. "This is Chad."

Chad smiled and nodded. "Hello."

The mom from the family who had checked in the day of the poisoning poked her head in. "Breakfast ready? We've got hungry kids." Young voices wafting in from the café accentuated her point.

LuAnn looked up from the sink where she was washing a pan. "Just about ready. The big table's all set." She pointed into the café to the long harvest table. Then she peered at Tess and the others. "You all go ahead and check the computer. I'll see to our guests."

"All right." Tess motioned to Brad, Janice, and Chad to follow her to the office.

Arriving, Tess woke up the computer and pointed toward the chair. "Chad, we're so glad you're here. Can you help us figure out who used the computer on Saturday afternoon?"

Chad, lanky and serious looking, but with a pleasant smile, slid into the chair. "I can find out who logged on, but if it was already logged on, anyone could've used it, and you wouldn't know. I suggest looking at the web history. People have unique patterns for their web use."

Tess nodded. "That's what we thought might be a good strategy too."

"Any help you can give us..." Janice added.

After a couple of minutes of clicking, Chad's fingers slowed. "Okay," he said without looking up. "I've got the date in question. At 4:15 someone looked up home remedies for a sore back."

"That was probably Winnie," LuAnn said.

"Uh-huh." His fingers clicked again. "At 4:37, someone went to the grocery website." Chad clicked on it, and a website showing various grocery items came up.

"That's it," Tess said.

"The person went to the 'Place an Order' page. A minute and seventeen seconds later, Facebook was accessed."

"Facebook?" Tess met eyes with Janice and Brad.

"Yeah. Looks like someone accessed the page of a Kylie Morgan."

"Yes, she works here." Tess took in a breath.

"Five minutes later, the Facebook site was closed. The grocery site was still open. Four minutes after that, the grocery order was placed. There's no more activity till the next day." Chad removed his hands from the keyboard.

"That's all from that day?" Tess asked.

"Yeah."

Tess pursed her lips. "So, it was Kylie."

Tess pondered the possibilities of why Kylie would ask the grocery store about toadstools.

"Can I look up anything else?" Chad asked.

Tess sighed. "No, I think that's about it."

Chad pushed his chair back.

"Thank you so much for your help." Janice shook his hand as he stood up.

"No problem."

"Give me a minute," Brad said to Chad, "and we'll head back to the office."

"Help yourself to coffee or a muffin," said Tess.

Chad's eyes brightened. "Thanks."

As he walked out of the office, LuAnn walked in. "Those kids really were hungry!" She smiled. "Super cute though." She pointed at the computer. "What'd you find out?"

Tess slouched into the chair Chad vacated. "Kylie was on the computer that afternoon."

"Around the time the order was placed?" LuAnn asked.

"Yeah. And she was also on Facebook."

LuAnn's eyes widened. "Do you think she put that horrible post on our page?"

"I don't know." Tess shook her head. "She could have been on there for many reasons." She folded her arms. "The thing is, she shouldn't have been on the computer at all."

"Yeah." LuAnn pursed her lips.

"Do you think she placed that order? She must have." Janice leaned her cheek into her hand. "Sad to think she would do that."

Brad stood next to the doorjamb. "One of you should talk to her."

Tess sighed. "I will. Maybe there's a reasonable explanation." She hoped so, but what explanation could there be? "I'll talk to her caseworker first. Get a little background, if she'll give it to me."

"She probably won't tell you much," LuAnn said. "But since Kylie is working here, she can give information relevant to her employment."

"Worth a try." Tess searched the web for the Hope Life Youth Services number as the others moved out of the office. Finding it, she picked up the phone and dialed. After a few rings she spoke to the receptionist.

"If you come right away, she can see you. She had a cancellation."

"Thank you. I'll be right there." Tess joined the group that had moved to the kitchen. "Do you guys mind holding down the fort for a bit?"

"We'll work on the rooms," Janice said.

Brad, holding a muffin in his hand, said goodbye, and he and Chad left.

Fifteen minutes later, Tess sat across the desk from Julie Williamson, the social worker handling Kylie's case. "Thank you for talking to me, Miss Williamson."

"I'm happy to." The woman in her thirties smiled. "And please, call me Julie."

"Thank you."

"I realize Kylie didn't have much—any—restaurant experience. It was so nice of you all to hire her." She pushed back a lock of her straight blonde hair.

"We were happy to. She's a very nice girl and seems eager to learn. I appreciate that."

"I noticed that about her too."

Tess fingered the chair's armrest. "I don't know if you heard, but we've had an incident at the inn."

Julie nodded. "I saw that on Facebook."

Tess's stomach clenched. "What, uh, did you see?"

"Oh, a terrible story about your cook. I don't believe most of the negative stuff I read on social media." She tilted her head. "I also follow your inn's page. I saw the prayer request that you all put up. I'm so sorry. That poor woman who got sick."

"Yes."

"Is she going to be okay?"

"We think so. We're hoping to visit her when she's strong enough." Tess leaned forward. "It looks like the soup was deliberately poisoned..."

"You want to know if Kylie has a criminal background. If she has done anything..." Julie raised her eyebrows. "I assure you, we don't send anyone into the workplace that we don't have every reason to believe is trustworthy." A tinge of irritation threaded her voice.

"I really like Kylie, but we need to rule out everyone who was there that morning."

"I get it, but I can't go into details about her history. I can tell you that she has no criminal background at all. No record. She was homeless when she came to us, but of course, that's not a crime."

Tess rubbed the back of her neck. She really wanted to believe the best of Kylie.

"I'd like to say one more thing." Julie's tone softened. "Sometimes kids who have been homeless have trouble trusting, so they hide who they really are. The attitude of I'll-hurt-you-before-you-hurt-me tends to color everything they do and say. I'm not saying I've seen this particularly in Kylie, but it's something to keep in mind."

What was this woman trying to tell her? Did she think Kylie was hiding who she really was? Tess wasn't sure. She stood and shook Julie's hand. "Thank you for your help. I really appreciate your time."

As she stepped out the door, Tess's phone buzzed. It was a text from LuAnn. *A new video has come up of Winnie. Come home.*

January 22, 1863

A midmorning powdering of snow fell outside the Riverfront House's kitchen window, like feathers lacing the banks of the Ohio. Inside, Prudence stoked the embers to ignite the wood in the stove, sending warmth throughout the room. She replaced the iron poker in its perch, then stirred the evening's lamb stew simmering in the cast-iron pot.

After filling a bowl with the stew and setting it and a cup of tea on a tray, Prudence headed down to the secret room for her most important task of the day—relieving Elizabeth, who was taking care of Angelica. As she entered the room, her thoughts tarried on the privilege she had to care for this and other freedom seekers. "It is more blessed to give than to receive," the Lord had said, and Prudence knew His words to be true. The souls she had helped truly gave more light to her life than she could hope to give back to them. She only wished she could do more. That her helping would make a real change to end the evil practice of slavery altogether.

"Good afternoon, Elizabeth, Angelica." She closed the door behind her.

Angelica sat up, and Prudence set the tray on her lap.

Elizabeth set her knitting down and turned bright eyes toward Prudence. "Angelica did well this night. She is a strong woman."

Prudence peered at Angelica sitting up against the pillows. She did appear stronger. Her eyelids no longer drooped. Her shoulders held their stature. Prudence took in her graceful beauty, which was coming through like a flower that pushed through winter's harshness. No wonder Angelica's Jermaine loved her.

Prudence glanced back at Elizabeth, who was waiting to take Angelica's dirty dish and cup back to the kitchen. "We have a special guest coming to the inn day after tomorrow, Judge Cyrus Graves from Pittsbugh."

"A judge? That is quite a privilege."

"He is known as a great supporter of the abolitionist cause. If only the Lord would send more honorable men like him to help us."

Angelica fell into a coughing fit. "I'm sorry," she said as it passed. "I swallowed the wrong way."

"Are you all right?" Elizabeth handed her the water cup.

Angelica nodded, but her chest still rose and fell rapidly. Prudence had learned to watch for signs of illness. "Thee is sure?"

"Yes."

Prudence turned back to Elizabeth. "He has a preference for a special soup. I left the recipe in the kitchen. Please prepare the meat tonight before thee goes home."

"Of course," Elizabeth said, and then with a smile at Angelica, she left.

As the door closed, Angelica shifted in her bed. "Excuse me. What kind of soup, may I ask? I do like recipes."

Prudence's face must have shown her confusion.

"I cooked for my mistress. I was in the house, worked with the children too. That's how I learned to read."

"It is such a blessing to be able to read." Prudence sat in the chair. "I will leave a Bible for thee."

Angelica's eyes iced over. "No. No Bible. My Jermaine, he loved the Good Book, as he called it. Loved your Jesus." Her lips tightened. "Now he is gone. What good did it do him?"

The chill in Angelica's eyes moved to Prudence's heart. Her own questions wavered close to the surface, yet she gave the young woman the most assurance she could muster. "I understand. We do not understand God's ways. I will leave thee a Bible anyway. Thee does not have to read it if thee does not care to."

"The recipe?" Angelica repeated her question.

Prudence smiled. "Oh, yes, of course. It is called Captain Sanderson's Pork and Navy Bean Soup. It is a pretty simple recipe, actually. Not that much different than my own pork stew. Apparently, the judge's son who died in the war preferred it, so he orders it to remember him."

"I wonder if I could copy it down."

"I shall bring it for thee."

"Thank you." Angelica's body relaxed, and she curled onto her side.

"Thee is getting stronger if thee is interested in cooking soup. I shall see if I can make preparations to get thee passage to the next stop tomorrow."

Angelica straightened again. "I..." She took in a breath. "I don't know. I may not be ready."

"It is safer for thee to leave."

But Angelica's gloom deepened rather than lightened.

CHAPTER TEN

As Tess drove home, she couldn't imagine what new video could have come up about Winnie. What more damage could someone want to do to Winnie's reputation? The inn's?

After parking in the freshly plowed parking lot, she crossed the path to the back door. With a sigh, she hung her coat and hat in the mudroom and moved to the kitchen where LuAnn and Janice sat at the table, their faces looking as wilted as winter leaves.

"That bad?" Tess asked as she sank into the chair next to LuAnn, who scooted her laptop for Tess to see. Since the Facebook page was shut down, the nasty propaganda now resided on the website winniethemurderer.com. The video link showed a grainy picture of Winnie at a store. The caption read: *You wanted evidence that Winnie Washington is the one who poisoned the soup at the Wayfarers Inn? Click here to see for yourself!* Tess took a deep breath, then clicked on the picture.

The timestamp read January 23, 9:22 a.m. Tess could clearly see that it was Winnie, even though the video was grainy. And she recognized the store.

"It's All Pro," she said.

Janice nodded and pointed back to the screen. Winnie walked up to a woman Tess didn't recognize. The woman handed her a small plastic bag filled with a brown substance. Then, without going to the cash register, Winnie handed her some money. She appeared to thank the woman, and then they parted. After that, the video restarted.

Tess massaged her neck. "Winnie never mentioned she went to All Pro. I can't believe…" She studied the video. "Who is she talking to? It's not Saffron."

"We were trying to figure that out," LuAnn said. "She doesn't have a name tag on, but I'm wondering…"

"If it's the woman Jack mentioned?" Janice asked. "The one who dries toadstools."

"Cheyenne, I think he said." Tess sat back in her chair.

At that moment, Winnie and Kylie entered the kitchen. "I don't give a fig if you don't like folding the towels. It's part of the job." Winnie's eyes narrowed at Kylie, who planted her feet in front of her boss.

"Fine." Kylie rolled her eyes. "I'll do it." Her voice sounded less than convincing.

"That means every morning we make sure clean towels are ready in the kitchen. Using dirty towels spreads germs. We don't want the health department after us. We didn't get that excellent rating for nothing."

"I said I'd do it." Kylie put on a smile to replace her pout. "Don't be mad."

Not taken in by Kylie's innocent act, Winnie peered over her glasses. "Get on back to work. I'll put these away. There's another load to fold in the basement. Go on."

Kylie slumped around and headed back out the kitchen door.

With a sigh, Winnie spoke to the Inn Crowd. "That girl. I'll make a good worker out of her if it kills me." She laughed.

"You're so good with her," Tess said.

"You really are." Janice smiled. "If only all young people had someone in their lives like you."

Winnie laughed nervously. "Now, now. I'm just doing what my grandmother did for me. Taught me the value of hard work. Not that I'm doing my job very well right now. You all are missing coffee cups. Ready for a late morning wake-up cup?" Her bright smile filled the room.

Ever since they met last year, Tess had admired Winnie's kindness, her willingness to serve others, and her amazing skill as a chef. The video troubled her. She couldn't figure out why Winnie had gone to All Pro or why she was talking to that woman. What she was buying?

One thing she knew, Winnie didn't have anything to do with the poisoning. The truth would show this. Tess would do whatever it took to get to the facts.

"Thanks, Winnie. We're fine." Tess peered at her friends.

Winnie inched backward. "You got quiet when I walked in. Weren't telling tales out of school about me, I hope."

"Have a seat." Tess pulled a chair from the table. "We were wondering..." Words wouldn't come, so she simply pointed to the screen and clicked the link.

Winnie gasped and watched the video with her hand over her mouth. Tess could see the regret in her eyes.

"Oh," she moaned. "You all have been so good to me. This is like home. Almost like home. The inn, the café—I'd never do anything to harm them. You don't think I...poisoned the soup, do you?"

Janice grasped Winnie's hands. "Of course we don't think that."

Tess shook her head. "We absolutely don't think you would ever do anything like that. We just wanted you to know about this video. And, well, who is that woman, Winnie?"

"That's Cheyenne. She works there, but I..."

"Why did you buy something from her and not through the store?" LuAnn asked.

"And what's in that bag?" Tess held her breath, waiting.

Before Winnie could answer, Janice interrupted. "You might want to see this." She pointed out the window. A police car was pulling into the parking lot. "It's Officer Randy Lewis."

"The one who was in your Sunday school class?" LuAnn asked.

"Yes. I sure love seeing those kids make good lives for themselves."

"What could he want?" Tess asked.

"Probably a warm place to drink a cup of coffee." Janice stood.

Within moments, a knock sounded on the back door. Tess moved to open it, but Janice beat her to it. "Randy." She greeted him. "How are you? Stopping by for some coffee? A muffin?"

They backtracked into the kitchen.

"That sounds great, Mrs. Eastman, but I'm good."

"How's your sweet wife doing?" Janice continued. "That baby coming soon?"

His eyes lit up. "I can't believe I'm going to be a dad. Sharon's doing great." He folded his hands. "I'm afraid I'm here on official business." He looked at Winnie, who was wiping the tile on the island.

The police had seen the same video. Of course they had. The person who posted it probably showed them.

"Mrs. Washington?" Officer Lewis stepped toward her.

"Yes."

"We have been given evidence that you bought certain ingredients from someone at All Pro Nutrition on the day of the poisoning. You were also in the café the morning of the incident."

Janice moved next to Winnie. "You think Winnie did this?"

"It's impossible," LuAnn added.

Tess strode forward. "She wouldn't do anything like this."

"We're not charging her with anything." He eyed the three women, then turned his attention to Winnie. "We just want to talk to you."

Winnie's brows furrowed. "Okay."

"We were made aware of a video of you buying something from All Pro Nutrition."

"Is it a crime to buy something at All Pro?" Tess asked.

He kept his focus on Winnie. "It's not." He pulled a computer tablet from its case and set it up on the island. He turned on the same video they had seen.

"We've seen this." Tess looked at him. "We discovered it online."

"Thank you. I still need Ms. Washington to make a positive identification."

He played the video. This time it seemed even more ominous.

"Yes, that's me," Winnie said when it finished.

"And that's All Pro Nutrition?"

"Yes."

"Can you identify this woman?"

Winnie glanced at Tess. "I don't want to get her in trouble. She didn't do anything wrong."

"If she didn't do anything wrong, there's nothing to worry about. We think she's an employee named Cheyenne. Is that right?"

"Yes, Cheyenne. I don't know her last name."

"Thank you." He rewound the video to the part where Winnie gave Cheyenne the money. "Did you give her money?"

"Yes, twenty dollars."

"And why didn't you go through the store's cash register?"

Winnie frowned. "It's something she makes. She doesn't normally sell it. Just doing me a favor."

"Now, we don't know what the foreign substance in the soup was yet. But we do know there was a recipe calling for—" He pulled a notepad from his pocket and flipped through it. "Five toadstools." His eyes hinted compassion as he looked at Winnie. "Our witness says she saw toadstools in the bag. It's not clear on the video."

Winnie's shoulders slumped.

Janice touched her arm. "What was it, Winnie? Some new cleaning product?"

"A beauty concoction?" Tess offered.

Winnie looked at the three women, then to the officer. "I did buy toadstools."

Chapter Eleven

"What?" Tess stepped forward.

"I'm sorry I didn't tell you." Winnie leaned against the island.

With a quick step, Janice moved to the table and pulled out a chair for her. "Sit down."

Winnie took a seat, the women gathering around her. The officer sat across from her. He didn't seem as shocked as Tess felt. But then, there had to be an explanation.

"You bought dried toadstools from the employee, Cheyenne," Officer Lewis stated. "Why?"

Winnie took a deep breath and released it. "I feel so foolish. I was putting laundry away the afternoon the ladies found that recipe. Kylie was in the kitchen prepping for breakfast the next morning."

"Kylie?" Officer Lewis asked.

"She's the kitchen help I'm training. She was there when they found the recipe, so she knew about it. And she brought up that Mason—"

"Mason?"

"Her boyfriend." Tess answered.

"—uses toadstools for rat killer at the Ski and Skate Shack—he's the new owner. More natural," she said. "Eco friendly."

"Rat killer?" LuAnn frowned. "Do we have a rat problem?"

Winnie shook her head. "We don't here, but at home, we've got this nasty intruder. Marcus and I have been trying to get rid of it for a month now. It evades traps, and I don't want to use conventional poison. I was about to call an exterminator, but I do hate to pay for someone to do what I can do myself. I can't stand the sound of that rat's tiny claws moving through my walls at night. Likes the warmth of the house, I guess. When Kylie mentioned toadstools worked for Mason, I thought I'd try it."

"So you reached out to him?" Officer Lewis asked.

"No, he stopped by, of course." She clucked her tongue softly. "Always hanging about. He's the one who told me about Cheyenne. I called her that night, and we set up a time for me to pick it up the next morning. While the soup was cooking, I went out and picked it up."

Tess knew Winnie was telling the truth. She simply wasn't the kind of person who would lie—much less poison someone. But she had to ask. "Why didn't you tell us?"

"I would have, but then when the soup was poisoned, I was afraid I'd get blamed." She gazed at the three women. "Not by you all, of course." She wrung her hands. "But I know it looks bad. I was the cook. I had toadstools—that recipe."

Officer Lewis sat back in his chair. "Mrs. Washington—"

"You can call me Winnie. How long have I known you?"

He smiled. "From what you're saying, you have a reasonable explanation for obtaining the poison—"

As he spoke, the back door opened, and in a moment, Marcus walked in. Spotting Winnie sitting at the table, he stalled, taking in the situation. "Grandma?"

"Everything's okay," Winnie said.

"Why is a policeman here?"

The officer stood to greet Marcus. "I'm Officer Randy Lewis. I don't think we've met. I've known your grandmother for years."

"He was in my Sunday school class," Janice piped up.

Officer Lewis turned back to Winnie. "Does this young man live with you?"

Winnie nodded, then her eyes flashed toward Marcus. "Oh! Marcus, tell the officer about that ornery rat we've been trying to kill."

"Uh...why?"

"We're trying to determine the reason Mrs. Washing—" Officer Lewis threw Winnie a polite glance. "Winnie bought the toadstools."

Marcus sighed and shook his head. "Her idea to get rid of the rat. I don't know why we can't get real rat poison. It would do the trick in one day."

Winnie's lips tightened. "This way is better for the environment, so I've been told. I thought it would be worth a try, but I never got the chance."

"You confirm the rat problem?" Officer Lewis asked Marcus. "And your grandmother told you she was going to buy toadstools for the purpose of killing rats?"

"One rat in particular."

Randy wrote something in his notebook and stood. Tess, LuAnn, Janice, and Winnie followed.

"I'll file this report," he said. "But my superiors will decide what to do."

"Is there..." Tess didn't know exactly what to ask. "Anything to worry about?"

She hoped his face would reveal complete confidence that Winnie would be cleared, but instead his lips formed a slight frown before forming a less-than-convincing smile. "No need to worry—ever. Right, Mrs. Eastman? That's what the Bible tells us."

Janice nodded unenthusiastically.

"But she was here when the incident happened, and she did possess a toxic substance."

Tess's heart raced. They had to find out who really did this. Too much was at stake—it seemed like everything was at stake. She returned her gaze to the officer.

His eyes lightened with a touch more hope. "We still don't know for sure the poison was toadstools, so until we know what actually poisoned the soup, just hang tight, okay?"

Tess had no intention of hanging tight.

The officer's radio buzzed. "I do have a couple more questions," he said, but before anyone could answer, a knock sounded on the back door, and Tess went to answer it. When she turned the knob, the door was slammed open by the wind.

"Clint. Hello," Tess said, letting him in.

"Boy that wind," he said breathlessly as he entered. Tess had been so entranced by the officer's interview of Winnie, she hadn't noticed the wind howling outside.

"Excuse me," Clint said, noticing the police officer. "Hello."

Officer Lewis nodded.

"I, uh, wanted to let you know a storm's coming," Clint continued. "They've been watching it but thought it would veer east of us. Looks like it changed direction and will hit Marietta tonight or tomorrow morning."

LuAnn glanced out the window. "It's really windy. And there are snow flurries."

Tess shivered. "How bad is it going to be?"

"Supposed to be forty-mile-per-hour winds. Lots of snow. Power outages."

Janice wrapped her sweater tighter around herself. "Maybe we should hook up the generator, just in case."

"I'd be happy to do that for you," Clint offered.

Tess tilted her head. "That would be kind of you, but shouldn't you be getting back to your farm?"

"I'll be fine. My truck can handle just about anything."

"Then I'd be grateful to take you up on your offer. I'll show you where it is." She looked at Officer Lewis. "But was there something else?"

He stepped forward. "First of all, how many toadstools did you buy? I'm not even sure how Cheyenne sells them. By the ounce? Or whole?"

Winnie sighed. "She sells them whole. I bought three of them. I thought if five would kill a person, surely three would take care of a rat. Mason thought so too."

Officer Lewis wrote something down in his notepad. "It would be helpful if we could examine the toadstools you bought, Winnie. I'm not confiscating them, but if you don't mind."

"'Course not." Winnie looked around. "After the poisoning, I didn't want anything to do with them, so I left them in my bag." She took a knapsack from the hook in the mudroom. "I put them in this pocket." She unzipped a pocket and reached her hand inside. As she felt around, her forehead bunched. "I thought I put them in here." She reached in another outside pocket and all through the bag. Finally, she stared at the group. "They're not there." She looked at Marcus.

"I didn't take it," he said. "I never touch your bag."

Officer Lewis frowned. "You don't know where it is?"

"No," Winnie said. "The toadstools are gone."

"This way," Tess said to Clint as she stepped down the stairs to the basement, Huck close on her heels. After Officer Lewis left with no toadstools to show for his trip, all Tess wanted to do was focus on finding out who had poisoned their soup. Not only were the inn's and Winnie's reputations at risk, now the police were investigating Winnie. What if they charged her with a crime? Tess couldn't bear the thought. This storm was interrupting her investigation.

"I'm sorry about your friend." Clint followed behind, his boots thudding on the wooden steps.

"There's no way she did it." Tess noticed an edge in her own voice, not meant for Clint.

"I'm sorry," Clint said. "I didn't mean to pry."

Tess took a breath. "I'm worried about her. She's a dear, godly, wise woman who deserves respect and trust. Not to be accused of something she didn't do."

They reached the bottom, and Tess moved to the storage room. "It's in here." She opened the door, and Huck trotted into the well-organized room.

"There." Clint noticed the generator first, tucked in a corner beneath a shelf of tools. "It's good that you thought to keep one handy. I was at the hardware store earlier. Got the last one for my place."

"It was Thorn's idea." Tess pushed her hands in her pockets against the cold basement air. "We've had great help with the inn."

"You care about the people who work for and with you, don't you?" Clint asked as he pulled the generator from its spot.

"We really do." Tess watched him working to maneuver the generator. "You seem to be handy with tools and, well, horses. I'm assuming you know what you're doing with the farm. How did you adjust from the business world to the farming world?"

Clint chuckled. "I was born on a farm. My family's from Dallas—the outskirts."

"I thought I detected an accent."

"Not a very big one anymore. I left when I turned eighteen. My parents were God-fearing people. Loved Jesus and their ranch and family. I didn't want any of it. Exchanged my tools for golf clubs." He looked at her for a moment, then scooted the generator toward the door. "I'm glad to be back to it though."

"I can imagine. I've enjoyed the simple routines of helping run this place." Tess guided him to the door leading to the loading area. Huck still scampered around her feet. She scooped him up and opened the door. "I know what you're thinking," she said to the pooch. "You're not getting out this time." She scratched his chest, growing fonder of the little guy every day, despite her initial resistance to letting another furry friend into her heart.

"Is the inlet box out here?" Clint asked.

Tess nodded toward the wall. "It's just around the corner there."

Clint nodded. "Great." He muscled the generator out the door and parked it, then turned back to Tess. "I know you've got plenty to do. You go on. I'll get it set, so all you have to do is turn her on if the power goes out."

"Maybe it won't."

"Let's hope it doesn't."

Tess folded her hands. "Thank you so much, Clint."

"No problem. Let me know if you need anything, okay?"

"We will."

As Tess headed toward the stairs, she noticed a clean load of towels waiting next to the dryer. Even when life's pressures seemed crushing, laundry persisted. She took a few minutes and folded the soft towels, letting her thoughts float into problem-solving mode. Her thoughts hadn't gotten far when Huck started sniffing the basket. As she neared the bottom, she saw what was interesting the dog's nose—a small plastic zipper bag. The zipper was closed, but the bag was empty, except for some brown, earthy-looking remnants.

CHAPTER TWELVE

The sound of "Great Is Thy Faithfulness" playing on the piano drifted to Tess as she trudged up the stairs from the basement. Tess always enjoyed Janice's music. She knew playing comforted her friend, as did the words to the songs. They comforted Tess too.

Reaching the top of the stairs, she found LuAnn standing next to the piano in the parlor as Janice played. Tess paused to rest in the moment, to trust that all their troubles were safe in God's faithful hands. When the song finished, she leaned on the piano.

"We need to have a powwow, don't you think?" she asked.

LuAnn nodded. "I agree."

"Is everything ready for the storm?"

"I think so," Janice answered. "I gave the guests extra blankets and candles."

"Clint has the generator ready in case we need it," Tess said. "We'll still have some lights and heat."

"I made sure the windows were all securely closed and the fireplaces had plenty of dry wood," LuAnn said.

"And Winnie prepared her hot chocolate mix in advance. If the power goes out, we'll still at least have the stove," Janice added.

"Sounds good." Tess's arms got a chill as the wind howled through the rafters. "Should we move upstairs? I have something to show you."

Janice stood. "Definitely. Let's go where it's private and comfy and we can talk."

"About poison and the police and a sick guest." Tess threw a mock smirk.

"Now, now. It'll all work out," LuAnn scolded with a smile. "Especially with the Inn Crowd on the case."

A few minutes later Tess sat in their common area on the fourth floor waiting for the others. She lit the fire that now crackled and popped, and Tom had seized the opportunity for a warm lap to cuddle on. Tess scratched around his ears to his delight. She relished the sense of home she felt even more in these rooms than the rest of the inn, but right now, her mind was focused. She needed to talk to LuAnn and Janice. Make a plan. Her shoulders released a touch of their anxiety when she heard both her friends' doors open and close.

"So," she blurted before the others had completely settled in. "The most important thing we need to talk about is—"

"Clearing Winnie," Janice jumped in. "We have to figure out how to do that before the police charge her."

"By finding out who poisoned our soup." Tess accentuated her words with a soft pound on the couch, causing Tom to shift his position with an irritated glare. Her frustration had been growing all day. She drew a calming breath. "I don't know why someone is doing all this."

LuAnn opened her notebook and pulled a pen from behind her ear. "What are we going to do?"

"First, I want to show you something." Tess carefully picked up the bag she and Huck had found from where she had set it on the lampstand next to her chair.

"A plastic bag?" LuAnn asked.

Tess passed it to her. "I found it in the laundry room."

LuAnn examined it. "It was zipped?" She passed it to Janice.

"Yes."

"What's that stuff inside?" Janice asked as she tucked her feet beneath her. "It's not . . ."

"I think this was the bag that contained the toadstools." Tess exhaled. "I don't know how it got downstairs."

"Whoever put them in the soup went downstairs?" LuAnn asked.

"It was in the laundry basket," Tess added. "Maybe the person accidentally dropped it in there."

Janice leaned her head against the sofa cushion. "Or it could have been wrapped up in one of the sheets or towels and fell out into the basket when we loaded the washer."

"Whoever did it may have been rushed, or . . ." Tess pointed at Huck who was circling on the floor trying to get comfortable.

"Maybe Huck found the empty baggie," Janice finished their thought.

"He is known to get into things and places he's not supposed to." Tess received the bag back from Janice and examined it again. "Look." She pointed to a canine-tooth-sized puncture mark.

"So, it's been dragged by him all over who knows where," LuAnn commented. "I doubt the police could get any fingerprints from it."

"We should probably give it to Randy anyway," Janice said.

"Yes," LuAnn agreed. "He'll want to know where it turned up."

Tess set the bag back on the lampstand. "Now, we have the issue of Kylie being on the computer when that order was placed."

"But why would someone want to poison Bonnie?" LuAnn wrapped an afghan around her shoulders and moved closer to the fire.

"The only thing I can think of," Janice said, "is they wanted to stop her from doing the program."

"But she would simply do the show another time," Tess said. "It seems like if they wanted to stop the program about the judges, they would have found another way." She stared at the fire, pondering. "Unless we find out something new about Bonnie, I think we should assume it wasn't an attempt to hurt her."

LuAnn nodded. "More likely it was an attempt to hurt us or—in light of the flyers and website—Winnie."

Janice tilted her head. "You're right."

"Well, it seems to be working," LuAnn observed.

"True, sadly." Tess tapped her fingers on the armrest of her chair. "We don't have any idea how many toadstools were actually used in the soup. Did the person use all three? We're pretty sure whoever poisoned the soup knew about the recipe, and would know it said that five toadstools would be deadly. We need to find out more about what happens when someone ingests them."

"Now you're talking." Janice smiled.

LuAnn perked up. "We could talk to the botany professor at the college. I think they call it plant biology now."

"Perfect," Tess said. "Let's try to do that."

"I can call the college tomorrow," LuAnn offered. "See if he'll talk to us."

"Great. Thanks, Lu." Tess noticed LuAnn writing in her notebook, and was grateful for her careful attention to detail. "Back to Kylie," she said. "I'll plan on talking to her as soon as I can. We need to get the grocery order cleared up, and if nothing else, let her know it's not okay for her to be on the computer for any reason."

"She shouldn't have been in the office. How did she even get the door unlocked?" LuAnn asked.

Tess studied her friends. She could tell neither of them felt any more settled than she did. "I think these things are a good start, but we still don't know who put those flyers out."

"Too bad the printers was a dead end," Janice said.

"And we still have more questions than answers about the poisoning," LuAnn added. "There must be some way to get a clear picture of what happened. We're missing something."

Tess again watched the fire, her thoughts circling LuAnn's comment. "I've got an idea," she said, cautiously. "What if we reenact what happened that morning? Get with Winnie and go through everything that happened, step by step. I don't know what we'll find out..."

"It can't hurt," Janice said, then interrupted herself with a yawn. "Sorry, I'm getting tired."

"I think reenacting that morning is a brilliant idea," LuAnn agreed. "Maybe we can figure out the timeframe when the toadstools—or whatever it was—were put in." She massaged her temples. "I'm getting tired too."

"Should we call it a night?" Tess stood. "So far no power outages."

"We can be thankful for that." LuAnn stood also. "Do we have everything planned for the skate-a-thon?" she asked as they moved down the hallway.

"I know Winnie's got the soup planned out. She's also making her cinnamon rolls," Janice answered.

"What a great idea!" Tess opened her door. "We should try to get a few more sponsors too."

"Indeed," LuAnn agreed as she went into her room. "Good night."

Tess crawled into bed. Trees creaking in the wind as well as her mind wrestling with unanswered questions delayed her rest. Finally, after an hour or so, she fell into a shallow sleep.

Early the next morning, a loud crash jolted Tess awake, followed by a door slamming. She bolted up in her bed. A glance at the dark clock told her the power had gone out. She listened, expecting to hear LuAnn and Janice moving around, but they must have slept through the noise.

She slid to the side of her bed and felt with her toes for the slippers she kept there. She slipped them on, crossed to the door, took her robe from the hook on the door, and moved to the common room.

A peek out the window showed her what caused the noise. A tree branch had fallen on the trash cans, tipping them over. Bags had ripped, and trash was spread all around them. "Ugh." She moved back to her room to dress. She needed to go down and turn the generator on, anyway. She supposed it wouldn't be too hard to get that trash cleaned up. She thought better of asking for help. She'd let her friends sleep. She could handle this.

Five minutes later, she had donned jeans and a sweater, and with the flashlight on her phone lighting the way, she descended the stairs. When she got to the bottom step she noticed a light coming from the kitchen. Probably Winnie, coming early to start preparations for the day. But when she opened the kitchen door, she didn't see Winnie, but Kylie. After her conversation with her friends last night, and knowing that Kylie had been on the computer, a pang of anxiety hit Tess's stomach. Confrontation was never fun, but especially in this case, it was necessary. What had Jeffrey taught her about handling tough conversations? Be understanding, don't give them anything to react against, speak the truth in love. He may have gotten that last one from the Bible.

"Hi there." Tess tried to sound bright.

Kylie must not have been expecting to see anyone, because she jumped. "I didn't know you were down here." She twisted her ponytail. "Winnie wanted me here early. I guess we're going to be prepping food for the skate-a-thon."

"It's only a few days away."

"I'm excited to be a part of it." She tilted her head and smiled. "I love to skate, plus to help foster kids—close to my heart."

Were her eyes moistening? Tess's heart softened toward the girl, but she was hard to read. "We're all looking forward to the skate-a-thon. Even though there's a lot to do for it." She waved at the packed pantry. Winnie had been preparing. "And now with the storm."

"Yeah. That wind is crazy!"

"Did you hear that loud crash a few minutes ago?"

"I did. And then when I came in the wind slammed the door behind me."

"How did you get in, if Winnie's not here? The back door wasn't locked?"

Kylie's eyes widened. "Oh, when Winnie wants me here early, she gives me a key card, in case she's running late." She glanced around. "Like today. She's never this late though. Anyway, I give it back to her as soon as I see her, of course."

Kylie was an employee, not a random person. Tess could see the logic in Winnie's method. They wouldn't want Kylie waiting alone in the cold, dark parking lot.

"So, that crash was a tree branch that broke and knocked over the trash cans. Would you come help me pick up the trash?" Tess grabbed a large black trash bag from under the sink.

"Sure."

Tess led Kylie outside, got her started gathering up the scattered trash, then switched on the generator. It really was a matter of simply "turning her on." She smiled to herself, grateful for Clint's help, then joined Kylie.

As she picked up trash alongside the young woman, Tess pondered the best way to approach the issue of her using the computer. She didn't want to spark an argument. She really wasn't sure what Kylie's personality was. Was there a way to get the information—why Kylie asked about the poisonous ingredients—from the girl without being obvious? Before confronting her directly, Tess had another question.

"Kylie? Did you ever try chess, like I suggested?" She grinned. "Not that you have to, but..."

Kylie paused in picking up trash. "Oh, I'm sorry." Her face deflated as she seemed to be thinking of what to say. "I didn't tell you the truth. I do play chess. It wasn't Mason's app."

"Why didn't you tell me? I wouldn't have cared."

"My mom taught my sister and me to play. I haven't seen my sister in years, so chess has some painful memories connected to it. Plus, when I was younger, it wasn't so cool for girls to be into chess. Kind of a nerdy game, I guess." She shivered and started picking up the last few pieces of trash.

That was unexpected—a confession without prodding. The inactivity made Tess even colder than she already was. She joined Kylie finishing the chore, then they moved inside where she turned on the now-powered coffeemaker.

"So you thought I'd judge you for playing chess?"

"I guess I'm used to people judging me."

Tess wondered what had happened to Kylie. Homelessness couldn't have been easy. She hoped at some point the girl would be comfortable sharing more, but she didn't want to push. Plus, she still had to talk to her about the computer order. Now she felt even more reluctant to do that.

After pouring herself a cup, Tess leaned against the counter. "Would you like some coffee?" She reached for a mug from the mug tree.

"Thanks," Kylie said. "But I only drink tea, mostly green tea. For the antioxidants."

Didn't coffee have antioxidants too? "Okay, I'll get the water started." She set the kettle to boil while Kylie read a note from Winnie.

When the teakettle whistled, Tess poured the water into Kylie's mug and plopped a teabag in. She set it on the kitchen table. "Hey, Kylie, why don't you sit with me for a minute?"

"Winnie left me a list. I should probably start on it."

"You don't want to slack off on Winnie," Tess agreed. "But don't worry. I'll help you with the list. I was wondering something." She sat down and pushed a chair out for Kylie, who then joined her.

"This smells good!" She picked up her tea.

Tess took another swig of coffee. "So, the Saturday before the poisoning..."

Kylie's face grew somber.

"I was wondering, um, was there any difference in the routine?"

"I don't think so. Everything was normal, as far as I can remember."

"Well, I mean, did you do your normal duties?"

"Yep."

"Nothing different?"

"Nope."

This wasn't working. She'd try another angle. "Kylie, the Saturday before the poisoning…" She waited, hoping Kylie would take the hint. When she continued staring, Tess ventured. "Were you on the computer?"

A quiet gasp escaped Kylie's lips. She hung her head. "I did go on the computer. I'm sorry."

"How did you get into the office?"

"Winnie went downstairs for a few minutes. The office rug had bunched up. The door got stuck on it."

That rug did get bunched up sometimes. "So you decided to go in?"

"My phone died." She paused as if Tess should grab her meaning.

"I needed to check my Facebook messages."

"You wanted to talk to Mason?"

"I was waiting for a message from him. The door was open, so I snuck in."

"And the computer?"

"Winnie had been working on the grocery order, so it was still on. I mean, it was already past the password."

Tess's heart raced. She admitted to being on the computer. "And the order? Did you see the grocery order?"

"Yeah. It was on the screen."

"Did you, uh, add anything to it?"

Kylie's forehead crinkled in confusion. "No. Why would I?"

It didn't make sense. She admitted to being on the computer but nothing else? Why?

Kylie must have seen the concern on Tess's face. "Is everything okay?" Her eyes narrowed slightly as her thoughts seemed to land somewhere unpleasant. "Whatever you're trying to ask. Just ask."

"There was a note on the order, questioning about toadstools. Since you were on the computer, we wondered..."

"You already knew before you asked me. Why didn't you say so?"

"I was trying to understand."

"This is like what always happens to me. I think I have something good—different. And then I end up being judged."

"I'm not judging you. It's hard to understand, though. You were on the computer during the time the note was added."

"I can't believe this. You think I poisoned the soup." Her voice choked up. "I need this job. I wouldn't do anything like that."

Tess didn't want to hurt the girl's feelings, but someone added that note. It wasn't the three partners or Winnie. The only other person on the computer was Kylie.

While Tess was still thinking, Winnie blew in. "What's going on in here?" she asked, out of breath.

"She thinks I put some note on the order—about toadstools." Kylie's lower lip quivered. "They think I poisoned the soup."

Tess shook her head. "I didn't say that."

"Oh dear." Winnie donned an apron she'd brought from home. They still hadn't gotten their aprons back from the health inspector. Her smile drooped into a frown. "Was this the Saturday before the soup was poisoned?"

Tess nodded. "She admitted to being on the computer."

"You already knew," Kylie put in. "But it was only for a couple of minutes, and I promise I didn't add any note to the order."

Winnie's eyes narrowed. "You went into the office? On the computer?"

"I'm so sorry," Kylie pleaded. "I shouldn't have. I'll never do it again. But I didn't put that question on the order."

Winnie shook her head. "It was wrong of her to go into the office and on the computer, but she couldn't have been in there more than a couple of minutes. I had her busy all afternoon. Other than a couple of minutes when I ran to the basement to fetch kitchen towels, I was with her the whole time."

Kylie eyed Tess. "See."

"I don't think she could've been on the computer long enough," Winnie reiterated.

Tess went over what Chad had said. He had seen her name. Someone had been on Kylie's Facebook page. Her story didn't contradict Chad's. And it also matched what Winnie said. Tess sighed.

"I'm sorry, Kylie."

"I told you it wasn't me," Kylie said.

Tess shifted her stance to face the girl. "I needed to figure out who put that note on there. I'm sorry I assumed it was you."

"It's okay." Kylie smiled.

"It doesn't feel good to have someone make false assumptions about you."

"No, but it's okay. I can understand why I was the only logical person to have done it." She looked at Winnie. "Can we get to work on those cinnamon rolls?"

Winnie had started foraging through the pantry as Tess and Kylie spoke. Now she poked her head out. "We've got a problem," she said, her eyes widening.

"What is it?" Tess asked. "Are you okay?"

"No. I'm not."

CHAPTER THIRTEEN

W innie?" Tess asked.

"We're out of cinnamon!" Winnie exclaimed.

Tess placed a hand over her heart. "You scared me."

"What are you scared of?" LuAnn entered the kitchen and poured herself a cup of coffee. Janice followed.

Winnie released a worried breath. "We're out of cinnamon."

"Really?" Janice asked. "We usually have that large container."

"I used the last of it over Christmas."

"Can't we get you some more?" LuAnn took a sip of her coffee.

"I only use the best organic brand. I ordered it from the store where Marcus works, but the freeway's out down in Davisville because of the storm, so their delivery is delayed."

"No one else has it?"

Winnie shook her head. "That's why I was late this morning. I was calling all the markets in town—that and the fact that I couldn't get my car out of the driveway. The storm left two feet of snow. I almost fell down several times walking here."

"Winnie." Janice stepped closer to her. "Your knee. You shouldn't be walking on it so far."

"Especially on ice," Tess added.

"It's not that far." Winnie rubbed her leg. "It does hurt some, though."

Janice grabbed a chair and had her sit down.

"Anyway, no one had any of the good organic brand. I even double-checked our pantry. I can't believe I ran out. How am I going to make my cinnamon rolls for the skate-a-thon? I need to start prepping today, or I won't have time to make enough."

The women sat in silence. After a moment, their thinking was interrupted by Kylie, who had been chopping potatoes again, this time probably for Winnie's fresh morning potatoes.

"Did I hear that farmer guy say he was opening a store with gourmet foods and stuff?" Kylie tilted her head.

"That's right!" Tess smiled. "Good thinking, Kylie."

Kylie shrugged.

"Do you think he would have it?" Janice asked. "Isn't he just getting started?"

"He's been stocking up," Tess said. "He mentioned he wants to open as soon as he can. It's worth a try."

Tess took her phone out and found Clint's name.

"I hope he has it!" Winnie said as Tess called. "I can hardly bear the thought of using plain old cinnamon in my rolls."

The phone rang once, and Clint picked up. "Hey there, Tess."

A tinge of nervousness hit Tess when she heard his voice. "I, um ..." Suddenly asking for organic cinnamon in the middle of a storm seemed like a crazy request. "We were wondering if you, in your shop, have any cinnamon?"

"Organic," Winnie stage-whispered.

"Cinnamon? I have been stocking up on things. Got a shipment of spices in the other day, actually. It's still in the box."

"Winnie is making cinnamon rolls for the skate-a-thon. Do you know about that?"

"Can't say that I do." Tess could hear rustling on the other end of the phone like he was searching for the cinnamon.

"Oh, it's coming up on Sunday, and it's for foster kids. We're helping with food and publicity . . . and getting sponsors." Might as well ask since they were on the subject.

"That sounds like a worthy cause. I used to participate in charity golf tournaments during my business days."

"Really? My husband worked at a golf course. He organized many such events. I wonder—"

"Do you skate?" Clint interrupted.

"I'm not very good—well, I kind of am." A blush warmed her cheeks, but she continued. "I can even skate backwards."

"Very impressive." Clint chuckled. "I'd be happy to sponsor the skate-a-thon."

"We'll put you on the list then," Tess said. "Thank you."

"Oh, hey. I opened the box, and I've got cinnamon."

Tess smiled at her friends and gave a thumbs-up.

"Is it organic?" Winnie whispered even louder than last time.

Tess mouthed "okay" to Winnie, then returned to Clint. "Do you know if the cinnamon is organic?"

"Sure is. 'Poppy's Organic Ceylon Cinnamon.'"

"Hold on a second, Clint." Tess turned to Winnie. "It's Poppy's Organic Ceylon Cinnamon. Will that work?"

Winnie smiled for the first time Tess had seen that morning. "It's perfect."

"I'll bring it to you, okay?"

Tess took a breath. She hadn't considered that issue. If Winnie's car was stuck, theirs probably were too. They'd need the snow removal company to come clear the parking lot. "How are you going to get here?"

"My truck can handle pretty much anything. Leave it to me."

"That's so kind of you. Thank you."

"No problem. I'll get there soon as I can."

Tess hung up and sent a big grin to Winnie. "It's going to be okay."

Winnie smiled. "That's a relief. After breakfast we'll get started on the rolls." She moved to the counter where Kylie was chopping potatoes. "Looks good, but next time they need to be a little smaller."

Kylie frowned. "Okay, Winnie. I'm trying."

"I know. You're doing much better."

Tess could see the young woman was improving. The skills she was learning would serve her in the future. She wished Kylie could get a handle on that attitude that popped out every so often. As exacting as Winnie could be, she showed Kylie a lot of patience. Not all supervisors would be so understanding.

Winnie grabbed a bowl out of the cupboard and set it on the island. "Potato and egg scramble this morning."

LuAnn sidled up next to her. "One of my favorites. I'll set the table."

As she was talking, the phone at the desk rang, and Janice went to the desk to answer it.

"I'll help with the table," Tess said as she took silverware from the drawer.

After a couple of minutes, Janice returned. "Are we just going to set the harvest table for our guests?"

"Yes," said LuAnn. "Counting them and us, we need to set about a dozen places."

"I thought since the café's closed, we'd make it extra special for them. Do you like the snowflake folded napkins?" Janice picked up a white napkin from a stack on the table and handed it to LuAnn. "Would you like to help?"

LuAnn pulled up a chair.

"That call," Janice said as she folded, "was from Bonnie's assistant."

Tess, who had finished placing the plates and silverware on the table in the café, joined the snowflake folding. "News of our resident radio reporter?"

"Yes. His name's Jeremy Parker. He's coming to help with her story about the Civil War-era judges. They had planned on Bonnie coming first for research and then he would join her."

LuAnn watched Janice carefully and mimicked her movements. "Does he know she's in the hospital?"

"Yes, he does. He said she's going to be released in a couple of days."

Tess flipped her napkin over to arrange the folds. "We better go visit her today, then."

"We really should," Janice agreed.

"I wonder if we could help with the research too. We know the date he stayed here…"

"We could look in Prudence's journal," LuAnn offered. "I always love reading her words. So full of hope and perseverance. Never wavering from her faith. Let's finish these and go over to the museum. We can see the original that way." LuAnn finished a snowflake and grabbed another napkin.

"You're forgetting something." Tess pointed to the window.

"We can't drive anywhere until the driveway's plowed," Janice said. "I called the snow removal company after I talked to Jeremy. They're pretty backed up today."

"That's okay," LuAnn said. "We can use our copies of the journal and take a look. If we run across something we can't make out, we can call Maybelline."

LuAnn and Janice agreed, and after serving and eating breakfast, they sat at the kitchen table and opened their copies of Prudence's journal.

"Bonnie said her grandpa Graves stayed here in January of 1863," Tess said as she and the others turned to the month.

"What was the exact date?" Janice asked.

"January twenty-third," LuAnn answered.

Tess scanned the pages. "It looks like the river froze over that year too."

"I wonder if Prudence skated," Janice pondered.

The thought brought a smile to Tess's face. "She and her husband and little Moses skating on the river. What a lovely thought."

"On the same river where we're having a skate-a-thon for foster kids," Janice added. "In a way, we're both working for worthy causes, aren't we?"

Tess relished the connection to past faithful ones who lived and worked in the same town where she and her friends did. "Yes, but aren't we blessed that we don't have to risk our lives to help the kids? Just a little skating." She smiled.

"Indeed," Janice answered.

"Here, look at this," LuAnn, whose head had been buried in the journal, said. "From the day before the judge stayed at the inn."

A parcel came two nights ago. The precious girl's name is Angelica, and she is an angel—though perhaps a broken angel, if such a thing exists. She lay unconscious in our barn, nearly frozen. And more, she is with child. A meager wedding ring was on her thin finger. Alas, her husband did not reach those who could help, but instead was brutally forced back into servitude. I do not understand why Thee, Lord, allows such pain, yet, I strive to trust.

LuAnn closed her eyes as if visualizing the scene. "She must have escaped somehow and then crossed the river without any help. In an icy January like this one."

"I imagine her slipping and sliding across the river, carrying a child in her womb." Janice rested her chin on her hand.

"I wonder whatever happened to her husband," LuAnn said. "To taste freedom and then be sent back to bondage. I can't imagine."

"Look at this part." Tess pointed and read aloud, "'I do not understand why Thee, Lord, allows such pain...' She sounds more despairing than she ever has before."

"It must have been heartbreaking to watch so much suffering, especially for a kind heart like hers," LuAnn said.

Tess thought about the suffering in her own time. People all over the world endured more than she could imagine. A sorrowful pang nudged her. She'd suffered too. She thought about her friends. So had they. God's ways were hard to understand, probably for all people of all times. Someday, all would be made right, she knew. She prayed for faith in the meantime.

"This woman came a few days before the judge was there," LuAnn commented.

"Yes. What else does Prudence write?"

LuAnn continued to read.

More difficult still is knowing that a man so highly esteemed, an "honorable" judge, is the one who broke her poor soul. He falsified documents allowing wretched slave catchers to haul rightly freed slaves back to misery. Both this woman and her husband were victims, he giving himself so she and their child could flee. How many others has he hurt for his own worldly gain? Will justice ever come?

"What?" Tess sucked in a breath.

"'An honorable judge'?" Janice asked. "Could that be the one Bonnie's been talking about?"

"It could be," LuAnn answered. "Her famous abolitionist grandfather."

"If it is, she's totally misinformed about him." Janice eyed the page.

"Unless she was lying," Tess suggested.

LuAnn straightened her reading glasses. "I don't think she'd do a story about him being an honorable judge if she knew he was corrupt. What good would that do?"

"Maybe she's trying to cover up the truth?" Tess offered. She thought about the secret room, imagining Angelica cowering there. The terror she must have felt. The hatred toward those who treated her so unjustly. And her thoughts shifted to Bonnie. She didn't seem to be trying to cover anything up. She appeared to truly admire her great-great-great-great-grandfather. He'd been the honor of their family. "I think we should give her the benefit of the doubt. We have no reason not to. Besides, we don't know for sure that he's the judge Prudence is talking about."

"Well…" LuAnn looked skeptical. "It makes a pretty good case for it being Bonnie's grandfather when Prudence talks about a judge one day and we know he comes to the inn the next day. Still, we can find out more when we visit Bonnie. I'm so glad she's feeling better."

"Me too," Janice said.

"Telling her the truth about her grandfather—that's going to be hard to take, if she admires him as much as she seems to," Tess added.

Janice took out her phone and shot pictures of the pages. "So she'll believe us."

"Good idea." Tess studied the page. "Wait. What's this?" On the margin in small writing, Tess spotted words she hadn't noticed before.

I lay justice at the foot of the cross.

The women eyed each other.

"What does that mean?" Tess asked. "What justice?"

"Do you think she's talking about the girl's situation? Her husband maybe?" Janice suggested.

"But why write it in the margin and in such small print?" LuAnn asked. "It's got to have something to do with the judge."

"The more we know about him the better." Tess stood. "Maybe Bonnie can shed some light on it."

"We have a lot to talk to her about," Janice said. "Should we visit her today?"

"What do you think, LuAnn?"

"I'm meeting Brad here for lunch—if he can make it through the snow—so you two go ahead."

Janice nodded. "That sounds good. I need to be back by three. Stacy is bringing Larry by—if they can get out of their driveway."

"That should work," Tess agreed. "This all depends on if the parking lot gets cleared."

"Good point," Janice said. "Can't drive if our cars are closed in."

"And it's too slick to walk."

"Let's just hope the removal guys get here soon."

They picked up their copies of Prudence's journal and passed through the café toward the check-in desk.

"I'll meet you back here," Tess said to Janice, who had situated herself at the desk. But before she took a step upstairs, something outside the window made her gasp.

CHAPTER FOURTEEN

Was that a...?" Tess gaped at Janice.

"I think so."

LuAnn burst in from the kitchen where she had gone to help Winnie and Kylie clean up after breakfast. "Did you see that horse?"

"We did!" Tess answered.

Janice moved from around the desk. "A beautiful white one."

Tess opened the front door, and the three women stepped outside.

"Hello there, ladies!" Clint sat atop what looked like one of the horses Tess had seen when he'd given them a ride on the sleigh. He dismounted, reached in his pocket, and held out the longed-for item. "I brought your cinnamon."

"Yay!" Janice exclaimed.

Tess shook her head as she received the spice. "You rode here?"

"All my bragging about my truck handling anything..." He grinned. "Couldn't get her out of the driveway. I knew you needed the cinnamon, so I thought a morning ride was called for." He rubbed the horse's neck.

"You didn't have to do that," LuAnn said.

"But I'm glad he did!" Winnie had made her way outside. "I appreciate it." She received the spice from Tess and examined it. "This looks like good quality. Just what I needed." She smiled at Clint. "Thank you very much."

Clint tipped his hat.

"Would you like to come inside?" Tess asked. "Warm up before you head home?"

"I'd like that." He tied his horse to a tree and followed the ladies inside.

"Quite a storm last night," Clint said as they stepped through the inn toward the kitchen. "Did your power go out?"

"It did," Tess answered. "Thanks for your help with the generator. Saved us the trouble of doing it."

"No problem."

"I guess your shop is getting close to opening," LuAnn observed as the four reached the kitchen. "If you were stocked up with spices."

Winnie had already set out mugs for each of them and was heating up the hot chocolate.

"We're hoping to open by Valentine's Day. Got a lot to do still."

As he spoke, a rumbling sounded from outside the back door. Tess guessed the snow removal crew had arrived. She sighed in relief. They'd be able to visit Bonnie.

"We understand the hard work it takes to get an inn open." Janice sat down at the table.

"Yes, I'm enjoying it though. The store's going to be a lot of fun too."

Tess took a seat across from Janice, and Clint sat next to her.

"We found that—" Tess started to share her thoughts about marketing, but Clint's phone rang. She glanced at it, and saw the name Bonnie Bradshaw.

"Excuse me," he said, and moved to the café.

"Hey," Tess couldn't help but overhear Clint say. "How are you doing?" Pause. "I'm glad to hear that...That would be great...I'll see you then. Okay, bye."

Odd. Why was he talking to Bonnie? And was he going to see her later? What about? Her mind raced.

"Sorry about that," Clint said as he re-entered. Without sitting down he picked up his mug and emptied it. "I should be heading back."

Tess stood. "We're really grateful for the cinnamon."

The three women walked him outside to his horse.

"She sure is beautiful." Janice scratched between the horse's ears. "Thank you for bringing her. It's a treat to pet a horse."

Clint mounted. "No problem. Will you save me one of those cinnamon rolls?"

Tess smiled. "Of course."

They watched as he rode off.

"It was kind of him to bring it like that. The hero on a white horse." LuAnn grinned.

"It really was," Janice added. "He certainly went out of his way." She peered at Tess, also with a grin.

Tess shook off her friends' obvious meaning. "It was strange," she said. "I noticed that call he took was from Bonnie."

"Really?" LuAnn asked. "Why would he be talking to her?"

"I don't know," Tess responded. "He said he was going to meet her later."

"I can't imagine why," Janice added.

"Anyway." Tess moved to a different subject. "He mentioned playing in charity golf tournaments. That made me wonder if I could find Jeffrey's old files. He had a list of sponsors he would regularly ask. We could ask them about the skate-a-thon. What do you think?"

"Great," LuAnn said. "Do you know where to look for them?"

"I think so. I still have a lot of his business files on my laptop. I never got around to deleting them."

"It's worth looking," Janice added.

"Let's get back to work. It's almost eleven o'clock now," Tess said. "We need to go visit Bonnie."

As they stepped inside, the phone rang. Tess moved to the desk to answer. "Wayfarers Inn. Tess Wallace speaking."

"Yes, this is Inspector Hancock. I'm calling to let you know the results of the toxicology report."

Tess waved her friends to her. "Yes." Her heart raced.

"It was toadstools. We've confirmed that. There are many varieties. We're still identifying the exact type. Not something we often search for."

LuAnn and Janice must have seen the distress on Tess's face because their expressions mirrored her worry.

"The good news is since we know what the substance is, and since you got an excellent standing otherwise, you are free to open the café."

"Oh, that's wonderful news."

"We'll let you know what we find."

"Thank you," Tess said and hung up, then turned to her waiting friends. "The good news is we're open for business again. The bad news is it was toadstools."

"Ugh, I thought those toadstools were the culprit," LuAnn said. "But I hoped it wouldn't be. It means the toadstools Winnie bought—"

"And which were found by our sleuthing dog—" Janice put in.

"Were most likely what caused Bonnie to get sick." Tess finished the thought. "We really need to figure this out. Should we go to the botanist's today after we visit Bonnie?"

"I have to get back to watch Larry for Stacy, remember?" Janice said.

"How about you and I switch out?" LuAnn offered.

"That'll work," said Tess.

"Should we ask Brad to come along?" LuAnn asked. "He knows his way around the school pretty well since he's taught real estate classes there. Janice, could you drive your car to the hospital and then drop Tess off at the college? Then after lunch, Brad and I can meet her there."

"Of course." Janice threw LuAnn a grin. "It's always fun, and beneficial, to have your dapper gentleman come along."

"My dapper gentleman." LuAnn blushed. "I'm not sure I'd call him that. But I have to admit, he's a pretty good friend. To all of us."

Janice grinned. "A great friend, especially to you."

"We never know who God will bring into our lives, right?" Tess said.

"Or what adventure," LuAnn added. "Like this inn and the café. We have some good news to tell Winnie."

"Do you think she'll have the café opened by tomorrow?" Janice asked.

Tess chuckled. "If anyone can do it, Winnie can."

Sitting in the car with Janice on the way to the hospital, Tess yawned. "What a morning." The pre-dawn wake-up because of that loud crash from the storm was catching up with her.

"Yeah. A storm and a cinnamon crisis and a hero on a horse." Janice smiled.

"That storm. Thank goodness we have the generator."

"Yes." Janice adjusted the heater. "You were out in the storm picking up trash. Did you say Kylie helped you with it?"

"That's right." Tess's conversation with Kylie seemed so long ago. "We talked after we got inside."

"I was wondering," Janice said. "Did you ask her about the toadstool question on the order?"

Tess nodded. "She admitted to being on the computer, but—"

"She did? I thought Winnie made it pretty clear she wasn't supposed to be. Maybe she didn't understand the rule."

Tess appreciated her friend's willingness to give Kylie the benefit of the doubt, however misguided. "She admitted that she knew she wasn't supposed to be on the computer."

"Oh."

"But she didn't admit to putting that note on the order." Tess shook her head. "Also, Winnie said she was with her the whole afternoon other than a few minutes. I don't know what to make of it."

"Yeah, that's really strange," Janice said. "If it wasn't Kylie, then who? Also, if the poisoner used the toadstools Winnie got from the gal at All Pro Nutrition, why would they put that note on the order?"

"The order was placed before Winnie went to All Pro. Maybe they were checking around to find them."

"Could be." Janice turned onto the street for the hospital. "Honestly, I'm glad to hear she was with Winnie most of the time. I like Kylie."

"Me too. Even though she does have a smidge of an attitude at times."

"Oh yeah, and none of *us* ever cop an attitude?" Janice grinned.

Tess smirked.

"You're sure Bonnie's still at the hospital?" Janice asked.

"Yes, I called. She'll be released tomorrow, apparently."

"Poor woman. I feel so bad that she got sick at our café."

"At least it wasn't because of anything we did."

"True," Janice replied. "Are you ready? We have some unpleasant things to talk to her about."

Tess took a deep breath. "Yeah. Maybe we can end up being a blessing to her if we break the news about her grandfather gently."

"I like that, though I think our gift basket will help too."

"And the flowers."

A moment of silence passed, and Tess took out her phone. She hadn't checked the anti-Winnie site in a while—not wanting to face the negativity. With a sick feeling in her stomach, she opened the site and saw a post.

Talked to police officer. I happily handed over the evidence of the Wayfarers Inn cook who tried to murder their guest and I told him all I knew about what a horrible person the Wayfarers Inn cook is. Do you wonder where that betrayer Winnie Washington will spend the night tonight? Check the county jail.

Winnie in jail? Tess gasped but then checked the date and realized the post was from before Officer Lewis had talked to them.

"What are you reading?" Janice asked.

"That website." Tess frowned. "There's a post I hadn't seen. Before you freak out, it's from a few days ago." She read it aloud.

"Whoever's posting these things really has something against Winnie."

"I know. Did you notice how it says, 'that betrayer'? Sounds personal. It must be someone Winnie knows."

"But who?" Janice's voice was tinged with frustration as she pulled into the hospital's parking structure.

"We've got to find out."

Janice parked, and the two walked through the hospital's glass door. Like an assault, the pungent odor of disinfectant, institutional food, and hand sanitizer plunged Tess back in time to other hospital visits. The time in high school when she broke her ankle...when she delivered Jeff Jr. And there was that one night, a Saturday, in the Emergency Room when Jeffrey...

She stopped herself. She was not going to ruminate over *that* right now. Hanging back in the registration area while Janice inquired about Bonnie, Tess removed her hat and shoved it into her bulky bag. The modern room had a sweeping curvy counter. Neutral colors. Nothing cozy about it—opposite of the inn.

After a moment, Janice pivoted toward her. "Room 412."

Their boot heels clicked against the hard floor as they strode down the corridors.

"This is it." Tess halted in front of a door with 412 next to it. She knocked.

"Come in!" A voice from inside yelled over the sound of talking, like from a TV.

Tess poked her head in. "We're sorry to interrupt."

A pale-looking Bonnie quickly pushed the remote to turn off the TV and smiled. "Hi. How nice of you to come."

"We're glad to hear you're doing better." Tess pulled a chair next to the bed and sat down. Janice did the same.

"Yes, me too. That was some soup." She smiled weakly.

"We've been worried about you, praying, hoping you'll get better." Compassion shone from Janice's face. "We brought you flowers."

Bonnie tilted her head. "That's so kind. You really didn't have to. I'll be released tomorrow."

"That's great news."

"I'll be coming back to the inn, getting to work on that story. Jeremy will be joining me."

Tess set the basket on a counter next to a sink. "We got a call from him this morning."

"Good. It'll be a rush to get everything done, after losing so much time due to this illness." She took a drink of water from a clear plastic cup sitting next to her bed. "But I'm up for it. Being in a hospital is boring, and I'm aching to find out what happened to my grandfather. I have a suspicion, but I really want to investigate. I have this photo of Grandpa Graves with his wife and entourage—being a prominent judge, he traveled with a pretty large group of people. Anyway, he's at the inn in the photo. There's something strange about it though. There's a woman wearing an apron, looking like she works for the inn. Now, I know no one smiled in those old photos, but her face..." She paused, seeming to search for a word. "She seemed angry." She took another drink of water. "I found that photo and the purse in my grandmother's attic. I've been itching to investigate ever since. I'd love to show you the photo. Maybe you could give me some insight on it. I left it in my room at the inn. Wasn't expecting to be gone."

Tess felt her face warm. "I actually noticed the photo when I was cleaning your room. I'm sorry, the drawer was stuck open, and when I tried to shut it... The photo case was unfolded... I couldn't help but notice."

"I completely understand. I'm actually glad. Can you tell me anything about it?"

Tess nodded.

"The woman in the picture is someone we know very well," Janice put in. "As much as you can know someone who lived one hundred and fifty years ago."

"Her name was Prudence Willard," Tess said. "She worked at the inn, and she was also a volunteer in the Underground Railroad. Our inn—it was called the Riverfront House back then—was a stop."

"I'd heard something about that. That's so interesting. I've wondered if that's why my grandfather came here. He was known to be a strong supporter of the abolitionist movement. I'd sure love to find out more." She took a deep breath. "But that woman. Did she work in the kitchen? Maybe she's the one who poisoned him. Not everyone in Ohio supported the abolition of slavery. Some fiercely opposed it. Maybe she was actually part of the opposition. Maybe she wanted to stop such a powerful judge from helping escapees."

Tess took in a breath. Telling Bonnie what they'd found would be more difficult than she expected. She thought the best way was to be direct, but with compassion. She leaned forward. "Bonnie, do you know for sure the judge was poisoned?"

"No, they say it was a heart attack. But how do you explain that recipe? 'Five toadstools in this will kill him.' Sounds like a murder plot to me."

Tess nodded. "It really does, but we have Prudence Willard's journal."

"You do? I'd love to see it."

"Of course," Janice answered. "We'd be happy to show it to you. We have copies at the inn, and the original is at the museum."

"Thank you."

"Prudence was a godly woman," Janice said. "She wouldn't have poisoned the judge."

"She was also a Quaker," Tess added. "Violence went against everything she believed in."

Bonnie furrowed her brow. "You never know about people, though. I've learned that from doing so many radio stories about individuals. Sometimes they do things you would never expect."

Tess didn't want to argue about Prudence's virtue. She'd let Bonnie read the journal. She would come to her own conclusions.

"There's something else we need to tell you." Tess needed the conversation to shift toward the judge's character.

"Yes?"

"The purse and your story about the judge sparked our interest...."

"Also, we wanted to help you research if we could," Janice added.

"We looked up the date you mentioned he was at the inn in Prudence's journal. We found—"

Before she could finish, a knock sounded at the door. "May I come in?"

CHAPTER FIFTEEN

January 23, 1863

Prudence smoothed a quilt over the bed in one of the inn's rooms. She placed a chocolate on the down pillow, reserved only for the most important guests. The honorable judge had arrived late last night. When he checked in, Prudence thanked him for his support of the cause. He said he only wished he could do more. So did she. If only there were more righteous men willing to fight for those unable to help themselves. She prayed, once again, for justice in this worldly kingdom, for peace in her own heart. With a final glance around the room, she opened the door. Footsteps sounded in the hallway, but by the time she looked, the person was gone. A guest must have slipped into his room.

She finished her chores and went to the kitchen where the pork and bean soup simmered, its aroma filling the inn. She filled a bowl for Angelica, and a cup of water, placed them on a tray, and headed to the secret room. She had hoped her "parcel" would be able to leave by now, but yesterday when she had delivered her meal—along with the soup recipe which Angelica insisted on copying herself—the young woman's recovery had stalled, even reversed. Prudence prayed the child within her fared well.

When she arrived, Angelica was alone, resting in her bed. She seemed out of breath.

"How is thee?"

Angelica's chest rose and fell more rapidly than Prudence had seen.

"I've been waiting for you to come, Miss Prudence. Ever since I heard that judge's name—"

"Judge Graves?"

Angelica cringed. "Yes. A plan came to me the first moment I heard he was comin' here. The plan's been stirring in my mind, bubbling like that soup." Her eyes pierced Prudence's. "Him coming here's a sign. Do you see? God brought him here, so we could make him pay for what he done to me and my Jermaine."

"I do not know what thee is talking about."

"The judge." Angelica's eyes widened. "I told you about the great injustice done to Jermaine and me. It was because of Judge Graves. We had our papers. Abolitionists paid for our freedom, but he signed us over to the bounty hunters." Her hand formed a fist. "It's his fault."

"But I thought…he is an abolitionist."

"He is a liar. He sure enough gets paid by the bounty hunters to authorize them taking slaves back to their own-ers—even the ones whose freedom's been bought." Her jaw clenched. "He did that to me and Jermaine." She rubbed her stomach. "Now we have a chance for justice. I have a plan, Prudence. We can give him justice. You have to help me."

"Angelica, I cannot do that. Only God or the law can mete out justice."

"God? The law?" Angelica grasped Prudence's arm. "It's up to us! No justice will come unless we do something. Why else would God bring him here?"

Prudence did not know what to think, but one thing she knew. She believed Angelica. No one ever appeared sincerer than this young woman. The image of scores, maybe hundreds of others, who had fought their way to the Free State of Pennsylvania only to be sent back in shackles to a desperate life? But what was Angelica suggesting? What could she do?

"I've heard of abolitionists poisoning rebels. Even talked to one once." Her eyes rounded large. "We could do it, Prudence."

Prudence fought the doubt this desperate woman's words quickened. All the waking hours she'd prayed for the suffering of slavery to end. The prayer meetings, the church services, the nights alone on her knees. Did the Prince of Peace even hear?

Angelica leaned forward. "Justice for the judge will not come by anyone else. It is up to me." Her muscles tensed. "To us. It is the right thing to do. It is!" Her exhausted voice grated, and she relaxed back into the pillow, holding her belly.

"Be still."

Angelica pushed herself forward again. "Promise me. Please. We have to do something. He's here."

"I make thee no promise, but I will...think on it."

Angelica squirmed in her bed, reaching for something. Then she retrieved an envelope. She took Prudence's hand in hers. "The abolitionist I spoke of gave this to me." She handed it to Prudence. The envelope was lumpy, and Prudence turned it over before peeking inside. She cast a questioning look at Angelica.

"Dried toadstools. Five of them," Angelica said. "Drop them in his serving. No one else will be hurt. He will get sick and die, and no one will know it was you, but you will know you got justice for my Jermaine." She rubbed her belly. "For us."

Prudence placed the envelope in her pocket, then pulled up the chair and sat with Angelica until she fell asleep.

Clint?" Tess stood.

"Oh, hey, ladies," Clint said as he slipped inside the room. "I'm sorry to interrupt." He looked at Bonnie. "Should I come back later?"

Bonnie glanced at Tess and Janice. "Are we almost done?"

Not really. Tess didn't want to share the news about Bonnie's grandfather with Clint in the room. "Uh..."

With a nod, Bonnie waved Clint in. "It'll just be a few more minutes. I'm eager to talk to you."

"Thank you. Are you sure? I can come back."

"That might be best," Tess asserted.

Bonnie's brows bunched, but Clint smiled graciously.

"No problem. I'll come back in, say, twenty minutes?"

Tess nodded and sent him a grateful smile as he slipped back out the door. He carried a briefcase.

Bonnie looked at Tess and Janice. "What were you going to tell me about that woman's journal?"

Tess refocused her thoughts. "Your grandpa Graves may not have been the abolitionist he seemed."

"What do you mean? We have records of him being a judge in Pittsburgh. His gravestone says 'Friend of Runaway Slaves.' Plus, my grandmother heard stories from her grandmother about Grandpa Graves. I have it on pretty good authority that he was an abolitionist."

"Sometimes people aren't as they seem." Janice repeated Tess's words.

"We found a few pages in Prudence's journal. They say he falsified papers, so the bounty hunters could capture former slaves—even those who had bought their freedom legally."

"That's not possible," Bonnie insisted.

"I took a picture of the pages from the journal." Janice stepped forward and handed her phone to Bonnie. "When you get back to the inn, you can see them for yourself."

Concern crept over Bonnie's face as she read. Finally, she looked up. "This is very interesting. Not what I was expecting to find, I admit." Her expression hardened. "But I'll need more than a page from this woman to prove your allegations are true." She gave the phone back to Janice.

Tess folded her hands. "We understand. We wanted to let you know what we found. I'm sure it's hard to hear."

Bonnie nodded. "Any doubt about the integrity of a man I've admired for so long is disappointing—what would I tell my grandmother if this is true? But I'm not afraid to find the truth. If he really was corrupt, I'd rather know. But I'll need more evidence than this."

"Of course," Tess said. She really didn't think anything other than Prudence's word was needed, though she could understand why Bonnie wanted to be sure.

"Sometimes a story leads to places you never expected. That's part of the adventure of being a reporter. No different because it's about my relative." A strange hint of anxiety washed over her face. "I need the story to be the best I've ever done. This twist and the delay may put a wrench in my plan…" The machine next to Bonnie's bed suddenly rumbled, and the blood pressure cuff on her arm went into action. Bonnie exhaled wearily as she sank into the sheets. "Who would've thought toadstools could cause so much trouble—if that's what it was. Did you ever find out?"

"Yes, the police say it was toadstools," Tess said. "We should let you rest. I'm sorry we had to bring such unsettling news." She stood.

Janice followed and grabbed the goodie basket from the counter. "Oh, and we brought you this." She displayed it so Bonnie could view the treasures. "A *Guideposts* magazine, amazing lavender bath soaps, and yummy-smelling candles."

"You ladies are so sweet. Thank you for coming. And for your help. I have a lot of research to do when I come back tomorrow."

Tess and Janice angled out the door and headed down the hallway. Coming their way was Clint, carrying the briefcase. He stopped when they approached him.

"What a coincidence to bump into you here," he said.

"You're visiting Bonnie?" Tess asked. Why would he be visiting her? She couldn't puzzle it out.

"Yes, I heard she was doing a story here, and I have a business proposal for her. She wanted to meet here since she'll be so busy with the story once she gets back." He tilted his head and grinned. "I should probably get in there."

Clint's answer confused Tess even more. What kind of business proposal could he have? Was he trying to get her to promote the Butterfly B&B? The Inn Crowd had hoped she would at least give a shout-out to Wayfarers. Maybe he was more competitive than he let on.

"It's very kind of you to come see her," she said, hoping her skepticism didn't come through her tone.

"And it's always good to see you both," he replied.

"Thanks," Tess answered as he continued his trek down the hallway toward Bonnie's room.

Tess looked at Janice. "What was that all about?"

"I can't imagine what they're talking about." Janice started walking toward the elevator. "A business proposal for a radio reporter..."

"He's got a new business he's trying to promote. Must have something to do with that."

"Yep." Janice pushed the button for the elevator. "What do you think about Bonnie?"

"She's very gracious, considering she's here because of our soup. I half expected her to be angry with us. I don't know how I would react if the roles were reversed."

"I know. Very nice of her. I guess I wasn't expecting her to want more evidence."

"I know what you mean. It didn't even occur to me to not take her at her word." Tess sighed. "I wonder where Bonnie will find more evidence. I'll be interested to hear her story when it comes out." Before they reached the parking garage, Janice's phone rang. She checked the display, then showed it to Tess. The call was from Officer Randy Lewis.

They reached the car, and Janice unlocked it. They both slipped in.

Janice put the phone on speaker. "Hello?"

"Mrs. Eastman?" the officer's deep voice asked.

"Hello, Randy. How are you?" Tess could tell Janice was keeping her voice as light as possible as she pulled out of the garage and onto the street.

"I'm here too. It's Tess," she said. "If that's okay."

"Yes. This concerns you as well. I'm calling to let you know—I suppose you heard about the toxicology report. It being toadstools that poisoned the soup?"

"We do know about that," Janice said.

"I wanted to give you a heads-up. Since Winnie had possession of toadstools, and she was there at the time of the poisoning—"

As he said those last words, a car cut in front of Janice. Janice put on her brakes, but the icy conditions sent her car sliding toward a mound of snow on the shoulder. When the car came to a standstill, Janice put it into Park, closed her eyes, and took a deep breath. A police vehicle flashed by after the other car, which finally pulled over across the street from where Tess and Janice watched.

Tess put a hand over her heart. She turned to Janice, who was catching her breath.

"Is everything okay?" Officer Lewis asked through the phone that had fallen to the floor.

Tess moved it back to the space between her and Janice. "Yes. We're okay. Just had a little incident." She smiled nervously at Janice.

"Okay." He took an audible breath and hesitated. Finally, he continued, "As I was saying, I'm really sorry, but my boss wants us to start working toward a warrant for Winnie."

CHAPTER SIXTEEN

Janice's usually rosy cheeks paled at the officer's words. A bolt of anxiety hit Tess's gut.

"Thank you, Randy," Janice said. "I really appreciate that you let us know."

"No problem. Take care, okay?"

"Okay."

Janice hung up and looked at Tess. "I can't believe this."

"Me neither. It's getting out of control. Winnie didn't do it."

"Maybe the botanist will have some insight," Janice offered.

"Don't you mean the plant biologist?"

"I suppose, if that's what they call them now."

Tess nodded, then noticed something up ahead. "Do you see the woman in that car who the police are talking to?"

"Yeah."

"She looks familiar."

Janice leaned forward, studying the scene. "I don't know that I recognize her."

"I recognize that," Tess said. "She looks like the girl LuAnn and I saw at Marty's Print Shop. The hair, the scarf."

"Wow," Janice said. "I wonder why the police were chasing her."

"Who knows, but running from the police is never a good idea, I would think."

Janice looked at her watch. "I need to get back to the inn. Stacy and Larry will be there soon."

Tess glanced around, scoping their stuck-in-the-snow situation.

"I never asked you if you were okay," Janice said.

Tess's neck ached, but that could be from the bad news as easily as from their sudden stop. "I'm fine, but how are we going to get out of here?"

"Pray we can pull right out." Janice closed her eyes and turned the engine back on.

"Praying!"

Opening her eyes, Janice turned the steering wheel away from the snow and gently stepped on the gas. The wheels spun, and the car stayed in place. She put the car in Reverse and rocked it backward slightly, then back into Drive and tried again. The wheels spun with a whining sound once more. "Come on!"

The third time the tires somehow caught traction, and Janice was able to steer away from the snowdrift and back onto the road.

"You did it." Tess blew out the breath she was holding. "Now, to the college to meet LuAnn and Brad."

Fifteen minutes later, Tess was wandering through the beautiful, historic campus of Marietta College, surrounded by red brick buildings and leafless trees. Rather than sprawling green grass, blankets of snow covered the lawns. LuAnn and Brad walked beside her.

"It's always fun to visit this place," she said. "Don't you think?"

"I do," LuAnn agreed. "Brings back our own college days. The learning, the friendships—" She grinned at Tess.

"Long-lasting ones!" Tess smiled.

"Lifelong ones." LuAnn chuckled. "And the adventure of starting out in the world."

"I feel that way too."

"Me too," Brad said.

"It's a beautiful campus," Tess observed. "An awesome place to go to college. It's what university campuses should look like."

"It really is," Brad agreed.

They reached the end of a long brick walkway, salted to keep pedestrians from slipping, and came to a brick building with a slanted roof on one side and a bell tower on the other.

"Rickey Science Center," Brad said. "This is the place."

They stepped inside, and Tess shivered as a whoosh of heat hit her after the cold. She paused. "I need to tell you something," she said. "Not that we can do anything about it right now, but I know you'll want to know."

LuAnn's eyes widened. "What is it?"

"Janice got a call from Officer Lewis."

Both LuAnn and Brad frowned.

"What did he say?" Brad asked.

"They're close to getting a warrant for Winnie."

LuAnn moaned.

"The toxicology report must have pushed them in that direction," Brad conjectured.

"It makes all this investigating so important," LuAnn said.

"It sure does." Tess nodded. "We should get on with this. Hopefully we'll find some information to help us figure this thing out."

"Is the professor expecting us?" LuAnn asked.

"Yes. Doctor O'Neill is his name. I made an appointment for two o'clock."

"Do you know him?" LuAnn asked Brad.

"I actually did cross paths with him once," he answered. "During a lunch break, I sat with him at the student union. He's a little..."

"He's a little what?" Tess asked.

"Um, intense. You'll see what I mean." Brad raised his eyebrows as he grinned.

On the wall, they found the professor's office number and headed that way.

Coming to the door, Tess knocked, causing it to open, so she pushed it the rest of the way. A tall, lanky man with receding white hair sat at a desk writing something in a notebook.

"Excuse me?" Tess said. "We're here to see Dr. O'Neill."

"That would be me," he said without looking up. "Come in. Just one second."

Tess and the others walked through the door and waited in his white-walled office. Shelves with plants lined the wall behind him, bookshelves the others.

Dr. O'Neill finished whatever he was writing and stood up. "Mushrooms!" he said enthusiastically. "You want to know about mushrooms?"

Tess stepped forward. "Yes, well, toadstools, actually. We have a few questions."

"Same thing. What most people don't know is that what are commonly called toadstools are actually wild mushrooms." He moved from behind the desk. "You've come to the right place. I wouldn't say I'm an expert on fungi, but others do!"

Tess smiled. "We don't want to take too much of your time."

"I always have time to talk mushrooms with anyone interested," he said. "Just ask my wife."

Tess and the others chuckled.

"Come with me." He pushed past them and out the door.

Tess raised her eyebrows at LuAnn and Brad.

"Where is he taking us?" LuAnn whispered.

Tess shook her head and shrugged. "I don't know."

"I guess we'll find out when we get there," Brad offered.

They walked down the corridor to a door, and then moved outside to a square tucked between corners of the building. The space was filled by a large greenhouse with a spired section in the middle and a wing on one side.

The professor led the way through the glass door. A musty warmth hit Tess.

He turned to go down the wing. "Mushrooms right this way."

As they reached the middle of the wing they came to a section that was closed off with a solid door and walls—not glass. He opened it and held it for them to walk through. The glass roof was covered with what looked like puffy foil, so the only light was the sunshine creeping through the cracks in the foil. It was dim, but light enough to see what lined the walls all the way to the end of the section.

"It looks like a Dr. Seuss book," Tess commented.

LuAnn whistled. "It sure does."

Tall, thin mushrooms. Short, fat mushrooms. All different colors.

"Are they not beautiful?" Dr. O'Neill asked. "This is the place to talk about mushrooms, am I right?"

"Absolutely," Tess answered.

"What is it you want to know?" He took out a misting sprayer and started spraying the mushrooms. "They like moist, cool places. We usually grow them in the dark, so the heat doesn't get in. The greenhouse effect."

Tess nodded. She remembered something about that from her college science classes.

"They don't have chlorophyll, so the sun has no effect on them—other than the heat." He pointed to a four-foot long tray of orange mushrooms. "You see, they're not green. None of them are. They have no chloroplasts to collect the sunlight."

LuAnn was jotting notes in her notebook as fast as she could write. "So how do they get nourishment, if not from the sun?"

The professor stopped midspray and eyed LuAnn. "You were a star student, weren't you?"

Brad threw her an approving grin.

"I did like school," she said.

"They get their nourishment from the decaying organic matter they are grown in."

LuAnn nodded. "I see."

"So, we have a couple of questions," Tess said.

"Ask away," he said.

"We're wondering about lethal mushrooms."

"Ah, the amanita bisporigera, the destroying angel." He walked to the end of the mushroom section to another area marked with Danger: Poison signs. He pointed at, but didn't touch, a box of slender white mushrooms. "Deadly," he said. "Never eat or even touch these foul ladies. Gorgeous though, aren't they?"

"So, if someone ate them, would they die immediately?" Tess asked.

"No, they wouldn't feel the effects for five to twenty-four hours. That's one thing that makes it so deadly. She does her damage in silence, and by the time her victim realizes he or she is sick, it's too late."

Tess, LuAnn, and Brad exchanged glances.

"It must not have been the destroying angel in our soup," Tess said.

"What other toadstools—wild mushrooms—are poisonous?" Brad asked.

Dr. O'Neill sprayed the angels, then pointed to another section filled with a variety of different specimens. "All of these are toxic, but none as lethal as that lady."

"Are they found around here?" Tess asked.

"All of these are. Not this time of year, of course. They have to be grown specially." He pointed toward a section along the opposite wall. "Those over there are our international mushrooms."

"What would happen if someone ingested some of these?"

"Just about any of these would make a person very sick in a short time. They would vomit, grow instantly weak, salivate..."

Tess's mind flooded with possible scenarios. "Thank you so much, Professor. I think that answers about all of our questions." She turned to LuAnn and Brad. "Can you think of anything else?"

They shook their heads.

"I'm always happy to share these glorious creations. The health benefits of the simple mushroom you get at the store are immeasurable. They also help restore soil damaged by pollution, and I bet you don't know this." He picked up a short orange one with white bumps. "This little guy kills rats."

"Really?" LuAnn asked.

"Yes, really. A large amount, say fifteen caps, will kill humans too, but fewer than that usually just makes them very sick. Only takes a small amount to kill rats. Others have incredible medicinal uses." He patted his head. "I could go on all day."

"My mind is reeling with all the wonderful mushroom facts we've learned," Tess said. The others nodded in agreement. "But we really should get going."

They headed out of the greenhouse and back through the science center. The professor turned into his office. "Good-bye," he said. "Let me know if you have any more questions."

"We will." Tess shook his hand. The others did too, and they made their way back to Brad's SUV.

"That guy knows his mushrooms," Brad said as they climbed into his car.

"He really does," LuAnn agreed. "And he certainly is intense." She grinned at Brad.

Tess slid into the back seat. "He certainly loves his work. I guess everyone has a passion for something." As she fastened her seat belt, she noticed her empty stomach. "You'd think being surrounded by all that fungi would temper a person's appetite, but I'm actually pretty hungry. You guys already ate lunch though, didn't you?"

LuAnn eyed Brad and chuckled. "You know Winnie's on a mission to get the café open by tomorrow. She had us scrubbing the floors..."

"Making sure the firewood was stocked up," Brad put in. "Ambience is important, you know."

Tess's jaw dropped. "She put you to work, Brad?"

Brad smiled. "No worries. It feels good to stack a little firewood every so often."

"I'm glad she's keeping busy," Tess said. "Because Janice is going to be breaking the news to her about the call we got from Officer Lewis."

"If anyone can tell her with the perfect words and compassion, it's Janice." LuAnn sighed.

"Anyway, so you guys are probably hungry too. Should we go to Nacho Average Taco?"

"That's a great idea," LuAnn said. "We can ask the owner if she'd like to sponsor the skate-a-thon."

Ten minutes later, as Tess opened the glass door to the tiny restaurant, the rich aroma of tacos wrapped around her. She eyed the line waiting in front of the wide counter to order. "I can't believe how busy this place always is."

"We'd better grab a table." LuAnn scanned the room. "There."

Tess and Brad followed LuAnn to a small circular table near the window. Tess's chair screeched as she scooted it out and sat down.

"It is busy." Brad slid into his chair. "They have stellar tacos, though. It's worth battling the crowds."

"I wonder what they have today. I love how they change their menu every week."

Tess lifted the marbleized menu from next to the napkin holder. Scanning the dishes, she spotted the one she wanted. "Cajun fish tacos for me. You guys ready to order?"

"Yup," Brad said, standing. "Shall we?"

They left their coats to save their table and went to the counter. Chelsea, the owner, took their order. "Hey," she said. "Why don't you all have a seat? I'll bring your food."

"Thanks," LuAnn said. "That's so nice of you. And, we have a question to ask you before we leave. If you have a minute."

Chelsea scanned the busy restaurant, and Tess realized she may not have a moment to spare.

"I'll stop by if I get a moment," she said.

"Sounds good," LuAnn responded.

They returned to their table, and as they did, a woman in a blue flannel shirt and jeans stopped them.

"Um, hi." She flicked a blonde wavy lock from her pockmarked cheek. "You ladies are from the Wayfarers Inn. Right?"

Tess nodded. "Yes, we are."

"I'm Mason's mom. Jeannie, as in, 'I Dream of...'" She laughed nervously. "My mom used to sing that to me. Anyway, I was leaving when I saw you all, and I just, I want to say thank you." Her raspy voice slowed, as if pained. "His Shack—don't you love the name? Kind of hippie throwback, y'know? Anyway, it means so much to my boy. After he got out of prison, he had a hard time getting his life together. I wanted to thank you ladies for using his Shack for your skate-a-thon. The years he spent in foster care when he was a child didn't help." Moisture pooled in her eyes. "I made so many mistakes when he was young...I'm sorry. I didn't mean to babble on."

"Don't worry about it." Tess felt for the woman. "You're in his life now?"

"As much as he will let me be. I follow him on Facebook. He'll talk to me, which is progress. Still a long way to go."

"You're making strides," LuAnn said.

"That's all you can do," Brad added.

"And pray." Jeannie's hand moved to a cross necklace she wore. "I do that now."

"Yes, that too." Tess smiled.

"It was sure nice to meet you folks. And thank you again for using the Ski and Skate Shack."

"Actually," LuAnn said, "we're just helping with the skate-a-thon. That decision was made by the foster agency. You should really thank them..."

"Oh, yes, he did mention that, but he said if you hadn't put in a good word for him..."

LuAnn tilted her head. "I was happy to recommend him. He's gone out of his way to get as many pairs of skates as possible. I suspect it wasn't easy."

Jeannie beamed. "That's nice of you to say. I won't keep you any longer," she said, and left.

Tess and the others stared at each other for a moment, taking in what happened. While she pondered, Tess studied the menu, remembering that woman from Marty's Print Shop she'd seen copying the menus for this place. They'd seen her get pulled over by the police too. As she inspected the menu, she realized it looked familiar.

"Lu!" She held it in front of LuAnn's face. "Look at this."

"A menu?" she asked, but looking at it more closely, her eyes widened. "It's the same paper as the flyers." She gaped at Tess. "That means..."

"The woman we saw at Marty's. She could have also made the nasty flyers. And..." Tess's heart raced. "I don't think I mentioned that Janice and I saw her being pulled over by the police today. She seemed to be trying to get away from them when they finally cornered her right in front of us."

"Oh, my!"

Just then, Chelsea arrived with the tacos. "I can probably talk for a few minutes now." She set their plates down.

"Thanks," Tess said, grateful for her timing. "We wanted to ask you about sponsoring the skate-a-thon, but something more important has come up."

Chelsea tilted her head. "Everything okay?"

"Yes, but we were wondering." Tess held up the menu. "The woman who made these copies. Does she work here? She has dark blonde hair, wears a red scarf?"

Chelsea frowned. "She did work here, but she stopped showing up. I honestly don't know what happened to her."

Tess looked around and spotted a bulletin board. Sure enough, the mean-spirited flyer was pinned to it. She resisted the urge to bolt away from the conversation and tear it down. Instead, she pointed. "Someone's been putting up flyers accusing our cook of poisoning someone at Wayfarers."

"That's terrible. Reputation is so important. I'll take that down right away. I'm so sorry. I didn't know it was up there." Chelsea shook her head. "And you think since it's on the same paper as my menu, my former employee made the flyers?"

Tess nodded. "It's at least worth checking into."

"Lina Klein's her name. I'll call her right now." She took out her phone and dialed. In a moment, she hung up. "Number's no longer in service. Sorry."

"You've helped us more than you know," Tess said. "Thank you."

"No problem. I hope you find her." Chelsea pointed at the tacos waiting on the plates. "You better eat before your food gets cold. Oh, and put me down to sponsor the skate-a-thon. We'd be happy to."

"Great!" LuAnn answered. "Will do."

They finished the tacos, which lived up to their name of not average. As they strode out of the restaurant with a wave to Chelsea, LuAnn's phone rang.

"Oh, hi!" LuAnn answered.

A few seconds later, Tess's phone also rang. A male voice came through. "Uh, hey, Tess. I got your number from Kylie at the inn. I tried to call LuAnn, but it went to voice mail."

"Mason?"

"I'm afraid I have some bummer news. My Shack got broken into. The skates are gone."

CHAPTER SEVENTEEN

Tess stared at the phone, then put it back to her ear. "What?" Was Mason joking? If he was, she didn't think it was funny.

"It's true. Losers busted in last night. I'm so sorry."

"Did you let the foster agency know?"

"Yeah. I just thought you guys would want to know too."

"Can you get more skates? Order them? Borrow them?"

"The skate-a-thon needed so many, I already nabbed them from all over the place. I don't normally stock so many. I mean, I only got skates this winter because of the freeze."

Tess's stomach ached at this news. "Okay," she said. "You reported it to the police?"

"Uh, one of my employees did."

Of course he wouldn't want to talk to the police. With his record he'd want to stay as uninvolved as possible. "Let me know if you hear anything."

"Will do. Sorry again."

By the time she hung up, they had reached the car. Tess slid into the back seat. As Brad started the engine, LuAnn finished up her call.

"Good news." Her eyes beamed. "That was my contact at the foster agency. They have a hundred and forty-seven people signed up for the skate-a-thon. It's way more than they expected. Winnie's going to have to make a lot of cinnamon rolls."

Tess stared out the window, not wanting to tell them.

"What was your call about?" LuAnn asked.

Tess sighed. "It was Mason. He had some 'bummer' news."

"What is it?" LuAnn asked.

"His Shack was broken into."

"Oh no. Was anything stolen?"

"All the skates are gone. And apparently he had been gathering skates from any other shop he could."

"This is so unfortunate. Who would steal skates for a foster kid benefit?" Brad frowned.

"There's got to be something we can do," LuAnn said.

"I know." As worrisome as this was, Tess tried to stay positive. "Even though Mason said he had checked most stores, I think that's worth a try anyway."

"I'll start working on that today," LuAnn agreed.

"I'll help however I can," Brad said.

"Between the Inn Crowd and its honorary member"—Tess glanced at Brad—"I'm sure we'll figure something out."

"I agree," LuAnn said.

Twenty minutes later, Tess and LuAnn were sitting with Janice in their common area.

"How was your time with little Larry?" Tess asked.

Janice's face softened into a warm smile. "Such a sweet boy. I sure enjoy playing dinosaurs with him."

"And Stacy's doing well?"

"She is."

"We had a busy day." Janice leaned into the sofa.

"No doubt," LuAnn said. "And we still have work to do getting ready for the skate-a-thon."

"Winnie and Kylie have been working hard on the cinnamon rolls and soup ingredients," Janice said.

The ache Tess felt when telling LuAnn and Brad the sad news came back, but fortunately LuAnn spoke before she could.

"Mason's Shack got broken into. The skates are gone."

Janice gasped. "That's terrible. Does it mean the skate-a-thon's canceled?"

"Nope. We just have to find a solution." Tess smiled.

"Like what?" LuAnn's eyes held worry. "I've been trying to think of something."

"It will come to one of us."

"I like your positive attitude," Janice said. "Let's pray the answer comes soon!"

"Speaking of Mason..." Tess's mind still mulled over their encounter with Mason's mom. "Did Lu tell you we ran into his mom?"

Janice nodded. "She did. Interesting."

LuAnn wrapped her hands in the afghan on her lap. "There seems to be a lot we don't know about Mason."

"I feel sorry for him." Janice said. "But why did he mislead us about his family?"

Tess mentally scrolled through past conversations with him. "He said they 'had to move' because they were 'shafted.' But he didn't mention his jail time or the troubles that sent him to foster care—whatever they were."

"His mother seems to be trying to better her life," LuAnn said.

"And what about Mason's criminal record?" Tess asked. "Do you think his mom was telling the truth about that?"

"She seemed to be," Janice said. "I guess we can't know for sure since we don't know her."

Tess tapped her pen on her leg. "Don't forget, Mason was in the kitchen the morning of the poisoning. I didn't think much of it, since I had mentally ruled him out as a suspect, but ..."

"He had the opportunity to place the poison," LuAnn finished.

Janice sat back to let Huck snuggle next to her. "How could he have known about the recipe, though?"

"Kylie knew about it. Maybe she told him," Tess answered.

"A lot of things seem to point to Mason," LuAnn said.

Janice sighed. "He barely knows us. I don't get it."

"Yeah," Tess said. "That's the question. Maybe something from his high school days with you, LuAnn."

"Actually, I was thinking," LuAnn began. "I mean, I was curious about Mason. You know he said he went to Robert C. Byrd."

"Yeah."

LuAnn stood and moved to her room, then returned carrying a blue-and-green yearbook. "I dug this out."

"It's from the time Mason would have been there?" Janice asked.

"It is."

"Brilliant!"

Searching for Mason's class picture amongst the myriads of photos, Tess spotted something she wasn't expecting. "Is that?" She pointed to the page. "It's Kylie!"

Mason and Kylie sat on the back of a gray pickup— the same one he still drove. His arm hung around her, and she leaned her head against his chest.

"He said they hadn't known each other in high school. He said they met a few months ago."

After studying the picture, Janice sat back on the sofa. "Why would he lie about that? It doesn't make sense."

"It really doesn't." Tess rubbed her shoulder. "There must be some reason he lied. I'm starting to wonder about the skates."

"Me too," LuAnn agreed. "Maybe he stole them to sabotage the skate-a-thon."

"We just don't know why," Tess said.

"I don't think we're going to figure that out tonight." Janice sighed.

As they were finishing up their discussion, the bell on the front door rang.

"That's got to be Bonnie's assistant," LuAnn said. "I wondered when he would check in."

"Let's give the Mason issue more thought," Tess suggested. "Get back to it later? Maybe go talk to him?"

LuAnn and Janice agreed.

"We better go get Jeremy Parker checked in," Janice said, and the Inn Crowd headed down the stairs.

Waiting at the desk was a thin, dark-haired man with a short, professional haircut. He wore an overcoat and black jeans.

"Welcome to Wayfarers Inn," Tess said as she scooted behind the desk.

"Jeremy Parker. I talked to someone on the phone. I'm Bonnie Bradshaw's assistant."

Janice smiled. "You talked to me. We're so glad you made it through the snow. You'll find a cozy place to work here."

He looked around. "I can see that. Looks great." He sighed. "It was a long drive through the weather. But it's worth it for this story."

"About the Civil War–era judges?" LuAnn opened the reservation book.

He nodded. "Yeah. Bonnie probably didn't tell you, but our boss wants her to enter this story for an Edward R. Murrow Award." He unbuttoned his coat. "I have to say, I'm sorry she got sick, but it'll add to the story." He raised his eyebrows. "Sorry. Journalist thinking."

Tess didn't know how to respond to such a foreign mindset. "She's doing much better."

"You must think I'm terrible." He smiled as he handed LuAnn his ID. "I am truly glad she's better. It's the journalist instinct in me."

"Not at all," Janice said.

Jeremy gazed around the inn, seeming to take a closer look. "This is the place where her grandfather might have been murdered. So fascinating. I know she was looking to research those 'five toadstools.'"

LuAnn shook her head. "There's no evidence he was murdered."

"Personally, I think that woman in the photo poisoned him. Have you seen it?"

"We have," Janice answered.

"That look on her face. Of course, we'll need more evidence. That's why we're here. To uncover the truth. I love my job."

Tess considered explaining to him about Prudence and what they'd learned about the judge being corrupt but figured Bonnie could fill him in. Something else he said struck her. "Did you say Bonnie was going to research the toadstools?"

"Oh yes. She wanted to start there."

Tess met eyes with LuAnn and Janice. "It's all very interesting."

"We're happy to help any way we can," Janice offered.

"That's very kind of you."

LuAnn handed him his room key. "You're in Woodsmoke and Pine on the third floor. It's across the hall from Bonnie's room, Woodbine and Roses. Would you like help with your luggage?"

He patted his single carry-on sized bag. "No thanks."

With a smile and a nod, he strode up the stairs.

Tess and her friends looked at each other. "Bonnie's up for an award?" Tess asked. "And she's been researching toadstools."

"We have a lot to talk about." LuAnn grabbed her notebook. "I could use a cup of hot chocolate, though. Do you want to join me?"

"I need to check something in the office," Tess said. "Want to bring them in there?"

"Sure."

Even though they had the stolen-skates obstacle to overcome, Tess wanted to keep finding sponsors. Surely, they'd uncover a way to make it happen, and the more sponsors, the more foster kids they could help.

Tess unlocked the office door but before stepping in, she inspected the rug. Sure enough, there was a crease in it near the door. Kylie said the day she had used the computer the door had been stuck open by the rug. Tess could see how that could have happened. She straightened it and moved to the bookshelf.

Earlier, after using it in the office for some personal correspondence, Tess had put her laptop on the shelf in an enclosed cupboard. She retrieved it, set it on the desk, and opened to a file marked "Jeffrey."

Seeing his name brought a wave of longing. She missed him. It also brought a breath of gratitude for the years they walked life's path together. Right now, she was especially grateful for his organizational skills. She scrolled to a file marked Charity Golf Tournaments and found a document titled "Sponsors." "Thank you, Jeffrey," she whispered.

She skimmed the first column of names, then out of the corner of her eye she noticed an object on the floor. It was on the end of the rug that was closest to her. When she had straightened the rug, she must have exposed the object. She picked it up. A pen, with a glossy black top and a forest-green bottom, and on it was a logo: the letters PNR in white script. Tess had never seen it before. PNR?

Tess was still studying it as her friends came in with the hot chocolate. They pulled up chairs.

"Have you guys seen this pen?" Tess held it out for them to see.

They shook their heads.

"It's nice," Janice commented, as she handed Tess her hot chocolate.

"I found it under the rug. If it's not any of ours, how did it get in here?"

"Could it be Winnie's?"

"Possibly."

"What do you think PNR stands for?" LuAnn asked.

Then it came to Tess. "PNR. Public News Radio. Isn't that right?"

"Oh, that's right," LuAnn said.

"You think it's Bonnie's pen?" Janice asked. "What was she doing in here?"

Tess replayed her conversations with Kylie and Chad. "Kylie said she got in because the rug kept the door open."

"When she left, it could have stuck again," LuAnn said.

The others stared at her. Finally, Janice said, "Jeremy said Bonnie was researching toadstools."

"Maybe she wanted to ask the grocer if they had any. She saw the screen already open, and went for it," Tess said. "Do you think?"

"Think about what we learned from Dr. O'Neill," Tess commented.

"The mushroom doctor?" Janice asked. "I've never heard what you guys found out from him."

Tess exchanged a glance with LuAnn. "A lot about mushrooms." She smiled.

"It was interesting though, don't you think?" LuAnn asked.

"Actually, it was. He was definitely passionate about his fungi," Tess said. "The interesting thing was that the lethal kind, at least the one that's really lethal—"

LuAnn flipped through her notebook. "The destroying angel."

"It couldn't have been that one. It takes too long to show symptoms. Bonnie got sick immediately. He said it would take a lot more than three of the one she had to kill someone."

"That's good, right?" Janice asked. "The poison wasn't meant to kill Bonnie."

Tess's mind circled around the question. "Right, like we talked about before. They just wanted to get her sick." She paused to think.

LuAnn gazed at her. "I was thinking. Once when I was teaching, a girl in my American History class left to go to the bathroom. The bathroom was next to my classroom, and we could hear her throwing up. I went to check on her, and she told me she had bulimia."

Tess sent a silent query to LuAnn. Where was she was going with this?

"It turns out she was faking an eating disorder."

"Why?" Janice asked.

"Because people with severe mental illness get to be inpatients."

"Uh-huh." Tess slowly grasped her meaning. "For whatever reason, she thought being in the hospital—even the mental health ward—would be better than her home life? Is that what you mean?"

LuAnn nodded. "I'm wondering…"

"If Bonnie poisoned herself?" Tess peered at LuAnn.

"Why would someone do that?" Janice asked.

Tess pondered. "I hate to say it, but for the story? You heard what Jeremy said about the journalist mindset."

"I don't know." Janice shook her head. "She was pretty sick. I wouldn't put myself through that kind of yuck—for any reason."

Tess took a sip of her hot chocolate. "Maybe she misjudged how much to put in."

"Still seems farfetched," LuAnn commented.

"Desperation sometimes leads to all kinds of irrational behavior," Tess said.

LuAnn wrapped her hands around her mug. "Is she that desperate?"

"Maybe there's more to the need for a great story than just winning an award," Tess proposed. "Maybe her job is on the line. Anyway, I'll try talking to her again."

"Good thinking." Janice stood. "It must be hard living under so much pressure to create a compelling piece."

"Yes." LuAnn also stood and pushed her chair in. "I do respect her dedication."

"I do too," Tess responded. "But I'm glad we don't have that kind of constant pressure."

"Me too." Janice moved toward the door. "I left a load of linens downstairs. I'm going to get a little folding and ironing done."

"That's good thinking too," LuAnn said. "I'll help, if you like. And while we're working, we should be thinking about how to do a skate-a-thon without skates." She frowned. "I'm trying not to worry."

Janice tilted her head. "Me too," she repeated.

"And me," Tess agreed. "But in the meantime, I found Jeffrey's list of sponsors. I'm going to call them. No point in giving up too soon."

"That's right." LuAnn sent Tess a grateful smile. Tess knew how much this skate-a-thon meant to her friend—to all of them. But especially to LuAnn.

As the two women headed toward the door, Tess refocused on the list of sponsors. As she went down the list, one of the names jumped off the page.

CHAPTER EIGHTEEN

You're not going to believe what I found." Confusion and suspicion slid through Tess as she read the name over again. "Look," she said, pointing.

Janice and LuAnn returned to the desk and stood behind her, looking down at the computer screen.

"Clint Lowery?" Janice's eyes widened. "He was a sponsor for Jeffrey?"

LuAnn blinked and took a second look. "Did he ever say anything to you about knowing Jeffrey?"

Tess shook her head. "Never. I can't believe this."

Janice patted Tess's shoulder. "He comes across like a great guy. Was he trying to mislead us for some reason?"

Tess attempted to think of any reason why he would try to get to know his former associate's widow. She came up with nothing. "I don't get it."

"Maybe it didn't come up in the conversation," LuAnn suggested. "But still, it does seem like something a person would mention."

"I was beginning to think of him as a friend," Tess said. "Now I don't know what to think."

"Yeah," LuAnn added. "I'm wondering if he does want to sabotage Wayfarers."

"But why?" Janice asked.

"Maybe he had some grudge against Jeffrey. Maybe he wants his inn to be the most successful in Marietta. Maybe for some reason we don't know." Tess closed the files on her computer, then shut the laptop. "I'll call him tomorrow. Maybe there's a reasonable explanation."

"Let's hope so," Janice said. "Do you want to help us downstairs?"

"What a kind offer." Tess chuckled. "Sure. I'll help, but you know my ironing's not that great. I'll do the folding."

Darkness still prevailed when Tess's alarm woke her at six the next morning. Snuggled beneath the cushy softness of her quilt, her early morning fog-brain struggled to put two coherent thoughts together. Clint had not told them he knew Jeffrey. She'd call him today. What was going to happen to Winnie? She hadn't had a chance to talk to her since Janice told Winnie about their interaction with Officer Lewis. She stretched and shifted to throw her feet from the bed. Talking with Winnie was her number one priority.

An hour later, she found Winnie in the kitchen with cinnamon roll dough rolled out on wax paper on the kitchen counters. The café would reopen today. Winnie had gotten everything ready, like the Inn Crowd knew she would. Kylie stood at the stove stirring country sausage gravy.

"Good morning," Tess said as she entered. "It smells amazing in here."

Winnie smiled. "Biscuits and gravy for breakfast."

"One of my favorites." Tess's stomach gurgled in anticipation.

"Mine too."

"I see you're working on cinnamon rolls too. Are you going to bake them ahead of time?"

Winnie shook her head. "Oh, no. I'll freeze them until the morning of the skate-a-thon, and then let them rise and cook them up in batches, so they'll be nice and warm for the skaters."

Tess sent up a prayer that it would actually happen. "I can't wait."

Winnie frowned at her with mock sternness. "You'll have to."

Tess chuckled. "Is there anything I can do to help?"

"Of course. There's always something to do. Why don't you put the finished trays in the freezer? I made room."

Tess picked up a tray and slid it into the freezer. "You doing okay, Winnie?"

Winnie's brows creased. "I don't like the idea of going to jail for something I didn't do." She started slathering butter on one of the rolled-out rectangles.

"We're doing everything we can to try and find out what really happened."

Winnie looked at Tess. "I know. And you ladies are good at figuring things out. I'm trying not to worry." She took a deep breath and released it. "I'm grateful for the skate-a-thon keeping me busy."

Tess nodded.

"What also bothers me…" She wiped her hands on her apron. "Is the reputation of the inn…and me. Those flyers." She picked up the bottle of cinnamon.

Tess picked up the last tray and moved it to the freezer. "We're working on that too. We think that a woman who worked at Nacho Average Taco made them."

"I've never been there."

"You'd like it. Really good food." Tess smiled. "She doesn't work there anymore, but the owner was kind enough to give us her name. Lina Klein."

Winnie dropped the bottle of cinnamon onto the dough. "Did you say Lina Klein?"

"Do you know her?"

Winnie gaped at Tess. "I knew her very well many years ago."

Before Winnie could explain, the doorbell jingled. Tess looked at Winnie. "I want to hear more about this, but let me go check on the door. I'm not sure if anyone's at the desk."

Tess moved out of the kitchen. Across the parlor, she spotted Bonnie shuffling to the desk accompanied by Jeremy. LuAnn and Janice were making their way down the stairs.

"Hello, Bonnie," Tess said. "Jeremy."

"We're so glad you're back." LuAnn smiled.

Bonnie lifted her chin. "I am too. I had enough of that place." She nodded at Jeremy. "And I'm itching to get back to work."

"We're both looking forward to sinking our teeth into this story," he said.

Tess glanced at her friends, then to Bonnie. "Could I talk to you about something privately?"

"Oh, hey." Jeremy took the hint. "I'll take your bag upstairs. My room is right across from yours, okay?"

Bonnie nodded at Jeremy as he left, then tilted her head toward Tess. "What's up?"

Tess pulled the PNR pen from her pocket. "We wanted to give this back to you."

Bonnie tentatively took it. "You had to give it back to me in private?"

"We found it in the office," Tess said. "And we were wondering how it got there."

Bonnie narrowed her eyes. "I ... don't ... "

"Also," Janice jumped in, "someone added a question to the grocery order, and we've been scurrying around trying to figure out who did that."

"We're curious, since your pen was in there..." LuAnn trailed off.

"I'm sorry." Bonnie's cheeks flushed. "It was me." She folded her hands on the desk. "I came down to ask if you could ask your grocer if they sold toadstools or wild mushrooms. Maybe they have a health food section. I thought it would save me a trip to the markets around."

"Okay..." Tess said.

"When I got here, no one was around. I saw your help come out of the office. I saw the computer and went in to see if it was on. I wanted to google toadstools. I couldn't do it myself, because I didn't know your Wi-Fi password yet. Then I saw the order on the screen. I jumped on and asked the question myself. I figured I would tell you all the next time I saw you, but I forgot all about it."

Part of Tess was relieved it wasn't Kylie who put that note on the order.

"You were trying to research toadstools?" Tess asked.

"That's right. I know I should've waited to ask you to contact your grocer, but when I saw the order on the computer, I thought it would save time to ask myself."

"I guess I can understand that," said Tess. "But you understand, I'm sure, that we ask our guests not to go into areas that are off-limits to them."

"Oh, I do, and I apologize." Bonnie tilted her head. "And now I'm really looking forward to learning more about the woman in the picture."

"Prudence."

"Yes. You mentioned a journal?"

"Absolutely," Janice said. "You can borrow mine."

"Thank you. I'm hoping it will shed more light on what really happened to Grandpa Graves. I'm going to be looking for more historical evidence than just the journal, but it's a start." She looked at Janice. "I promise I'll take good care of it."

"I'll get it up to you. And no hurry. Keep it as long as you need it."

"Thank you. And again, I'm sorry about the order thing. Well, I'm going to head upstairs so I can get to work. Thanks, ladies."

As she moved upstairs, Bonnie's phone rang, and she dug it out of her pocket. "Hello, Clint. Yes, I did look that over. I've got some thoughts..."

Tess couldn't hear the rest of the conversation.

"Do you think Bonnie was telling the truth about the order?" she asked.

"Going into our office on the computer and writing a note on an order does seem a little...what's the word?" LuAnn narrowed her eyes.

"Bold?" Tess suggested. "Invasive? Audacious?"

"Yeah."

"Her reporter instincts took over." Janice opened the reservation book. "We've learned a lot about reporter instincts lately."

Tess snorted. "We sure have."

"I'm not sure what to think," LuAnn said.

Janice made a note in the book. "She seems like a nice woman. Should we give her the benefit of the doubt?"

"Well," Tess said, "I'm wondering how powerful those journalist instincts are. If she needs an incredible story to keep her job...I'm still not settled with that."

"Like that girl in my class," LuAnn put in. "It's not unheard of that people would harm themselves for personal gain."

"And we hear about journalists risking their lives all the time," Tess added.

Silence fell between them.

Janice closed the book. "It makes me sad to think she blames Prudence for her grandfather's death. That's not the Prudence we know."

"At least she's open-minded about wanting more evidence," LuAnn said. "She's not completely stuck on the idea that our Prudence did it."

"If he was poisoned," Tess added, "someone else must have done it."

"But who?" LuAnn asked.

"That woman Prudence was helping maybe." Janice shrugged. "We may never know."

"Now that we're talking about Prudence, I'm thinking about her journal," Tess said. "Remember that note she wrote, 'I lay justice at the foot of the cross'?"

"Yeah. I still can't figure it out," Janice answered.

"We need to investigate in the secret room." Tess waved toward the basement.

"Why?" LuAnn asked. "What would we look for?"

"I'm not sure." The mention of a cross associated with the secret room had stirred Tess's memory, but she couldn't nail it down specifically. "I'll know when I see it."

"Let's do it." Janice came out from behind the desk.

"We need to check out the secret room again, but I think we should do it later," Tess said.

"Why?" Janice asked.

"I asked Winnie about Lina Klein," Tess answered.

"You did?"

Tess nodded. "And she knows someone by that name. I didn't get to hear the story, because Bonnie and Jeremy came as I was asking her. We need to understand how Winnie knows the woman who's been trying to tarnish her reputation."

"So let's plan on investigating the secret room later," Janice suggested.

The three women walked into the kitchen where Winnie had finished the cinnamon roll prep and was helping Kylie wash dishes from breakfast.

"Hey again," Tess said as she entered. "If you have a minute, I'd love to hear about your association with Lina Klein."

Winnie dried her hands on a towel. "I've been waiting to tell you."

They sat around the kitchen table.

Winnie took a breath. "Lina Klein. That name brings back memories."

"When did you know her?" Tess asked.

"It was a summer cooking intensive in New Orleans a little over thirty years ago. She was my roommate. Healthy competition brewed between us, but for the most part we held each other up when the pressures of tests and homework beat us down. How I cherished that friendship. We both gave our lives to Jesus during that time. For a while we went to Bible studies together, but then a guy came along. She fell in love—Victor. That was his name. You know what?" Her gaze ascended to the ceiling, as if picturing him in her mind. "He wasn't that good looking!" She laughed. "But he had that thing, that charisma. Everyone wanted to be near him. The more she pined after him, the more a depression swept over her. I prayed for her, tried to talk to her..."

Tess broke in. "Didn't go well?"

"I just couldn't break through her pride. After that, her work suffered, but I did great. My grandmother had taught me to cook, so the intensive was easy for me. Lina resented that." Winnie sighed. "Part of the rift was my fault," she admitted. "When Victor expressed interest in me, I should've turned him away, for Lina's sake."

"You had feelings for him?" Tess asked.

"I really did. What's worse, we tried to hide it from her. When she found out, she was so angry. She dropped out of the intensive. I'll never forget what she said when she moved out of our apartment. 'I hate this school, and I hate you, Winnie. I hope I never lay eyes on you again.'"

"I'm so sorry," Janice said.

"I never forgot her." She sat in stillness for a moment. "I haven't seen her for all these years. She still must hold a grudge."

"Oh, Winnie," Janice said.

Tess reached out and squeezed Winnie's hand. "We'll just have to go talk to her."

At that moment Marcus rushed in the back door. "Grandma! You have to see this!"

CHAPTER NINETEEN

January 23, 1863

Moses swallowed his last spoonful of applesauce, and Prudence noted she would have to fetch another jar from the cellar before the day's end. She then put him down for his afternoon nap, trusting his care to Jason, and crossed the field to the inn.

After peeling what seemed like a thousand pounds of potatoes and making sure everything was set for dinner, Prudence moved into the saloon to wipe tables. Across the room, she spotted the tall, heavyset man she had checked in two nights before—the judge. What a different feeling she had toward him now.

His white hair was slicked over his scalp. He sported an expensive three-piece suit covered by a fur-lined overcoat. In his manicured hand he held a shiny new top hat. How many slaves could be saved with the cost of those clothes? How many slaves had he sentenced to misery to be able to afford them?

Elizabeth stood behind the desk. Seeing Prudence, she called her over. "Can you help the judge? He has a question."

Prudence turned to the judge. "Can I help thee?"

"A Quaker, are you?" He offered a glowing smile, as if his approval was the answer to her prayers. "We're going to use this area for a few minutes. It won't take long. You don't mind keeping other guests out, do you?"

Prudence shook her head.

The judge's wife, Prudence assumed, strolled up as he turned to her, a blonde woman, her hair in perfect rolls, probably arranged by a servant. Her dress could have been worn by Mary Todd Lincoln. "We need extra blankets." As she spoke she waved a small, intricately detailed purse with a star quilt pattern on it, reminding Prudence of the North Star. The woman sized up Prudence's simple dress, then drifted away like a bored cat.

The judge took out his pocket watch, the gold chain gleaming in the sunlight shining in through the window. Prudence felt sick at the indulgence.

As Prudence was about to fetch them more blankets, another man, shorter than the judge and wearing frayed trousers, entered, carrying a large case.

"You're late." The judge crossed the room and slapped the man on the back. "We need publicity. What are the papers going to put on their front page if not a picture of me?" He pointed to the man's case. "Come on, what're you waiting for? Get one of us right here in this lovely inn's saloon." He glanced around, his gaze landing on Prudence. "I have an idea! Wouldn't it be dandy if a highly respected judge had a picture made with the humble folks who run this place?" He nodded toward Prudence. "Come on over here, sweetheart."

Before she could make an excuse to leave, Prudence was having her picture made with the man who had betrayed Angelica and his family and friends. She longed to face the villain, accuse him in front of everyone, but would anyone believe her? It would only put her friend at risk. So, hardly suppressing a strong anger, she stood and stared for the long wait until the photographer was done.

Still sitting at the table in the kitchen, Tess gazed at the young man, whose eyes brimmed with anger. "What's wrong, Marcus?"

"They're saying the police have a warrant for Grandma's arrest." He held out his phone. He had it opened to the anti-Winnie web page. "And they talk about you ladies too."

"What?" Tess took his phone and looked at the screen. A warped photo of Winnie appeared on the page. Tess scrolled up. The headline said, "Stay Away from Wayfarers Inn." There was a picture of the inn along with an unflattering picture of Tess, LuAnn, and Janice. Under the photo, it said, "These women, the betrayer's bosses, must enjoy getting a single mom fired from her job. Thanks a lot."

Tess looked up from the screen. "She must have gone back to Nacho Average Taco, and Chelsea fired her."

"Yeah," LuAnn said.

"It wasn't our fault she was fired." Tess handed the phone back to Marcus. "Chelsea said she'd been missing work."

"Exactly," LuAnn agreed.

"We need to talk to her." Janice turned to Winnie. "Do you want to come with us?"

"I don't know how she'd react if I suddenly showed up after all these years. It might be better if I don't. Maybe only two of you should go. I need one of you at least to stay and help with the prep work."

"That makes sense," LuAnn said.

"I hope you'll convince her to come talk to me," Winnie added. "I would love that."

"Do we know where she lives?" Janice asked.

"In the old days we could use the phone book." LuAnn chuckled.

"Hard to find those anymore," Tess said. "Here." She pulled out her phone, and the others huddled around.

"This person-search site charges you." Janice shook her head. "They charge for everything these days."

Tess continued searching for one that didn't charge. "There." She put in Lina's name, and the address came right up.

"Okay, we have her address." Tess gazed at LuAnn and Janice. "Which of us should go?"

"Tess and Janice," Winnie answered. "I've got Kylie." She pointed at the girl, still scrubbing an apparently stubborn pan.

"But I still have a lot to do. With LuAnn here, I may get a two-for-one deal…in case that *friend* of hers stops by."

LuAnn smiled. "You put Brad to work last time. I'm sure he'd be happy to help if he can."

"What do you think?" Tess asked Janice.

"I like the idea." Janice looked at Winnie and LuAnn. "You'll pray for us?"

"Of course," Winnie said.

After getting changed, Tess had one more item on her to-do list before she and Janice could leave. Call Clint.

Sitting in her study, phone in hand, she didn't know why she was nervous. He had been very kind to her—bringing the cinnamon on a horse? Who does that kind of thing? And he seemed to show her special attention. She admitted, she didn't mind it too much. It cracked open a window she'd kept closed since Jeffrey died. She certainly wasn't ready for a relationship yet, but maybe someday. She took in a breath and released it. "Maybe," she whispered to herself.

But now, she had to figure out why Clint had not told her about knowing Jeffrey.

She scrolled through her contacts and pressed his name.

"Hey there, Tess," he answered. "What can I do you for?"

"Hi, I was calling…I want to thank you for bringing the cinnamon the other day. That was a lifesaver."

"No problem."

Enough stalling. "I wanted to ask you about something."

"Sure."

"I was going through some of my late husband's files, and I actually found your name on a list of sponsors for his golf tournaments. I—"

"You were trying to find information on me?" His voice was calm, but his question seemed more like a statement.

"No, no. I was looking for possible sponsors for the skate-a-thon."

"I see. So you're wondering why my name was on there?"

"Actually, yes, I was. Why didn't you tell me you knew Jeffrey? Especially when I even mentioned the golf tournaments the other day."

A long silence passed. "I'm sorry. I really am, but I can't talk about that right now."

"What do you mean?"

"I've got to go," he said. "I am sorry."

And he hung up.

Tess stared at her phone. Why wouldn't he explain himself? Why would he hang up like that? She decided to talk it over with Janice. She'd do her best thinking while talking to a friend.

It was after noon by the time they left.

Her conversation with Clint still played on her mind as Tess drove down Front Street toward Lina's. Janice must have read her thoughts.

"Did you ever call Clint to see why he didn't tell you he knew Jeffrey?"

"I did. Right before we left."

"What did he say?"

"He wouldn't answer my question. He hung up."

Janice turned toward Tess, incredulous. "He hung up?"

"Yeah. He said he couldn't talk about it right now."

"That's strange. What do you think about it?"

"I'm not sure, but I did sort of catch him off guard. Maybe he needs time to process whatever he has to tell me. At least I hope that's what it is, and not that he will never explain it to me."

"Yeah. Or..."

"Or something more troublesome." Tess sighed. "I have no way of knowing right now, so I suppose I should focus on the task at hand." She lifted her chin.

"I like that plan." Janice smiled. "How should we approach Lina?"

"I think we should simply state who we are and see what happens."

"Keep it simple," Janice responded. "Good approach. I was thinking about something. We saw the police pulling her over. You don't think she got arrested, do you? She might not, uh, be home."

"I thought of that too. But we know she got fired and had the opportunity to put up that nasty post. I don't think she's in jail."

"Good point."

Tess slowed as she searched for the house number. "It's 321. Do you see it?"

Janice peered out the window. "There's 304. Must be on the other side of the street."

Tess drove a little farther, then saw the number painted on the curb. She parked on the street. The small house had dark brown siding and white trim. Two trash cans sat on the side of the cleared driveway leading to a closed garage. Snow covered the walkway.

Tess opened her door. "We get to tromp through the snow."

The two women trudged down the snow-covered path. Reaching the front door, Tess noticed through the window that the TV was on. She spotted a sofa, but she couldn't tell if anyone was sitting on it. She turned to Janice. "Ready?"

"Yep."

Tess knocked. After a moment, the door opened.

A teen girl appeared. She had light brown hair and beautiful eyes. "Hi."

"Hi." Tess wondered if this was Lina's daughter. "Is Lina here?"

The girl took in a breath. "No, she's uh—"

Before she could answer, a woman came and stood next to her. "You asking for Lina?" She let out a scoffing laugh. "I'm her landlord. She doesn't live here anymore."

The girl hung her head, not meeting their eyes.

"Never paid her rent," the woman continued. "So I had to send her on her way. I'm letting Nat here stay for a couple of days, but she has to go too, eventually. Sorry to do it, but I got a mortgage to pay."

Tess nodded. "I understand. Sometimes you have to do hard things."

"Who are you?" the woman asked. "Debt collectors?"

"Oh no," Janice reassured her.

"I'm Tess Wallace, and this is Janice Eastman."

They shook the woman's hand.

"What are you all doing looking for Lina?"

Tess eyed the girl. "We're the owners of Wayfarers Inn and…" She paused, waiting to see if they would react.

The woman and the girl stared blankly. Tess was relieved they seemed to not know about the flyers and the website. Lina must have hidden her shady activities from them.

"Is Lina your mom?" Janice looked at the girl.

"Yeah."

Tess glanced at the woman, then back to the girl. "And your name is Nat?"

"Yes."

"Are you, uh, do you have a place to stay?" Tess asked.

"I'm eighteen now. I'm a good student, so I graduated early—took the GED, actually. I'm going to college in a few days for spring semester." Nat's face beamed.

Tess smiled. "That's a great achievement. Where are you going?"

"Marietta. It's a good college. And I get financial aid, so…"

"What will you be studying?" Janice asked.

"Oh, probably something in the sciences. I love test tubes and chemical reactions."

"Can't go wrong with the sciences," Tess said.

"Lots of jobs in that field." Janice gave her an encouraging smile.

Nat nodded. "I hope so."

"If you meet Dr. O'Neill—he's in the plant biology department—tell him Tess Wallace says hi. He's a pretty great guy—if you like mushrooms."

"Okay…" Nat said with a confused grin.

The woman gripped the door as if she were about to close it.

Tess stepped forward. "Before we go, do you know where we can find your mom?"

"I don't know where she's staying." A hint of sadness came over Nat's eyes. "On the street, maybe."

Tess's heart ached. She could tell by Janice's face hers did too.

"She likes to be on the computer," Nat continued. "She's on it like, all the time."

"So she uses a laptop?" Tess asked.

"Yeah, goes anywhere they have internet, but mostly the library. You might find her there."

"Thank you so much, Nat. We wish the best for you."

Nat's eyes brightened. She seemed grateful for positive interaction.

"Thanks. Bye."

Tess and Janice turned around and heard the door close behind them.

"Should we head over to the library?" Janice asked

They climbed into the car and buckled their seat belts.

"Absolutely," Tess said. "All Pro's on the way to the library though. Should we stop by and see if Cheyenne is back? It'd be nice to confirm what kind of toadstools she sold Winnie."

"And Mason uses them in his Shack, remember?"

"Right."

Tess drove across town to All Pro Nutrition, and in minutes she and Janice walked inside. No one stood at the counter, so they roamed around until Tess spotted a woman with brown curly hair talking to Saffron in the corner.

When Saffron saw them, she looked up and smiled. "Hey."

"Hi, Saffron," Janice said. "How are you?"

"I'm good. What's up?"

Tess studied the woman standing next to Saffron. Her nametag read "Cheyenne." Tess cheered on the inside. They finally caught up with her. She turned her gaze toward the woman. "We were actually looking for you."

"Oh, right," Saffron said. "You guys wanted to talk toadstools."

Cheyenne eyed Tess inquisitively. "What can I do for you?"

"Well, there's this video with Winnie Washington and you. She bought toadstools from you?" Tess asked.

"I showed her that stupid video." Saffron shook her head.

"Yeah, it's pretty awful," Cheyenne said.

"We were trying to figure out what kind of mushrooms you sold to Winnie, and apparently also to Mason from the Ski and Skate Shack," Tess said.

"Yeah, Mason gets them too," Cheyenne said. "They're called amanita mushrooms. They're not nearly as deadly as some others. I wouldn't want to keep those ones around, much less try to dry them."

"Like the destroying angel?" Tess ventured.

Cheyenne nodded. "Right. You know your mushrooms."

"I've been learning about them lately."

"The ones I use have the orange top with little white bumps."

"Yes," Tess said. "We're familiar with it."

Cheyenne's strawberry-blonde hair fell into her face, and she anchored it behind her ear. "I'm sorry about what happened. I don't know Winnie very well, but she seems nice."

"Thanks," Janice said.

"No problem. Let me know if I can help with anything else."

Tess and Janice said goodbye to Saffron and headed back to the car.

"We finally know the type of mushroom Winnie got," Janice said as she slid back into her seat.

"Yes." Tess put the keys in the ignition. "Now, when the full toxicology report comes back, if the toadstool in the soup doesn't match what Winnie got, we can clear her."

"That would be awesome."

"I doubt that'll happen, though." Tess backed out of the parking spot. "The person who did the poisoning probably got them out of the bag Winnie had. Still, it's good to know what type it was."

"On to the library?" Janice asked.

"You bet," Tess agreed. As she turned toward the library, her phone buzzed, notifying her of a text. "Will you see who that is?" she asked Janice.

Janice picked up the phone, looked at the display, and glanced at Tess.

"What's wrong?"

"It's from Clint. He says he's sorry about the uncomfortable conversation earlier, and he wants to talk to you."

Tess let out a breath.

"He says he wants to confess something to you."

CHAPTER TWENTY

Tess had spent enough time contemplating what Clint could possibly want to confess. Right now, as she turned onto Fifth Street toward the historic brick library, she focused on Lina. "I hope we find her there."

"Me too."

Tess pulled into the parking lot, and the two women walked along the tree-lined path toward the front door. Entering, Tess admired the library's stately décor.

"People knew how to make libraries back in the day," Janice commented.

"So true." Tess scanned the room. No sign of the blonde-haired woman she and Janice had seen pulled over the other day.

"She could be tucked away anywhere," Janice said.

Tess nodded. "Yeah, they have chairs scattered throughout the stacks. She could easily plug her laptop in and hide."

"I love this huge library, but it's not helping our search." Janice bunched her eyebrows.

"Let's be intentional about this," Tess said. "We'll start on one end and work our way through."

"Okay. Should we start in those stacks against the wall?"

"As good a place as any."

They had worked their way from US History to Decorative Arts when, across the room, over by the wall of wooden bookshelves that held the fiction section A-E, Tess saw the back of a woman sitting in a cluster of chairs. "Is that her?" She pointed as discreetly as possible.

Janice squinted. "It could be."

They headed toward her. As they got closer, they saw she had an open laptop balanced on her legs. She appeared to be working on something.

Tess stepped closer. It was the anti-Winnie website. Tess's heart dropped. How was she going to confront this person who was making her and her friends' lives so difficult? She gathered a breath for bravery.

Tess met eyes with Janice, who nodded. They sidled next to Lina.

"Hello," Tess said as gently as she could.

Lina didn't look up, apparently not hearing, and Tess noticed she had earbuds in.

"Lina?" Tess said more loudly.

This time, Lina's gaze flitted toward them, then moved back to her computer. Tess looked at Janice, who shrugged. The woman seemed to suddenly register that her name had been called and finally actually looked at Tess and Janice.

"You?" she said. She rushed to close her computer and shove it in her bag. "I'm not talking to you." Hugging her backpack to her chest, she pushed past them, heading toward the front door.

"Wait, Lina. Please," Tess called after her, quietly yet loud enough for her to hear.

She didn't stop, so Tess and Janice rushed after her, trying not to disturb the silence.

Lina had almost reached the big inner door when she tripped on a book that fell out of her backpack. Apparently, in her rush, she hadn't closed it all the way. Tess noticed that it was a cookbook. So sad that Lina had given up that dream. Lina stumbled, and as she tried to correct herself, bumped into a book cart. She was scrambling to get her stuff together when Tess and Janice reached her.

"Please, Lina," Janice began. "We're not here to hurt you or…"

Lina scowled. "I know who you are, and I don't want anything to do with you." She narrowed her eyes and clenched her fists.

"We know about the flyers, Lina. And the website."

Lina's face reddened, and Tess wondered if it was from anger or embarrassment. Maybe both.

"We're not here to accuse you." Janice's voice dripped with compassion. "We want to ask you to please take that website down—"

"And stop putting up the flyers."

Lina held her ground. "Why should I? Winnie poisoned your soup. People need to know."

Tess shook her head. "No, she didn't. She would never…"

"You don't know her like I do. She's a betrayer."

"She remembers you," Janice said. "She'd love to see you again."

Lina unclenched her fists. "Why would she want to do that?"

"She cares about you. She said she never forgot your friendship." Tess picked up one of her fallen books and handed it to her.

"You're just saying that to get me to stop the website." She straightened her shoulders. "I know Winnie did it."

Tess's mind spun, trying to figure out what to say. The woman seemed impossible to convince. After thirty years of hating Winnie, she guessed one conversation with her and Janice wouldn't change everything. Were they being naive?

As she pondered these things, the door near where they stood opened, and Nat walked in.

"Mama," Nat said as she took in the situation. "You're here." The girl stepped up to her mother, and Lina's eyes softened for a moment. Nat turned to Tess and Janice. "You found her."

"What?" Lina said. "You told them where I would be?"

"They came to the house," Nat said. "They're the owners of Wayfarers Inn."

"We want to talk to you. That's all," Janice said.

Lina ignored Janice's words and looked at her daughter. "They're here to coerce me into taking down my website."

"Your cooking site?"

"No, the one that's standing up for justice." Lina frowned, and Tess thought she detected a hint of guilt. "I didn't want to show you, because I wasn't sure you would understand, but it's the right thing to do."

"What are you talking about, Mama?"

"If you look up winniethemurderer.com, you'll see," Tess said.

Nat typed the site name into her phone. "Mama! This is awful. Why would you post things like this? Who is Winnie Washington? And what do you have against these ladies' inn?"

Lina's shoulders slumped under her daughter's disapproval. "I knew you wouldn't understand."

"Will you explain it to me?"

"I knew Winnie when we were young. She hurt me. She's not a good person."

"Oh, Mama, even if she's not a good person, do you really think she poisoned that soup?"

"She could have."

"She didn't," Janice put in.

Nat gazed back at the site. "And did these ladies get you fired?"

Lina nodded. "That much is true."

"Lina, we asked your boss about the flyers you had put up," Tess said. "She told us you weren't showing up for work."

"I had to find a new place to live. It's not easy being a single mom."

"Mama, you have to take that site down." Nat touched Lina's arm. "You're better than this."

Lina took a breath.

"And you haven't even heard the news. I was accepted at Marietta College. The semester starts soon. Why don't we spend some time together before I get buried in schoolwork?"

This news seemed to put a dent in Lina's wall. Her eyes moistened. "That would be nice."

"And, Mama." Nat held out the phone. "You'll take the website down? Make sure there are no more flyers around town?"

Lina hesitated a moment before turning to Tess and Janice. "Yes, I will."

Tess relaxed. "Thank you."

"Winnie really would love to see you," Janice said. "Maybe you could come stay at the inn for a night. On the house, of course." She smiled at her unintended pun.

Lina smiled for the first time. "You would do that? After all—" She shook her head and turned to her daughter. "Want to get something to eat?"

"I'd love to." Nat looked at Tess and Janice. "Thank you. I'm really glad I met you ladies."

"You know that offer's good for you too," Janice said.

"Definitely," Tess affirmed.

Tess and Janice watched mother and daughter walk together down the library's snow-laden walkway.

"That was kind of amazing," Tess said.

Janice nodded. "Sometimes God brings us moments to remind us why we're here."

Tess and Janice got home about four thirty, enough time for Tess to grab a snack and freshen up for her meeting with Clint. When the time arrived, she crossed the entryway to the café.

Clint sat at a table, facing the entrance. When he saw her, he straightened the sweater vest he wore and stood. "Hello, Tess. How are you doing?"

Tess went to the coffee bar and poured herself a cup of coffee. "Fine, thank you."

Clint let out a breath. "Okay."

"Would you like a cup of coffee?"

"No, thank you."

Tess crossed to the table and sat down across from him. "Clint, I..."

"I'm sorry. You have questions. I have answers, but"—he blew out a breath and sat back down—"I haven't been completely honest with you."

"I figured that out. I found the list of sponsors. You knew Jeffrey. You're not denying that, are you?"

"No, you're right. I'm so sorry I didn't tell you. I was going to, and then when I had the opportunity, I guess I didn't want you to think ill of me, and I didn't know how to broach the subject. It's no excuse." He stared at his folded hands. "I should have told you the first chance I got. If for no other reason, to ask you for forgiveness."

"You must have known I was his widow when you first came to Marietta."

"Yes, that's true. I did."

"Then why didn't you tell me? It's as easy as, 'Hi, I'm Clint. By the way, I knew your husband, Jeffrey.'"

Clint's lips curved downward. "There's more to the story."

Tess couldn't imagine what it could be.

"I golfed at the club he managed."

"I wondered if that was how you met. He knew a lot of the businesses in Stow from his job there."

"Right. I told you I was a different person back then— self-centered, money hungry, power hungry. Really, insecurity plagued me, always seeking acceptance by being on top, by being right. One day at the golf shop I made a big stink over a set of golf clubs. I accused the guy who sold them to me of double-charging my credit card."

"That would be troubling. I'm sure Jeffrey would make it right though."

"I'm sure he would have if I'd given him the chance. I stormed into the resort, demanding to talk to the manager. Jeffrey came out, perfectly calm, accommodating. He apologized for the confusion, but he said the problem must be with my bank. Their records didn't show my card was double-charged."

"And you thought he was swindling you?" Tess asked. "Jeffrey?"

"He handled it like a real professional, even offered to give me a free game. I wouldn't listen. I yelled at him, like a fool, in front of all the customers."

Tess's hand moved to her chest. Her husband never said anything about the conflict. He rarely shared his work stress with her, to protect her from worry. He encountered incidents like this at times, but he prided himself on customer service and dealing with difficult customers in a way that resolved issues fairly and amicably. His sense of humor and sincere desire to serve could usually turn even the angriest client into a raving fan. The fact that he couldn't satisfy a customer—that would have been very stressful for him.

"I don't know what to say," Tess said.

"There's more." He swallowed. "The next week, I heard that he had suffered a stroke and passed away." His eyes moistened. "It was the same day I yelled at him."

Tess sucked in a breath. "What? The same day he..." Her throat choked up as memories of that day rushed back.

"I came to Marietta to start a new life, but I knew I couldn't do that until I apologized to you. That's one reason I tried to get to know you."

"So why didn't you tell me?"

"I wanted to. I've been carrying the burden of Jeffrey's death all these years. It really was the catalyst that pushed me to change my life." He wiped a tear. "I often thought about approaching you, to make it right—or as right as I could. But when I met you, I froze. I guess I was waiting for the right moment, but I should have told you when I first met you. I'm sorry I didn't, and..." He looked Tess in the eyes. "I'm so sorry about Jeffrey. He was a good man."

Tess's breath felt shaky. "He was. Very good." She knew Jeffrey's death wasn't Clint's fault. There was no way to prove any single event caused his stroke, but she struggled to calm her emotions. "Clint," she said, "I accept your apology."

"You do?" Gratitude shone in his eyes.

"But I need a little time to process this. Is that okay?"

"Of course. Take as much time as you need." He dipped his head. "I'm here if you need me. If you encounter any more spice emergencies."

Tess smiled. "Thank you."

As he left, Tess heard the inn's phone ring. Janice answered. When Tess joined her at the desk, her face had grown pale.

"It was the foster agency."

LuAnn approached from downstairs, carrying a load of towels.

Janice eyed both of them. "They're canceling the skate-a-thon."

CHAPTER TWENTY-ONE

W hat?" Tess knew the foster agency had no choice, but she wished they could have waited a little longer.

"They said if there's no resolution to the stolen skates situation by tomorrow afternoon, they'll have to cancel."

LuAnn frowned. "That's terrible. We got all those sponsors. I'm sure the foster kids were looking forward to it."

"My grandkids sure were," Tess said.

"So was Larry," Janice added.

"I've been thinking about this for a while," Tess began. "We should talk to Mason again. Take a look at the Ski and Skate Shack. Maybe we can figure out where those skates are." She lifted her chin. "What do you think?"

"I'm with you," LuAnn agreed. "Are they still open?"

Tess checked her phone. "It's six fifteen. They close at seven. Let's go."

LuAnn nodded, and started walking up the stairs. "Let me get my purse and keys. I'll drive."

"Grab my purse too," Tess called after her, then glanced at Janice. "Are you okay with this plan?"

"Of course. I'll stay and pray you find those skates."

Ten minutes later, they parked in front of the Ski and Skate Shack. Tess scanned the store. The Closed sign was lit. She sighed. "Ugh. They're not open."

"What time is it?" LuAnn asked.

"It's 6:25. He must have closed early," Tess answered. "Let's take a look around. Maybe it's a good thing he's not here to see us snoop."

LuAnn smiled. "I'm with you." She opened the door and stepped out.

Tess reached the door and peeked inside the well-lit store. Apparently, Mason kept the lights on to discourage thieves from breaking in.

Inside, everything looked the same as it had the last time she and LuAnn had visited. She moved to the side where he had shown them the skates. Sure enough, all the shelves were empty.

"That's a sad sight," LuAnn said, gazing at the same thing.

"It is." Tess stepped back. "Nothing's sticking out to me... wait." Tess eyed the door near the doorknob. "Do you see that?"

"The scratches? Must be from when it was broken into." LuAnn wrapped her coat tighter. "We should be going."

Tess agreed, and they walked to the car. As she slid into the driver's seat, Tess received a text from Chelsea.

Could you come by the restaurant? I have something I want to donate to the skate-a-thon.

Tess frowned as she showed it to LuAnn.

"We should stop, let her know that it's probably canceled," LuAnn said.

"It's just down the street. Might as well."

A few minutes later, they entered their favorite taco shop.

"Can I help you?" the cashier asked them as they approached.

"We're looking for—"

"Hi!" Chelsea walked up. "You sure got here fast!"

Tess chuckled. "We were down the street. Caught us at the right moment."

"Awesome." She signaled them to move to the side as the cashier helped a customer.

"What's up?" Tess asked.

"I was thinking about the skate-a-thon," Chelsea started. "I'm sure you guys are prepared, but I was wondering if you need any cups." She smiled. "Sounds kind of weird now that I say it. We've started using cups with our logo on them, and I have stacks of hot beverage cups in our storage shed out back that we won't be using now. I'd be happy to donate them. Let me show you." She headed down a hallway toward a back door.

Tess started to tell her about the possible cancellation, but Chelsea was already outdoors and heading toward the shed.

Pausing at the door to the shed, Tess said, "I'm afraid the skate-a-thon will likely be canceled."

Chelsea twisted toward Tess. "What? Why?"

"The skates—"

"What's this?" Chelsea pointed to the padlock on the door to her shed. "It's been snipped."

Tess fingered the lock. The neck was snipped right off. "When's the last time you were out here?"

"It was a while back. The lock was fine then. We don't come out here very often. It's mostly where we store our seasonal stuff." Chelsea took the lock off and turned the knob. "Let's see what they stole."

Tess and LuAnn stood back as Chelsea walked inside. She couldn't get far, because laid out across the floor were trays stacked on top of each other, ten high. Trays filled with...

"What are these doing here?" Chelsea asked.

"The skates!" LuAnn exclaimed.

"How did they get here?" Tess stepped closer. "They've got to be the ones from the Shack." Her mind spun.

Chelsea rubbed her forehead. "I have no idea how these got here. Like I said, I rarely come out here."

"I'm going to call the police." Tess pulled her phone out of her purse. "They'll be glad to know these were found."

"I'm glad too," LuAnn said. "As weird as it is that they're in this shed, at least we found them."

Tess and LuAnn returned to the hallway Chelsea had led them down, keeping an eye on the shed until Officer Lewis arrived. When they saw him pull up, they went back outside to the shed.

"Hello, ladies," he said as he reached them. "You said you found the missing skates?"

Tess and LuAnn showed him the skate stash.

Mason clomped through the snow toward them. "Hey," he said. "I heard you found my skates."

"On my way here, I called Mason," Officer Lewis said.

"Hello, Mason," Tess said, her mind spinning with all they had learned about him over the last couple of days.

LuAnn pointed into the shed.

"Oh, man," he said.

Officer Lewis faced him. "Are these the skates that were stolen from your shop?"

"They sure are. How'd they get here?"

Tess shrugged. "We don't know."

Mason grinned at Tess and LuAnn. "I bet you guys are happy. Skates for the skate-a-thon. I was so bummed for the foster kids." He sobered. "They deserve a break. Stealing skates from kids? That's messed up."

"It really is." LuAnn nodded. "And you're right. We are very relieved."

"Do you have a truckload of questions to ask me again, like you did when they were stolen?" Mason looked at Officer Lewis.

The officer shook his head. "Not as many. You still have no idea who took these?"

"No. Wish I did."

"Okay, well." Officer Lewis's eyes crinkled with compassion, which made Tess nervous. "I'm going to have to get a truck over here to gather the skates. We have to confiscate them."

"No! Really?" LuAnn's previous joy deflated.

"I'm sorry," the officer said. "They're evidence. A theft was committed." He grabbed his radio and stepped away.

Mason turned to the ladies, looking dejected. "Aw, man." He shook his head, his floppy hair swaying. "Foster kids can never get a break."

Mason left, and Tess and LuAnn said goodbye to Chelsea and Officer Lewis. As they drove home, LuAnn asked, "So, how on earth did the skates get in that shed?"

Tess frowned. "Lina?"

"That's what I was thinking too."

"I really don't want to think that," Tess said. "But she worked at Nacho Average Taco. Who else with a motive to ruin the skate-a-thon—and therefore hurt Winnie and us—would even know about that shed?"

"I was starting to think Mason stole them, but he wouldn't have known about the shed. How would Lina have gotten into the Shack, though?"

"She may have a criminal background," Tess offered. "We don't know why she was being pursued by the police. Maybe she has experience breaking into places."

"It did happen before you and Janice talked to her."

"I don't want her to get into trouble. It seemed like she turned a corner as we were talking with her." Tess entered the inn's parking lot.

When they reached the inn Tess was grateful for the lovely aroma of Janice's beef stroganoff that greeted them. She shrugged off her boots and coat in the mudroom and moved to the kitchen where Janice worked over the pot.

"You're back." Janice turned and smiled. "I thought you must be hungry."

"That smells amazing," Tess said as they approached.

"Have a seat. It's all ready, and by the way, I left the mushrooms out." She winked.

Tess and LuAnn chuckled as they sat at the table.

"Your good cooking is a blessing," Tess said.

"You know I enjoy fixing a hearty meal, and it's especially fun to feed my hungry and cold friends." Janice set the pan on a hot pad in the middle of the table, sat down, and after they had given thanks for the food, they served themselves. "How did it go? Did you find the skates?"

"We did…" Tess took a bite and sighed as the delicious warmth filled her.

"Really?" Janice clapped. "That's fantastic."

"It would be." LuAnn shook her head. "But they were confiscated by the police."

Janice deflated as LuAnn had earlier. "So the skate-a-thon's really going to be canceled?"

"Seems so," Tess said.

"Do they know who took them?" Janice asked.

"No," LuAnn answered. "We found them in the shed behind Nacho Average Taco."

"What?" Janice's jaw dropped.

"I know." Tess tapped her finger on the table. "It's so strange."

"They have no idea how they got there?"

LuAnn shook her head and took a drink of water.

"Well…" Tess hated to say it. "It could have been Lina."

Before Janice could respond, the front doorbell jingled.

Tess put her fork down. "Are we expecting a guest?"

"No," LuAnn said. She rose.

Janice stood and began heading toward the desk.

Tess followed and spied Lina, standing at the desk, gripping her hands together.

"Lina." Janice smiled. "I'm so happy you came. I'll be right back." She disappeared into the office.

"I'm glad you came also," Tess greeted her.

"I thought I'd take you up on your offer for an overnight stay."

Tess had assumed Lina would call to make a reservation. She hoped they had an opening. How awful it would be to have to turn her away. She turned to LuAnn, who opened the reservation book, looked through it, then nodded and smiled. Tess sighed in relief.

"This is our other partner, LuAnn," Tess said, nodding toward LuAnn.

LuAnn smiled. "Nice to meet you." She stretched out her hand, and Lina tentatively shook it.

"Is, um..." She started to say something but stopped herself.

"We have a room for you." LuAnn pointed to the stairs. "Lily and Lace. You'll like it."

Lina nodded. After a pause, she started again, "Is she here?"

"Winnie?" Janice came out of the office. "She's on her way."

Tess had guessed that Janice went to call Winnie. She was grateful for her friend's thoughtfulness.

"Oh, she's not making a special trip, is she?"

"Of course she is," Janice said. "She's been praying you'd come."

Tess stepped toward Lina. "Why don't I take you to your room and you can get settled, and when Winnie comes, we'll let you know." Tess scanned the area for a suitcase and noticed a small backpack. She picked it up and walked up the stairs with Lina to Lily and Lace. When she opened the door, Lina gasped with delight. "It's a nice room."

This was a good reason to own an inn. The best.

"Here's the bathroom. There's a tub if you'd like to relax. Extra towels are in the cupboard." She moved back to the room and opened the drawer in the nightstand. "The remote is in here. We have all the cable channels."

Lina seemed less tense than when she arrived. "Thank you." A hint of a smile slowly crept over her face.

"Let us know if you need anything. Just dial zero for the desk."

"Okay."

Tess meandered back down the stairs and rejoined her friends.

"Did she like the room?" LuAnn asked.

"She did. I think it must be something orderly in her chaotic life . . ."

"It's got to feel good," Janice agreed.

As they spoke, the door opened and Bonnie and Jeremy walked in.

"Hello," Bonnie said, her eyes wide. "You three wait here for all your guests to come back?" She laughed.

Tess smiled. "No, you just caught us at the right time."

"How did your research go?" LuAnn asked.

Bonnie exhaled, seemingly tired. "Not that well, I'm afraid. We went to the museum."

"You saw Maybelline?"

"We did." Jeremy set his equipment bag on the floor. "She was very informative."

"But she couldn't conceive of the idea that Prudence would kill someone," Bonnie said. "Not that we're sure she did either. We want to know the truth, and we should be open to that possibility."

"It could have been someone else." Tess had to put the idea out there. It seemed so obvious to her, but Bonnie didn't feel the same.

"Have you had time to read her journal?" Janice asked.

"I have read some. Thank you for bringing that to my room, by the way. She seems to have been a very devout woman."

"A mother, with a dear family," Janice added.

"Yes, that too." Bonnie nodded. "I'll read more tonight. We'll get to the bottom of it—no matter what the truth is." She looked at Jeremy, then back to the three women. "We did, fortunately, get some good sound bites from Maybelline as well as some recordings of me around the town. Being in radio, we have to use sound instead of sight. I love the challenge of that. We have a ton of editing to do before bed tonight, so..."

"You need to get to it," Tess said.

Bonnie and Jeremy ascended the stairs.

"I hope she does find the truth." Tess straightened the items on the desk. "I'd like to know what happened to the judge as well."

"History is so mysterious," LuAnn said. "It's part of what makes it fun."

"And nerve-wracking," Janice added.

"It's that, too, sometimes, I suppose." LuAnn smiled at Janice.

As they were heading back to the kitchen to finish eating, they heard a familiar voice. "She's here?"

CHAPTER TWENTY-TWO

January 23, 1863

Prudence strode to the kitchen, her hand in her pocket, holding an envelope with poison inside.

The scent of the pork and bean soup assaulted her. What would normally be a heavenly aroma smelled more like the other place to Prudence. The judge's boisterous laugh spilled into the kitchen from the café.

Elizabeth, who had seated the judge's party, came in, all smiles. "Such good people. Did you know he supports abolitionist legislature? He told me all about his work in the New York State government. Apparently, he's very influential, even with Mayor Opdyke and Governor Seymour." She placed the order slip on the counter. "And he's so charming too."

"What did they order?" Prudence asked.

"They want the soup."

Mechanically, Prudence ladled the soup into the inn's finest china bowls. Only the best for this important guest. She placed a slice of freshly baked bread on the plate next to each bowl. Then she set the plates on a tray for Elizabeth to deliver. Only four fit.

She watched as Elizabeth served the soup. She didn't give the judge his, but said she'd be right back with the rest. Was it God's Providence that she had waited to serve him? Now Prudence could so easily serve the last two herself, making sure the judge got the correct one.

She felt the poison in her pocket. He would never receive justice for what he'd done to Jermaine and Angelica, their child…all the others. "*It's up to us!*" Angelica had said. "*It's the right thing to do.*"

Prudence's hands quivered as she opened the envelope and poured the dried toadstools into the soup bowl on the left. She put the bread on the other plate, but left the judge's empty, so she would remember which was his. He would not need bread.

"Winnie." Tess smiled at her friend. "She came. Isn't that exciting?"

Winnie nodded, but her brow wrinkled. "It's exciting, but I'm a little nervous."

"Of course you are," Janice said. "You haven't seen her for years, and you didn't part on very good terms, but she came because she wanted to talk to you. That's pretty special."

"Should I call her room and let her know you're here?" Tess asked.

Winnie took in a breath and released it. "Sure. I'm ready."

"Why don't you sit on the sofa in front of the fireplace," LuAnn suggested.

"That sounds perfect." Winnie pulled her coat off, and LuAnn took it from her.

"We'll give you your privacy, okay?" Tess asked.

"Actually, I wouldn't mind if one of you sat with me. It might help with my nerves. If Lina doesn't mind." Her eyes narrowed. "Plus, I don't fully trust her."

"Sure." Tess got her point. "Just because she seems to have changed…It's only been one day. And she fostered enough anger to create a website against you—"

"Go around town putting up flyers," LuAnn added.

"Makes sense you'd want someone with you as a witness, just in case."

"It should probably be one of you two." LuAnn eyed Tess and Janice. "You were the ones who talked to her before."

Tess nodded. "I would love to sit with you, Winnie."

"Thank you."

LuAnn and Janice moved to the kitchen to clean up their half-finished dinner, and Tess called Lina's room. In a few minutes, Lina was sitting on the couch facing Winnie, who sat next to her. Tess sat in a chair beside them.

"I hope you don't mind that Tess is here. I thought she might be an encouragement if we need it," Winnie said.

"It's okay."

"I'm so glad you're here. It's been a long time." Winnie shook her head, showing her awe. "Time does go fast."

Lina's chest rose and fell rapidly. She didn't seem to want to engage in small talk. "I'm so sorry, Winnie," she blurted out. "What was I thinking?"

"I forgive you," Winnie said simply.

"The flyers were nasty. The website. I was so angry."

"Lina," Winnie said. "I forgive you."

"What?" Lina looked as though she didn't believe her ears.

"You've carried bitterness toward me for a long time. It can make you do things you never otherwise would. Warps your thinking."

"True. But when your friends found me and asked me to stop, it was like my eyes were opened. I saw how foolish I was."

Winnie smiled. "That may be because LuAnn and I were back here praying."

"Janice and I were praying even as we were talking to you," Tess inserted.

"For me?"

"Yes, friend. For you." Tess paused for a moment. "Lina, I'm wondering, how did you know Winnie would be at All Pro on Monday morning to buy toadstools?"

Lina looked at her, clearly puzzled. "I didn't know about that until I saw the video."

Tess's jaw dropped. "You mean you weren't at the store that morning?"

"No." Lina shifted uncomfortably in her seat, and she peeked at Winnie out of the corner of her eye. "I put an email address on the website for people to send me any negative information they had about the inn, and someone sent me the video. I turned it over to the police. I can't tell you how ashamed of myself I am."

Lina gazed at the fire for a moment before turning to face Tess. "I'm sorry too, about what I said about you and the other owners."

"We gladly forgive you."

She sat in silence another moment. "I feel freer than I have in years."

Tess noticed that her breathing seemed to have slowed, her jaw unclenched.

"That peace comes from God," Winnie said. "He's never left you."

Lina's eyes moistened. "I may need to talk to Him tonight."

"That's a good idea," Winnie said.

"It really is," Tess added.

"Thank you for finding me," she said to Tess. "And for the room. It's beautiful." A smile spread over her face. "I only wish my daughter were here too. She would love this place."

Thirty minutes later, Nat arrived.

"Would you ladies like some hot chocolate?" Winnie asked as Lina ushered her daughter into the lobby.

"We'd love that," Nat said. "Thank you."

They sat at one of the café tables and enjoyed Winnie's famous hot chocolate, then, arm in arm, they headed up the stairs to their room.

Tess made sure the front door was locked and joined the other three ladies in the kitchen.

"I never thought that would happen." Winnie wiped the kitchen island with a sponge.

"God still works, doesn't He?" Janice said.

"He sure does," LuAnn agreed and moved to the table, where she pushed in the chairs.

Tess fetched the broom and started sweeping. Something about the day nudged her thoughts. "It is strange though," she finally said.

"It is." LuAnn nodded, apparently the same thought nudging her. "The skates being found at the taco place."

Tess leaned on the broom. "It points to Lina."

"I can see that." Janice was wiping down Big Red. "But with how repentant she's been, you'd think she would have fessed up if she had done it."

Tess started sweeping again. "You're one hundred percent correct. She was sincere, I'm sure of it."

"I was." It was Lina's voice.

Tess and the others jerked toward the kitchen door. Tess hadn't noticed Lina approach.

Her face bore a frown, but it wasn't angry. Tess was grateful for that.

Lina stared inquisitively until Tess stepped toward her. "Did you know about the skate-a-thon?"

"I saw a flyer or two when I was putting up mine..."

"It was planned for Sunday," LuAnn said.

"Day after tomorrow?"

"Yes, but the skates that were going to be used were stolen," Tess said. "They were found in the shed behind Nacho Average Taco."

"There? That's so weird," Lina said. "That's why you thought I did it?"

"We wondered, to be honest." Tess tilted her head.

"Why would I do that?"

"We're helping with it," Winnie said. "The inn's name is on the advertising. We thought you might want to—"

"Hurt you all." She shook her head. "I can understand why you thought that. But I didn't do it. Not that I wouldn't have, if I had thought of it."

"We believe you," Tess said. "You've been so honest."

"It's new to me." Lina sighed. "Feels a little strange, but I think I could get used to it."

Tess smiled at her. "What brought you to the kitchen?" she asked. "Can we get something for you?"

"Nat and I were going to start a movie and were hoping for a snack to eat while we watched."

Winnie moved to the pantry. "How about I make you some popcorn? Have a seat, and we'll chat while I shake the pan." She emerged with a container of kernels.

Lina smiled. "Sounds perfect." She sat on a stool next to the island.

After saying good night to Lina and Winnie, Tess and the others moved upstairs. As Tess walked into her room, she heard Janice gasp. Seconds later Janice stood in her doorway, holding her phone. LuAnn stood next to her.

Without waiting for them to ask what was wrong, Janice spoke. "It's a text from Randy. 'Found out the type of mushroom in the soup sample was amanita. The same kind Winnie bought. We have all the evidence we need to arrest her.'" Janice looked up and then continued. "'I can't tell you when, but I wanted to give you a heads-up. I trust you'll be wise with this information. I wouldn't do this for anyone but you.'"

"Ugh." Tess sank onto her bed.

"This is getting distressing," Janice said.

"They don't know about Lina," Tess observed. "Their evidence of Winnie being the kind of person who would do something like this came from her."

"But she was still here when the soup was poisoned," LuAnn said. "And she had the toadstools in her possession."

"Don't they need a motive, even if she had means and opportunity?" Janice asked.

"I don't know, but we still need to talk to Officer Lewis first thing in the morning." Tess looked at the clock next to her bed. It was getting late.

"Should I ask him to come by?" Janice asked.

"I think it would be better if we went to see him," Tess answered. "And one more thing. It's high time we tried to reenact what happened that morning. How about we do it after lunch tomorrow?"

Overnight, Tess's mind flooded with unanswered questions. Most stayed unanswered, but as her mind relaxed, a few things started to come to light—not completely clear yet, but she was beginning to think they'd find the culprit. When they reenacted the poisoning later, she hoped things would become even clearer.

When morning came, and the light from her lamp lit her still-dark room, Tess sat up. One thing she'd realized was that Officer Lewis would need to talk not just to the Inn Crowd about Lina's confession that Winnie wasn't to blame, but to Lina herself. Tess had been swept away by compassion for Lina and Nat, wishing a bright future for them. She didn't like to think that Lina would have to talk to the police, because a part of her wanted to protect Lina from facing them—it could be a negative encounter. But as compassionate as Tess felt, there was no other way. Lina would have to answer their questions.

After dressing, she headed downstairs where Winnie, Kylie, and LuAnn were preparing for breakfast.

"Good morning," Tess said as she entered.

"Hey." Kylie smiled at her, then turned back to whisking eggs.

Tess stepped toward her. "I haven't seen you for a while, Kylie."

"I've been here."

"I know. I've been all over the place in the mornings. By the time I've gotten back, you've been gone already."

"Yeah."

"I wanted to make sure you knew about the, uh, order."

Kylie's eyebrows rose, and her whisking slowed. "What do you mean, that you found out for sure it wasn't me who put that question on the order?" She looked at Tess with a slight smirk. "Janice told me while you and LuAnn were out yesterday."

"I wanted you to know that we know it wasn't you." Tess released a breath. "And again, I'm sorry I accused you."

Kylie smiled at her. "I'm sorry I went in there."

"I know you won't do it again." Tess gazed at her.

"I promise," she said and went back to whisking the eggs. "I'm really grateful for you and Winnie and Janice."

"We're grateful for you too," Tess responded, a little perplexed that she'd left out LuAnn. "And I think those eggs are pretty thoroughly whisked."

Kylie chuckled and set down the whisk.

"Pour those in here." Winnie pointed to a steaming skillet.

Tess turned to LuAnn. "After breakfast, Janice and I will go to the police department."

"That's sounds good. The sooner the better."

"I was thinking we should see if Lina is willing to go."

LuAnn cringed. "I hate to make her do that. We don't know if she . . . if they're looking into her."

"I was thinking that too," Tess said, "but even if they aren't, she needs to tell them she's changed her mind about Winnie.

They might not believe she's had a change of heart just because we say so."

"Probably not," LuAnn said. "I guess you'll have to ask her."

They finished preparing breakfast, and soon guests began coming down, including Lina and Nat. Before they were served, Tess pulled Lina aside.

"I hate to ask this," she said. "But would you be willing to come to the police department with us today?"

Lina's eyes widened as she stepped back. "Why?"

"They need to hear from you that you don't think Winnie poisoned the soup."

"Since I'm the one that told them she did?" Lina asked.

"Yeah."

"Okay." She lifted her chin. "Whatever I can do to help clear Winnie's name. It's only right I tell the truth."

After breakfast, Tess and Janice, accompanied by Lina, drove to the Marietta Police Department. They entered the building and approached the reception desk.

"Can we see Officer Lewis?" Tess asked. "I believe he's expecting us."

As she spoke, the officer stepped out from the back. "Hello, ladies." He narrowed his eyes when he saw Lina. "Hello, Miss Klein." Then he pointed to the door leading to a side room. "Follow me."

They obeyed, and he led them inside a room with a rectangular table. He sat on the short end, and they sat on the long side.

"How are you, Randy?" Janice smiled. "I've been praying for your wife."

"Thank you," Randy said. "We really appreciate that."

"She's doing all right?"

"Yes." He seemed to want to get to business. "What can I do to help you?"

"We have information we think is important to Winnie's case," Tess said.

"Oh?"

Lina sat forward in her chair. "I want to retract my accusations. I was bitter. I blamed her for things in the past, and when I saw on the Marietta Community Facebook page that someone had been poisoned, I posted on their Facebook page that Winnie did it. I also put up a website. Went around posting flyers." She exhaled. "I'm sorry."

"Why are you coming forward now?"

"These ladies found me, and Winnie and I have reconciled. I don't believe she poisoned the soup."

"You said that she was a vindictive person who wanted to hurt people. You're retracting that statement?"

Lina nodded.

"Okay." He looked at Tess and Janice. "I will talk to my captain about this. We do have the fact that she was there and in possession of the poisonous substance, but lack of a motive may—and I'm not promising—*may* slow things down. *May.*"

Tess exchanged a smile with Janice, then looked back at Officer Lewis. "Thank you so much for your help."

"You're welcome." He turned to Lina. "Making a false accusation is a serious offense."

"I know," Lina said.

Janice patted her arm. "Whatever happens, we're here to support you, okay?"

As they walked toward the car, Tess thought about Winnie. What a relief it would be to give her good news. She wasn't free and clear, but at least her imminent arrest wasn't bearing down on them as it had been. She breathed in the cold air, and, as they reached the car, a thought that had started as she fell asleep the night before resurfaced. Perhaps it was the crisp air or getting the meeting with Officer Lewis out of the way, but the idea became clear.

She turned to Janice and Lina. "I know how to solve the skates problem!"

CHAPTER TWENTY-THREE

When they arrived at the inn, Lina hurried upstairs to rejoin Nat, and Tess and Janice found LuAnn and Winnie sitting at the table munching on muffins and sipping tea. They both smiled when she came in.

"You two are sitting down?" Tess asked. "I don't see that very often in the mornings."

Winnie stood. "It did feel strange, but it was slow again this morning, so..."

"We decided a five-minute tea break wouldn't hurt," LuAnn finished.

"Are people still not sure they want to eat at a place with a recent poisoning?" Tess asked.

"Guess so." Winnie frowned. "Disappointing."

"We've even had a few guests cancel," LuAnn said.

"Because they heard about the poisoning?" Tess asked.

"They don't say so, but..."

"A lot?" Janice placed a hand on her chest.

"Not a lot, but enough to know it's not a coincidence," LuAnn answered.

"Ugh," Tess said. "We've got to get this behind us."

"How did it go at the police department?" LuAnn asked.

Tess took in a breath and released it. "Good and not so good."

Winnie's brows furrowed. "What do you mean?"

"Officer Lewis said the fact that Lina retracted her accusation meant they don't have a motive for you doing it."

"That's good," LuAnn commented.

"It is," Janice answered. "He even said it would slow down the investigation—at least the part that has to do with Winnie."

Winnie exhaled and sank into a chair. "What a relief. I was trying not to worry, but…" She shook her head. "I was scared. I really was."

"We still have to figure out who actually did it," Tess said. "But at least you're not under the gun at the moment."

"Thank You, Lord," Winnie said.

"What was the not-so-good part?" LuAnn asked.

Tess leaned on the island. "Lina could be charged with making a false accusation."

"That's serious," Winnie said.

"Yeah," Janice answered. "It is."

"He's a fair police officer. I'm sure he'll do what he can to make sure the right thing happens." Tess pecked at the empty café. "So things were slow here?"

"They were." LuAnn tapped her pen on her notebook. "Actually, we weren't just having a snack. We were also trying to figure out how to keep the foster agency from canceling the skate-a-thon."

Tess scooted out the chair next to LuAnn and sat down. She threw each person a conspiratorial smile.

"What's gotten into you?" LuAnn asked.

"She figured out a way to solve the skate-a-thon problem." Janice peered at Tess expectantly.

"I know how to get skates. We have a day, right?"

"Yes." LuAnn sat back, eyeing Tess. "We've tried everything. I'm not sure what else there is to do."

"Well?" Janice sat down across from Tess. "How much longer do we have to wait? Let's hear it."

"My idea is three pronged."

"Okay," LuAnn said.

"First, we ask people to bring their own," Tess said. "It's so simple, right?"

"I like it." Janice smiled.

"And if they have extras they could share them," LuAnn added.

"Exactly," Tess agreed. "I could make a spreadsheet, so we could keep track of them."

Janice nodded. "I like it, but I don't think it would be enough."

"Right, that's where my second prong comes in. I have a friend, Maggie. She worked with Jeffrey at the resort for a while. Very sharp lady. Anyway, she works at Ohio State in Athens. She started a program at the school where, when students are done with their skates, they can donate them to the school, and she gives them to charities. I don't know why I didn't think of this before."

"Really?" Janice asked. "Does she have some now?"

"I texted her, and…"

"Yes?" Janice leaned forward.

"She said she has about fifty pairs!"

"That's awesome," LuAnn said, but a note of skepticism showed on her face. "Will they be the right sizes though?"

"The university's rink is also used for kids' lessons," Tess answered. "The students can donate their outgrown skates too, so they have lots of sizes."

"Still, will it be enough?" LuAnn asked.

"You forgot the third prong."

"Oh, right," Janice said.

"I was talking to Lizzie the other night, and she was remembering how her youth group used to play broomball when the river froze."

"Broomball?" LuAnn asked.

"Yes, it's like hockey," Tess explained. "But it's played with brooms, and you don't wear skates!"

"Our youth group used to play that too," Janice said. "The kids loved it."

"People could choose to skate or play broomball," Tess said. "It's all about the fun anyway, don't you think?"

"Broomball to the rescue!" Janice clapped.

Tess checked out the notebook LuAnn had been writing in. On the top of the page she read, "How to Keep from Canceling the Skate-a-thon." LuAnn crossed that out and wrote, "How to Combine Skate-a-thon with Broomball-a-thon."

"I like that," Tess said.

"I'll call the foster agency and let them know we have a solution," LuAnn offered. "They'll be so happy."

"They will," Janice said. "And do we need to figure out which one of us will drive to Athens to pick up the skates from Ohio U?"

"Actually, Maggie said she wanted to try to gather a group of skaters to join in the skate-a-thon. She'll bring the skates and—hopefully—a group of talented skaters. Isn't that awesome?"

"It is," Janice agreed. "I'm so grateful the skate-a-thon is back on."

"But we still need to figure out who poisoned the soup, and that means after the lunch rush, reenacting what happened that morning. See if it can shed any light on what happened." Tess looked at Winnie. "Can you stay a little later today?"

"Of course."

"We'll all be here," Janice said.

Only three parties graced the café for lunch, so by two, the kitchen was sparkling, and Kylie had gone home.

"Where do we start?" Janice asked as she leaned on the island. "I'm nervous, for some reason."

"I am too," Winnie said. "I don't know what we're going to find out."

"Don't worry," LuAnn reassured them. "This is mostly to help uncover details we might have missed. Right, Tess?"

"Exactly, and to put the events in the order they happened, so we can see who had the opportunity at the exact moment the soup was poisoned."

"Okay," Winnie and Janice said in unison.

Tess turned to Winnie. "I think we should begin with the soup preparation. When did you start preparing?"

"I had Kylie gather ingredients as soon as we decided to make the soup, on Saturday. I ordered the pork, and fortunately Marcus was able to deliver it that day. On Sunday night I cubed it, so it would be ready for boiling Monday morning. I also put the navy beans to soak."

"Okay," Tess said. "That all makes sense. When did you get here the next morning?"

"Around six thirty, as usual. First LuAnn, Kylie, and I prepared breakfast and served it to the guests. Once we finished cleaning up from that, I started on the soup."

"Nothing strange happened during breakfast?" Tess peered at Winnie and LuAnn.

They shook their heads.

"Then let's focus on the soup," Tess said. "What did you use to cook it in?"

Winnie stepped to the cupboard and pulled out a large pot. "I used a pot like this. The police haven't returned the actual one yet." She set it on the stove, and the others gathered around.

"I see," Tess muttered. "What did you do next?"

"I went through the steps on the recipe—boiled the pork, combined bacon fat with the vegetables. Waited till the broth was clear, then added vinegar and thyme. When that was ready, I added the pork." Winnie wiped her brow with her arm. "That's when I let it simmer and left for All Pro. And do I ever wish I'd never darkened its door."

"I can imagine," Janice said.

"How long did all that take you, do you think?" Tess focused on the process.

"Oh, at least an hour. I had to let it simmer between steps."

"I had gone upstairs for an hour or so," LuAnn said. "Do you remember who was here when you did all that?"

"Kylie was helping me."

Tess shifted her weight. "So only Kylie was around when you left for All Pro?"

"That's right."

"When you got back, I was here," LuAnn said. "And of course Kylie was still in the kitchen."

"I told her to stay in the kitchen and stir the soup every so often," Winnie added. "It smelled really good."

"So Kylie was in the kitchen alone with the soup for about an hour?" Janice asked.

"Yes, but that doesn't mean anything," said Tess. "She wouldn't have had access to the toadstools, because Winnie hadn't bought them yet."

"What time do you think it was when you got back from All Pro?" Janice asked Winnie.

"I'd say about ten, maybe ten fifteen." Winnie glanced at LuAnn.

"Yeah, that's about right."

The four women returned to standing around the island. Tess leaned toward Winnie, who stood across from her. "When you came back from All Pro, you had the toadstools in your bag, right?"

"Yes."

"What did you do with it?" Tess asked.

"I hung it on the hook in the mudroom. I always do. A customer would have to come through the kitchen to get to it. I thought it was safe back there."

"So, after you got back, someone must have seen the mushrooms in your bag and seized the opportunity to poison the soup," Janice offered.

"But was anyone back there?" LuAnn asked.

"Let's think about who would have had access to the bag," Tess suggested.

"The three of us, Kylie, and Mason—only because he had trouble respecting our boundaries." Winnie frowned.

"And Clint," Tess added.

Janice tilted her head. "Clint?"

"He came into the kitchen that morning," Tess said. "Remember?"

"You're right," Janice said.

Winnie nodded. "But no guests."

LuAnn shrugged. "Bonnie, maybe. She doesn't always respect our boundaries either."

"Okay, so that tells us who would have had access, but not who actually went back there. Did you see anyone?" Tess asked Winnie and LuAnn.

"I didn't," Winnie said.

LuAnn shook her head. "I didn't either, but I was washing dishes. My back was turned."

"Mine too," Winnie said. "I was focused on the soup."

"So someone could have snuck into the mudroom when you weren't looking," LuAnn concluded. "But how would the poisoner have known Winnie had toadstools in her bag?"

"I don't know for sure, yet." Tess's mind orbited the answer. She could feel it coming closer to light. She turned back to Winnie. "Okay, what did you do after you hung up your bag?"

"I found a clean apron and got back to work. I was excited to serve the soup. It smelled so good."

"Did you taste it at that point?" Janice asked.

Winnie gazed at the ceiling, pondering. "I did." She looked at Tess. "I always taste it—with a clean spoon each time, of course—as I'm cooking. I definitely did a few minutes before Bonnie poked her head in."

"And you didn't get sick," LuAnn stated.

"So the toadstools must have been added during the window of time between when you sampled it and when the soup was served," Tess said. "Did you leave the kitchen at all?"

Winnie shook her head. "No, but my eyes weren't totally focused on the soup pot either. I was taking the bread out of the oven and slicing it."

"I think we were all here at that point," LuAnn offered.

"Isn't that when Mason came in?"

"Yes. I have told him many times he is not allowed in the kitchen." Winnie's eyes narrowed. "But he came in, anyway. I'm afraid I snapped at him later. Told him if he stepped foot in my kitchen again, I would ban him from the inn."

"What did he say to that?" LuAnn asked.

"He flipped his hair—which annoyed me all over again," Winnie answered.

"Did Kylie react?"

"Of course. She reacted like you'd expect. I thought she might go after him to say goodbye or something."

"Did she?" Janice asked.

"No," Winnie said. "She came back and got to work."

"That's good to hear," LuAnn commented.

Janice shook her head. "It's hard to imagine that someone could have put the toadstools in the soup with all of us here."

"Let's keep at this. I think it's helping," Tess said. "What happened next?"

"So, then I remember Bonnie came in and asked if she could have the soup a little early," Janice said.

"All of us had our attention on Bonnie then, right?" Tess tapped her chin.

The other ladies nodded.

"So anyone who saw their opportunity could have taken it then," Tess continued. "We were talking to Bonnie about finding the purse, and there would have been ample time for the poisoner to drop the toadstools into the pot."

"So then you seated her, right, Tess?" LuAnn asked.

They walked into the café, and Tess pointed to the table. "I seated her here." She pointed toward another table in the corner. "Clint was already sitting there. He'd left the kitchen before Bonnie came in. So that could rule him out."

"And then I brought the soup," Winnie said.

"A few minutes later I took pictures of LuAnn and Janice with Bonnie, then Kylie and Winnie came out of the kitchen, and I got pictures of them too." Tess took out her phone and scanned the pictures from that morning.

"Then Bonnie got sick," Winnie said. "That's all that happened, right? We're not any closer to figuring this out."

"Don't forget Clint," Tess added. "He never took a bite of the soup. Then, after Bonnie got sick, he offered to help her, and when I told him we had it handled, he went outside to wait for the ambulance."

"So?" Winnie asked.

"So..." Tess wasn't sure yet. "Nothing. I think we're done."

CHAPTER TWENTY-FOUR

After Winnie left for the day, Tess, LuAnn, and Janice lingered in the kitchen pondering the reenactment. Before they could begin discussing it again, the front doorbell jingled.

"I'll get it," Tess said as she headed toward the desk.

Janice followed her. "I'll come with you. I need to clean Lily and Lace. Lina and Nat checked out a little late, so I didn't have time to before our meeting."

"I'll come too," LuAnn said. "Both to see who's at the door and to help with the cleaning."

"Bonnie." Tess greeted the reporter as she entered through the front door, Jeremy following close behind. "Hi, Jeremy."

LuAnn and Janice paused to greet them as well.

"Hello, ladies." Bonnie smiled. "We're only here for a few minutes to drop off some things, but I'm glad I caught you."

LuAnn smiled at them. "Have your rooms been okay?"

"Yes. Very nice," Jeremy said. He headed upstairs with a bag.

Bonnie set her backpack on the floor. "We've been at the museum researching Civil War–era judges, like Grandpa Graves."

"Did you find something about him specifically?" Tess asked.

"Yes, I found court records on cases he oversaw. He did preside over a lot of the cases in which former slaves were handed over to bounty hunters."

Tess exchanged glances with her friends but didn't say anything.

"It doesn't prove beyond a doubt he was guilty of corruption. He had to abide by the law, and the Fugitive Slave Act made it his responsibility to send them back, but..." She shook her head.

Tess recalled the picture of Judge Graves in his fine clothing. He could very well have been getting kickbacks from the bounty hunters, but she didn't want to say anything. She knew it was a sensitive topic for Bonnie.

"Between that and the journal you showed me...he may have been corrupt," she admitted. "I don't know if we will find positive proof, but I'm willing to concede that the evidence seems to point in that direction." She shrugged. "Gotta go where the story takes you."

"I'm sorry, Bonnie." Janice tilted her head.

What a relief she'd come to that conclusion on her own.

"I'm okay. In a way, it makes my story more interesting. Conflict. Corruption. Drama. I'm not looking forward to telling my grandmother though." Bonnie took a deep breath. "I wouldn't tell her at all, except she'll listen to my report. She always does."

"Grandmothers make great cheerleaders," Janice said.

"But I'm still not sure he wasn't poisoned," Bonnie said.

Tess's relief floated away. "You don't still think it was Prudence, do you?"

"I don't know." Bonnie shook her head. "If he was corrupt, that would make it more probable that he was murdered, not less. If Prudence was such a strong abolitionist, maybe she couldn't take the fact that he was getting away with hurting the ones she cared so much about."

Tess didn't want to argue. Bonnie would have to find the truth for herself as she had with the judge. Tess could wait.

Jeremy returned and picked up Bonnie's backpack.

"We should be going." Bonnie waved, and she and Jeremy left.

Tess eyed her friends. "How will we ever convince her that Prudence is innocent?"

"I don't know that we can," LuAnn said.

"I wish we could figure out that note in Prudence's journal. 'I lay justice at the foot of the cross.'" Janice rubbed the back of her neck.

"Justice..." Tess said slowly, then looked at her friends. Suddenly, a memory struck her. "There's a cross on a brick in the secret room."

Her friends gaped at her.

"What are you talking about?" LuAnn asked.

"In the secret room, down toward the floor, I've seen a brick that had a cross etched into it. Haven't you noticed that?"

Janice shook her head. "If I did, I don't remember it."

"Come on," Tess said. "Let's take a look."

January 23, 1863

Elizabeth re-entered the kitchen with a smile. "That judge is a character. He said I have pretty eyes." She batted her lashes as she put the last two bowls on the tray.

Prudence pushed in front of her and grabbed the tray. "I'll serve it."

Elizabeth held tight. "No, no, I will. They're my customers."

Before Prudence could stop her, Elizabeth had taken the tray to the dining room.

"No!" Prudence chased after her.

Elizabeth set the bowl with the bread in front of the judge's wife. Prudence let out a sigh of relief, but then her friend picked up the other bowl and aimed it toward the judge.

Prudence's heart raced, and her knees felt weak. Wiping her hands on her apron, she noticed the words that she herself had stitched on it. *Trust in the Lord with all thine heart and lean not unto thine own understanding.* Proverbs 3:5. She had memorized it—her favorite verse. So full of truth and love from the Father's heart.

"I cannot do this," she whispered. Before Elizabeth set the soup down, Prudence rushed to the table and grabbed the bowl from her hand. A dollop splashed out and landed on the judge's expensive-looking tie.

"I am so sorry," she said as she wiped it off. "I think I over-salted this. I will bring you another bowl."

But she didn't. She raced to the kitchen, threw the soup bowl into the sink, cracking it to pieces, washed the contents down the sink, and ran outside.

Kneeling on the dusty floor in the secret room, Tess wiggled the brick with the cross. "It moved."

"I saw it." LuAnn knelt, peeking over Tess's shoulder.

"Me too." Janice peered from Tess's other side. "Can you get the brick out?"

Tess jimmied the brick, prying her finger beside it to inch it out.

"You got it," Janice said when Tess finally lifted the brick from its spot, revealing a rectangular hole bordered by other bricks.

"Is anything in there?" LuAnn asked.

Tess peeked in. "It's so dark." She winced, then reached her hand in. "I feel something."

"What?"

"It feels like fabric of some kind." She wrapped her fingers around the item and pulled out a square fabric pouch, made of calico material.

"Do you think Prudence stitched this herself?" Janice asked.

LuAnn fingered the delicate stitches. "She probably did."

Tess moved it to her other hand and felt along the sides of the hiding place. "I'm guessing she dug the hole, then placed four bricks like walls and one underneath, to keep the pouch from being destroyed by insects or moisture."

"Such a resourceful woman." Janice inspected Prudence's innovation.

"I'm going to open it," Tess said as she carefully unbuttoned the triangle flap that held the pouch closed. Inside she found a piece of faded paper, rough like newsprint. "I'm afraid to touch it."

"Before we inspect it, should we take it to Maybelline, so it doesn't get ruined?" Janice asked.

"I think it's okay to take it out, as long as you're careful," LuAnn said.

Tess unfolded the paper. It was indeed a newspaper clipping. She held it out for LuAnn and Janice to see.

January 25, 1863
Judge Cyrus Graves Taken by Death

New York's shining son, Judge Cyrus Graves, has been taken beyond the Jordan. He was traveling home from a short excursion to Marietta, Ohio. This terrific loss, according to Dr. Nathaniel Miller, was due to a quick and unexpected attack of the heart. Although foul play was at first suspected, it has been thoroughly and definitively ruled out. All who know the great leader are requested to attend his funeral service at Trinity Church, 75 Broadway, on Friday, January 30 at 2:00.

Tess read it again. "'Thoroughly and definitively ruled out.' How could they know for certain back then?"

LuAnn was still scanning the article. "They had autopsies. For a prominent judge whose death was suspicious, they probably performed one on him. A doctor could tell if his heart was congested or inflamed. He would have been able to see stomach damage if it was poison as well."

"So he wasn't poisoned." Janice's eyes brightened. "Not by Prudence, of course, or Angelica. I'm so glad."

"Me too," LuAnn agreed.

"He died of natural causes," Tess added. "Bonnie will be happy to hear this."

Janice tilted her head. "Do you think so?"

"Do you mean she might like the drama of a murder?" LuAnn's eyes were wide. "For her story's sake?"

"Yeah, I was wondering..."

"Maybe," Tess said. "But she always said she wanted the truth. I think she'll be glad to finally know what really happened."

"You're probably right," Janice said. "She can use it all in her story."

"I sure love how we keep finding more historical tidbits in this inn of ours." LuAnn replaced the brick with the cross on it. "I can't wait to tell our guests the story of 'justice found at the foot of the cross.'"

"Now, we should get back to preparing for the skate-a-thon," Tess said. All three groaned as they straightened from the kneeling position they had been in.

Tess carefully folded the letter and slipped it back into the pouch. She held the pouch carefully as they climbed the stairs.

"I'll put this in the safe," she said as they reached the top.

CHAPTER TWENTY-FIVE

After attending the early service at church, Tess joined the others in the kitchen where Winnie and Kylie were placing ready-to-be-heated cinnamon rolls in insulated food carriers.

"How's it going?" Tess asked.

Winnie paused her work and sighed. "It's going good. Cinnamon rolls are ready. Hot chocolate is ready. Soup's ready. Just about time to load up and take it all to our booth."

"Cinnamon rolls, hot chocolate, and soup—three items. I like how you're keeping it simple," LuAnn said.

"Yep. Simple is best," Winnie said. "When Thorn and I set up the booth, I saw Grimes Realty is having a warming tent next to ours."

LuAnn nodded. "Yes. Isn't that a good idea? It'll have a space heater and blankets."

"Skaters can drink their hot chocolate in a warm, comfy spot," Tess said. "I love it."

"And eat their cinnamon rolls," Janice observed. "You've got plenty, I see."

"We do," Kylie put in. "I helped with a ton of them."

"Looks like you did a good job." LuAnn smiled at her.

"Thanks." Kylie looked away from her.

"What can we do to help?" Tess asked.

"There's lots you can do—" Winnie began.

Just then, Bonnie poked her head in. "I'm sorry to interrupt. We're ready to check out."

"Of course." Tess waved at LuAnn and Janice. "Could we talk to you first? It won't take long."

"Uh, sure. I have a few minutes."

"Why don't you all sit in the parlor," Tess suggested. "I'll be right there."

After retrieving the pouch from the safe, Tess joined the others and sat next to Bonnie on the sofa. She set the pouch on the coffee table.

"What's this about?" Bonnie asked.

"We have some really interesting news to share." LuAnn sat forward in her chair.

"Is it about that?" Bonnie asked, pointing to it. "I'm really curious what it is. It looks old. Actually..." She waved to Jeremy who was still waiting by the desk, seeming unsure whether he should interrupt. "Come here, Jeremy, and bring the recording equipment."

He lifted his bags and hauled them to the sitting area. He sat next to Bonnie on the sofa.

Bonnie gazed at the three women. "Do you mind if I record this?"

"We don't mind if you don't mind," Janice assured her. "Our news has to do with your grandpa Graves, so it's up to you."

As they were speaking, Jeremy set up his recorder. At Bonnie's cue, he turned it on.

"I have your permission to record you?" Bonnie asked again. "I have to have it on record. Could you state your names, and then answer the question?"

They each gave permission.

"Thank you," Bonnie said. "Now, you were going to tell me about some news."

A flurry of nerves came over Tess now that she knew she was being recorded. She took a deep breath, and Bonnie smiled. "Yes," she finally said. "We were in the inn's secret room." She peered at Bonnie. "Should I explain what that is?"

"No, I can do that with voice-over. Just pretend the recorder's not here."

"Okay, so a few days ago we found a note in Prudence's journal. It said, 'I lay justice at the foot of the cross.'"

"That's mysterious," Bonnie commented.

"We thought so too," Janice said.

"It baffled us for a few days until I remembered a brick in the secret room that has a cross etched into it," Tess continued.

"Oh?" Bonnie's eyebrows raised. "Interesting."

"It really is." LuAnn scooted forward in her seat.

"We found the brick with the cross and were able to pry it from its spot. Beneath it was a hole bordered by four bricks." Tess held up the pouch. "We found this pouch. And inside it we found something else." Tess put on a pair of cotton gloves, then pulled the paper out and unfolded it.

"Is that a newspaper clipping?" Bonnie's eyes widened. "About Grandpa Graves?"

"Yes," LuAnn said.

"What was it about? His life...?"

"His death," Janice answered.

Tess held it out for Bonnie to see. She read it silently, then lifted her eyes. "Wow." Her voice was thick with emotion. "You were right. Here, I'll read it."

She read the clipping for the recording, and herself maybe, just to make it real. "All this time, I doubted he really had a heart attack, but this proves it." She exhaled. "Justice at the foot of the cross." She paused, then tilted her head toward Tess and her friends. "I'm so glad to know the truth."

"We thought you would be," Tess said.

"I'm sorry I accused your Prudence." Bonnie smiled. "Now that I think about it, it's hard to imagine a Quaker woman that devout harming anyone."

"That's okay," Janice said. "It's like you said, you never know about people."

"That's right. I suppose the story will have a different ending than I thought."

"I hope it does well," Janice said. "In that competition."

"How do you know about that?" Bonnie chuckled with a hint of embarrassment.

"I may have told them." Jeremy grinned.

"To be honest, I hope it does well too," Bonnie said. "But no matter what, I'm so glad I finally know the truth. That's what reporting is really about." She nodded to Jeremy, and he stopped recording. "We should check out. We want to get a few more recordings from around town, and some from the skate-a-thon. Then we'll be out of your hair." She stood.

The others did too.

"It's been a pleasure having you here," LuAnn said.

"Did you ever find out who poisoned me?"

"Not yet," Tess said. "But we will."

"Let me know if you do, okay?"

"Definitely," Janice said.

LuAnn headed toward the desk. "I'll be happy to check you out."

"We'll go see if Winnie needs any help," Tess said as they parted ways.

As Tess and Janice reentered the kitchen, Tess's phone rang, and she answered.

"Hi, Tess, it's Maggie."

"Maggie," Tess said. "How's the drive?"

"Not too bad. We're here."

After all the worry about supplying skates, Tess's heart rejoiced. She looked at the others in the kitchen. "The skates are here!"

"Yay!" they all cheered.

Maggie chuckled. "I found the skate rental booth. We're setting it up right now."

"I'll be down there soon," Tess said.

"Sounds good." Maggie hung up.

"I can't fit any more trays in your car, Winnie." Kylie walked in from outside.

"Oh dear." Winnie's eyebrows furrowed. "I guess that means more trips."

"We can use our cars," Tess offered as she entered.

"Mason's in the back parking lot," Kylie said. "He came to see if I could have a break with him." She guffawed. "As if. We're way too busy today." She twirled her ponytail. "He's got his truck. I could ask him if he'd be willing to drive some stuff over to the food stand."

"That would be great," Winnie said. "He could transport the hot chocolate." She pointed to three large beverage dispensers.

"I'll go tell him."

Tess glanced at her friends, and they each picked up one of the dispensers. "We'll follow you."

"Thanks!" Winnie said, and they followed Kylie out the back door like a hot chocolate parade.

Mason was leaning on his pickup.

"Hey, Mason," Kylie said. "Would you mind driving these dispensers to the food booth for the skate-a-thon?"

Mason flipped his hair. "No problem." He paced to the back of his truck and opened it, then pointed. "Right in here."

The three women loaded the dispensers.

"Wait." Winnie emerged from the kitchen holding a small convection oven. "Can you take this too? We need to be able to heat up the cinnamon rolls."

"Sure."

Winnie smiled at Mason and loaded the oven into the truck. "I appreciate your help."

"No problem. It's for the kids, right?"

"How about I go with you," Tess said to Mason. "I'll show you where to put them."

"Sure thing." He climbed in.

"I'm supposed to go too." Kylie, who had gone back into the kitchen, returned holding a container of cinnamon rolls. "Winnie wants me to stay with the booth."

"I'll be back in a few minutes," Tess said as she slid into the passenger seat. "We only have an hour till people start showing up."

"Exciting!" LuAnn said.

They drove the short distance to the parking lot near the park where the skate-a-thon would launch from. The Wayfarers Inn stand was all set up, just waiting for the final details. The generator they shared with Brad's warming booth whirred in the background.

Mason hoisted the oven from the back, and Kylie pulled out a hot chocolate dispenser.

When Tess went to get another one, she noticed a blanket was pushed against it. She thought it might have moved when they were driving. She pushed it back to make room for her hand to grip the container. In the process she uncovered the tip of a black object. She didn't think anything of it, but as she pulled the dispenser, the blanket moved with it, and the whole object was uncovered. It was a skate. A small size, it would definitely not fit Mason. She then spotted an insignia branded on the side. It said, "Property of Clarksville Skate." It was one of the places Mason had borrowed skates from. It could have been left from when he first picked up the skates from Clarksville. She eyed Mason as he and Kylie returned to transport the last two dispensers of hot chocolate.

"You want a ride back to the inn?" Mason asked.

Tess took out her phone. "Maybe in a minute," she said. First she needed to text her friends before she confronted Mason.

"Okay, just let me know."

Tess thanked him and stepped away. She gazed out at the frozen river, then texted LuAnn and Janice.

Found skate in Mason's truck. I don't think we should leave them alone in the booth. I'll stay here. Okay?

Okay, LuAnn texted. *We'll meet you there soon.*

Tess pocketed her phone. When she walked back to the booth, Mason and Kylie were gone. She couldn't search for them, since she was now the only one manning the booth, and the skate-a-thon would start soon. She assumed they had returned to the inn, but it was strange that they hadn't said anything. As she was pondering what to do, Brad arrived at the warming tent.

"Hey there, Tess," he said as he approached. "You all by yourself?"

"It looks like it. I lost my helpers."

As she spoke, her friend Maggie, who was manning the booth on the other side of the inn's, approached.

"Maggie!" Tess said. "It's so good to see you."

The woman's curly brown hair bobbed as she spoke. "It's good to see you too." She pointed at her booth, which was being run by several young men and women. "I brought my peeps with me."

"So fun that you all came. It'll be a real treat watching your skaters do their stuff."

Maggie waved the comment away. "Oh, they love it. It's fun for them as well."

"Well, without you, this couldn't have happened."

"It's going to be a special day," Maggie said as she moved back to her booth.

A few minutes later, LuAnn, Janice, and Winnie arrived, carrying armloads of trays.

When LuAnn saw Brad, she smiled, and that made Tess smile. Made Brad smile too.

"Where's Kylie?" Winnie asked as she set her load down.

"Here I am." Kylie came from around the corner. "Mason and I were checking out the ice. It's so awesome when the river freezes. Now he's checking out the broomball area. He can't wait to play."

Winnie shook her head. "Well, I need you to stack these over here." She pointed to a rectangular table in the back of the booth. "I'll plug in the oven. We don't have much time. Marcus is coming to help. He should be here soon."

Tess glanced out at the river. The first skaters were starting to glide over the ice. Her heartbeat sped up with anticipation. This was going to be fun.

An hour later, satisfied grins shone from her friends' faces as they left the booth to Winnie, Marcus, and Kylie so they could take in the events. To Tess's left, kids and their parents competed in a high-spirited game of broomball, with Thorn refereeing. To her right, about seventy folks rounded the pylons marking the skate-a-thon route. In the center, students from Ohio University's skating team did spins and jumps to the cheers of spectators.

"To think yesterday we were going to cancel." Janice folded her arms.

Tess breathed in the fresh winter air. "I'm thankful everything worked out."

"Yeah..."

"Miss Sherrill?" Tess turned to see a thin, pretty teenager calling to LuAnn, but before Tess could figure out who she was, voices she recognized grabbed her attention.

Her daughter, son-in-law, and grandkids arrived, skating across the ice. Actually, Lizzie and Michael skated. Henry and Liam held their daddy's hands as they wobbled along. Harper pushed Lizzie's help away. Such an independent spirit—reminded Tess of herself.

"Mimi," the kids all called at once.

Tess wrapped them in a group hug. "You came!"

When Tess released them, Lizzie sidled up next to her.

"How are you doing, Mom?"

"Good, sweetie."

Harper, who was still clinging to Tess's leg, peered up at Tess. "We skate today."

"Let's go!" Henry said, and Tess's daughter and son-in-law rounded them up.

"We'll see you later, okay, Mom?"

"Yep."

As Tess finished basking in her joyful moment, she scanned the frozen river, alive with skaters and broomball players. "I need to find Mason," she said to Janice.

At Face Value

"Who are you looking for?" LuAnn asked, returning from her conversation. "Mason?"

"Yeah," Janice answered. "We need to find out why that skate was in his truck."

Tess pointed toward the broomball game. "There he is." He and Kylie hung on the outskirts, passing a red ball between them with brooms. Mason flipped his hair as he aimed a shot, but missed the ball and teetered, almost falling. In response, Kylie hugged her stomach as she laughed, mocking him. But Mason wasn't laughing, not even smiling. He slammed his broom on the ice.

"Why is Kylie not at the booth?" Tess asked, not waiting for an answer. She moved toward them, but LuAnn tugged her back to where Janice waited.

"I have something to tell you."

Tess turned toward her. "What is it? Everything okay?"

"Yeah, it's amazing really. The girl talking to me when your grandkids were here. Did you see her?"

"Oh yeah. Who was that?" Tess asked.

"You're not going to believe it." LuAnn beamed. "She's one of my former students."

Janice grinned. "That's awesome."

"There's more. Kaitlyn—that's her name—went through hard times. Her dad abused her, and her mom was addicted. She'd come into my classroom before school, and I'd try to have a snack for her—a muffin or apple. She loved chocolate chip muffins. It's amazing how a little thing like sharing a two-dollar treat can communicate love."

"So true," Tess responded.

"And we'd talk. When she finally opened up about the abuse, I had to report it as a mandated reporter. The authorities deemed it severe enough that she and her sister were to be put in foster care. At first, she freaked out about going. Honestly, I was freaked out for her. But what could I do? The morning before she had to leave, I took her to a coffee shop, and we prayed together."

"That's amazing," Janice said. "I can't believe you bumped into her here."

"She came because she saw my name on one of the flyers. She works with foster kids now, so she heard about it that way."

"She works with foster kids?" Tess asked. "I love when people who have overcome a hardship help those still going through it."

"I know. She's great," LuAnn said. "And you're not going to believe this. There's more."

Before she could continue, Winnie approached.

"Hey, Winnie," Tess greeted her. "What's up?"

"I left Marcus alone at the booth to find where Kylie ran off to."

"She's over there." Janice pointed to where she was talking to Mason.

Winnie's eyebrows raised. "They don't seem too happy."

"They don't," Janice agreed.

Tess turned to LuAnn. "I'm dying to know the rest of your Kaitlyn story."

"I know, but we'd better corner Mason while we can."

As they closed in on the young adults, their tense tones continued.

"I don't care!" Mason barked.

Tess walked up to Mason. "Excuse us. Could we talk to you a minute?"

Mason's eyes narrowed, but he nodded.

"We wanted to ask you a few questions," LuAnn said. "To clear up a few things."

"Uh, okay."

Janice edged toward him. "Mason, Tess found a skate in your truck."

"And, well, you lied to us about not knowing Kylie in high school," LuAnn added. "We saw you two together in the yearbook."

"We also know you spent time in jail." Tess tossed the final dirt onto the pile.

Mason squared his shoulders, and he looked Tess in the eye. "This all looks really bad. I'm sorry for lying, but—"

Kylie moved between Mason and the ladies. "I can't do this anymore," she interrupted. "I told you not to poison that soup." Tears welled in her eyes. "Just because LuAnn did that to your family—hurting people isn't right."

"What?" Mason stumbled backward, almost losing his balance on the ice.

Kylie gazed at him with pleading in her eyes. "They're going to find out anyway."

"You're crazy—I wouldn't do anything like that. Did you do it? You only came here because you hate Miss Sherrill."

"You're going to turn this on me?" Kylie went on. "Everything points to you."

A frustrated moan exploded from Mason's lips. "You're lying." He eyed the ladies. "I swear! She's the one who told me to lie about knowing her in high school. She was afraid you'd—"

"Not true," Kylie exclaimed.

"And I didn't tell you about my time in jail because—well, why should I? I'm trying to make a better life for myself, the Ski and Skate Shack, you know? If people knew about my record, it might be bad for business." Mason shook his head. "I honestly have no clue how that skate got into my truck. Why would I steal from my own store?"

"Why would they believe you, Mason?" Kylie turned to the ladies. "Everything he said is a lie. He's a major manipulator." She wiped away a tear. "I'm so stupid for believing he cared about me."

Beyond Kylie and Mason's drama, Tess noticed Officer Lewis walking toward them. The young people must have noticed too, because they quit talking.

"Hello, ladies." Officer Lewis reached them. "Winnie."

"Hi, Randy," Janice said.

Officer Lewis frowned. "I'm really sorry." He looked at Winnie.

Tess's stomach plunged.

"My captain doesn't believe Lina Klein's retraction. She's too unreliable. That, with possession of the toadstools, and the fact that you had opportunity, is enough to arrest you." He turned to the others. "But the most important evidence is the toxicology report on your apron."

"What?" LuAnn clenched her hands. "Is this real?"

Janice gasped. "Does this mean...?"

Janice gazed at Winnie, then looked back at Officer Lewis. "You found traces of the toadstools on the apron with Winnie's name on it? That's impossible!"

"The apron didn't have Winnie's name on it," said the officer. "But we did find a letter addressed to her and an All Pro Nutrition saver's card with her name on it in the apron's pocket."

"This isn't right," Winnie said. "I never put those things in my apron pocket. Why would I?"

Tess snapped her fingers. "Wait!" she said, turning to Officer Lewis and pulling out her phone. "Were there any distinguishing marks on the apron?"

The officer smiled. "Well, just the normal marks you'd expect on a kitchen apron. I do remember, though, that one of the toxicologists mentioned a "turtle-shaped" stain on the bodice of the apron. Seemed to think it was pretty funny."

Tess swiped her phone screen to open her photo gallery. "I took photos of everyone that day—and we had our aprons on." She scrolled until she reached a picture of LuAnn, Janice, Winnie, and Kylie standing behind Bonnie, all smiling, with their arms around each other's waists. She zeroed in on a particular apron and enlarged the photo. "Bingo!" she shouted.

Chapter Twenty-Six

Tess turned her phone around and showed the screen to Officer Lewis. "Look at Kylie's apron. There's a turtle-shaped stain on the bodice."

"What? Me? I never wore that—that apron." Kylie awkwardly twisted her hair, but the act wasn't working anymore.

Winnie stepped toward Kylie, her forehead creased. "You did this?"

Kylie raised her chin. "No, I didn't."

"You were trying to frame Winnie," Tess said.

Winnie peered at Kylie, her face painted with disappointment.

"Also," Tess went on, "when we went to the Ski and Skate Shack to talk to Mason, I noticed scrapes on the door around the keyhole. That's when I knew whoever stole the skates must have had a key."

"I don't have a key," Kylie said triumphantly.

"You did," Mason said. "Remember? I gave you my keys when you said you wanted to go on a taco run. I wondered why you were gone so long, and you said there was a line."

Tess took a deep breath as she went on. "So you loaded the skates in the back of Mason's truck. Then you scratched near the lock, so it would look like a break-in."

"Why would I do that? And why would I put the skates in that taco place's shed?"

Tess tilted her head. "We never talked about the skates being found in Nacho Average Taco's shed."

"I—"

"But we did talk about Lina when you were around. We mentioned that she worked at the taco place and was let go. You decided it would be the perfect way to sabotage the skate-a-thon and put the blame on someone else." Tess stopped talking, waiting for Kylie's response, glad Officer Lewis had heard all of that.

A storm of anger came over Kylie's face. Finally, she pointed at LuAnn. "That woman ruined my life. She's the reason I spent a year on the street. She's the reason my mom died. And who knows where my dad is. Because of her, I haven't seen my sister in years. When I heard she was having a fund-raiser for foster kids..." She scoffed. "I couldn't stand the hypocrisy. She doesn't deserve to have a happy life in her sweet little pathetic inn. I'm proud I poisoned the soup. I hope you have to close down the inn and live on the streets like I did."

Janice's brows furrowed. "How did you do it all? How did you plan it?"

"Easy. I overheard you talking about the recipe in that old purse, and about the toadstool note on it. I knew all I had to do was get Winnie to buy toadstools—so I had Mason tell her about how they kill rats and that she could buy some from Cheyenne. When she told me that morning she was going to All Pro and would be back in an hour or so, it was just a matter of following her and getting her purchase on video with my phone. I beat her back to the inn, and she was none the wiser." Kylie's voice was dripping with disdain as she mapped out just how she'd fooled them all.

"I knew exactly which pocket of her bag Winnie put the toadstools in. I just waited for my moment—when Bonnie came in, and you all were talking about that stupid purse. I went into the mudroom, grabbed the toadstools and a couple of things from Winnie's billfold, and got back to the kitchen. It took me all of about thirty seconds. Then it was just a matter of dropping the toadstools in the soup and her card and letter in my pocket. Easy as pie."

As much stress and heartache as she had caused, Tess pitied the girl. "You'll go to jail for this. A woman could have died. Was revenge worth throwing your life away?"

Kylie didn't answer, and Officer Lewis moved across the ice toward her. Before he reached her, Kylie took off running and sliding toward the park.

"Kylie!" A voice sailed across the ice. "Is that you?"

LuAnn pointed at a slender, brown-haired girl with big brown eyes. "It's Kaitlyn."

"Who is Kaitlyn?" Officer Lewis asked.

"She's—" LuAnn started.

"Please, wait!" Kaitlyn was wearing skates, so she easily caught up with Kylie, though she had nearly reached the park. Kylie slowed.

"It's me." Kaitlyn's voice trembled, like she was about to cry. "Is it really you, Kylie?" She slowed to a stop a few feet from Kylie.

Kylie twisted toward the voice as Kaitlyn edged closer. The fear and anger still etched in her features melted into confused wonder.

Tess turned to LuAnn with questioning eyes.

"I didn't finish telling you," LuAnn answered. "Kaitlyn is Kylie's sister."

"What?" Janice's voice was filled with awe.

"They were separated by the foster system. That's probably why Kylie blames me. My reporting the abuse is what caused the separation..."

Tess wanted to know more but was caught up in the scene before them.

"Kaitlyn?" Kylie stepped closer. "How are you here?"

"I heard about the skate-a-thon," Kaitlyn said. "But I didn't know you would be here. And then I thought I saw you..."

Kylie burst into tears and ran to embrace her sister. "I can't believe this. You're here."

"I found you!" Kaitlyn's cheeks also glistened. "I finally found you."

Chapter Twenty-Seven

January 23, 1863

Prudence sped to the river. Her chest ached from exhaustion and the harsh cold as she collapsed next to the shore. Snow-flakes began to fall around her, big, fluffy, pure, and clean, whitening the burgundy cloak she wore. A voice floated through the whiteness, calling her name. A familiar voice, a beloved voice.

Jason.

His limping gait echoed on the bridge above her. Like a shepherd, he searched, and when he spotted her, he rushed to her and took her into his arms.

"Jason...I almost...." She couldn't speak the words. "I am sorry." She spoke more to God than to her husband. "I am sorry."

Her wise husband caressed her head with his work-worn hand, then paused to reach in his pocket. "I found this." He produced the envelope that held the recipe. "Elizabeth said thee rushed out, upset."

"I wanted justice. I hungered for it, Jason. More than..."

"...God?"

"Yes, justice became an idol." Her hair, usually spun in a tight bun, had come loose and was strewn messily over her face. "I don't understand. Why, Jason, why does our Father not punish the wicked?" Again the verse embroidered on her apron spoke to her, the Holy Spirit's words. "'Lean not unto thine own understanding,'" she whispered.

Jason moved a strand of her hair away from her eyes. "He is good. I do not know His ways, beloved. But He is good, and His mercy endureth forever."

Tess scratched Huck's chin as she admired the river from the fourth-floor gathering-room window. An overnight snowfall had blanketed the ice once more, and no one would know over two hundred people had skated and played broomball on it only the day before.

After the police arrested Kylie, things had settled down, and the closing ceremony, though short because of the cold, had brought grateful tears to Tess's eyes. Cold from the window brushed her cheek, bringing her back to the present. As she turned away from the window Janice and LuAnn padded into the room.

"Clint's downstairs," Janice said. "He wants to see you."

Tess took in a breath. Yes, Clint. That situation had yet to be resolved.

A few minutes later, she sat at a table in the café with him, drinking coffee.

"Thank you for seeing me," Clint started.

"I was going to text you today." Tess leaned forward. "I didn't want to leave things the way I had."

"I wanted to apologize, again," Clint said. "I should have told you about my connection with Jeffrey."

"I understand," Tess said. "And Jeffrey's stroke wasn't your fault. You don't have the power to give someone a stroke." She smiled.

With a lowered head, Clint whispered, "Thank you."

"You're welcome. And I need to thank you too."

Clint's head came up. "For what?"

"Your friendship, or the start of a friendship maybe?"

"I hope so."

"I'm grateful for the sleigh ride, the help with the generator, the horse-delivered cinnamon."

Clint chuckled.

"I've also appreciated your honesty with me."

Clint lowered his eyes. "I'm sorry—"

"I mean your honesty about your life in the business world, and how God helped you change. That encouraged me."

"I'm glad."

"And even the part about Jeffrey," Tess continued. "I know it couldn't have been easy to tell me that."

Clint took in a deep breath and released it. "I'm glad I finally did."

"Me too." Tess sipped her coffee. "I think we're good then."

Clint's shoulders relaxed. "I'm so glad. It's been great fun getting to know you and LuAnn and Janice."

"We are a pretty fun crowd." She smiled at him. "So, Clint, I do have a question."

"Sure. What is it?"

"I saw you with Bonnie several times. You said you had a business proposal for her. It's none of my business." She grinned. "But I am curious…"

Clint grinned back at her. "I can see how that would make you curious," he said. "I think you're going to like it. I asked Bonnie to give me the name of the travel editor of their radio station. I thought it would be a good marketing opportunity if, when they did the story about the judges, their travel show also did a story about the sites—and inns—in Marietta. It would benefit both our B&Bs as well as the rest of the community."

"So why did you need to meet with her? It would have only taken a minute to get the name."

"She didn't want to give me the travel editor's information until she heard my idea."

"I see," Tess said. "I think it's a great idea. What did Bonnie think?"

"She liked it." Clint's eyes brightened. "They're looking into doing a story about us."

"Wonderful."

Clint sat back in his chair and finished his coffee. "I'd better let you get back to it."

"Thanks for stopping by, Clint." Tess stood.

"Thank you, friend."

As Tess walked him to the front door, she thought about Jeffrey. She liked Clint, and his friendship opened a door she'd closed since Jeffrey's death. Not wide open. She chuckled to herself. But a crack. Maybe someday, a relationship would come again.

"By the way, how'd it go when you visited Kylie?" Tess asked LuAnn, a couple of days later. She and her friends sat on the sofa in the late morning after the breakfast rush, before the lunch rush.

"Well," LuAnn began. "It turns out when she and Kaitlyn were separated by child protective services, Kylie ran away. She naively planned to break Kaitlyn out of her foster home, but she got caught and was put in a group home. She soon ran away from there too. That's when she lived on the streets. Kaitlyn's foster family relocated, and Kylie had no way of finding out where she was without being caught and put back into the system. Kaitlyn had an awesome foster family, apparently. Really good people who loved her like their own. Eventually, she was adopted."

"What different paths their lives went down." Tess soaked in the heat from the fire as Winnie entered to bring them hot chocolate.

"Maybe this will help Kylie turn her life around," Winnie said, pausing next to the fireplace. "She was doing better as a worker."

"You taught her some marketable skills." Janice reached out and squeezed Winnie's hand.

"I hope she has a change of heart. I think reconciling with Kaitlyn will do a lot of good." LuAnn tilted her head. "She still seemed bitter toward me for reporting them so long ago though."

Janice patted LuAnn's shoulder. "You had to, sweetie. It was the right thing to do."

"I know." LuAnn blew out a breath. "I should keep visiting her—"

"We will too, if you want," Tess offered.

"Me too," Winnie said.

"We'll love the hurt and bitterness right out of her." Janice sipped her hot chocolate.

"What about Mason?" LuAnn asked. "Do you think she was using him the whole time?"

"They had a strong history together, you know." Tess unfolded the afghan from the back of the sofa and handed it to Janice.

"He was duped too." Janice straightened the afghan over her lap. "And I think he really cared about her. Sometimes you just don't know who you can take at face value."

"Maybe she cared about him too," LuAnn added. "But bitterness destroyed that."

"He's got to be brokenhearted," Tess said. "But he really seems to want to do well, so I think he'll be okay."

"I heard from Lina this morning," Winnie said. "She got a new job and a place to stay. She hasn't heard if the police are going to press charges about making that false claim, but she's prepared to take the consequences of her actions."

When Winnie finished talking, the doorbell jingled. Tess leaned over to see who it was. Bonnie entered and scanned the room, then hurried toward them.

"Bonnie." Tess started to stand. "You're back?"

"No, no. Don't get up," she said. "You ladies look pretty comfy. I can't stay—I just forgot to give this to you." She handed Tess a small box.

"What is this?" Tess asked as she settled back down on the sofa.

"Open it and see," Bonnie responded.

Tess opened it and couldn't believe what she saw. "The purse?"

"You're giving this to us?" Janice, sitting next to Tess, looked at the purse. Its jewels sparkled in the sunlight coming through the window.

"I want to give it to you. It has so much history here. You can give it to the historical society if you want, or the museum, or keep it here. It's up to you."

"Thank you," LuAnn said.

"You're welcome. I've got to run now."

"Amazing," Janice said after she'd gone. "That was so kind of her."

"It really was," LuAnn agreed.

Tess removed the purse from the box and peeked inside. "The recipe's still here."

"What a story we have to tell guests," Janice said.

"So many stories in this old place." LuAnn sighed happily.

"And the best part? We're making our own too." Tess set the purse on the coffee table and grabbed her friends' hands.

As she did, Huck tromped into the room and jumped on the coffee table, the purse in his sights.

"Oh no you don't," Tess said. "You've caused enough trouble with that purse!"

CHAPTER TWENTY-EIGHT

June 22, 1873

Dear Miss Prudence,

I have a story to tell that you of all people will find amazing. I made it to Canaan. My daughter and I have a good *free* life. You saved me and my Harriet. Did I ever thank you? Not enough.

Yesterday, I was out in my garden—my very own—planting tomatoes. Harriet is ten years old now, a sweet girl. She knows how to read and write. What a tender heart she has, and she can sing. How we sing! As a matter of fact, we was singing that very morning. Guess what her favorite song is? Amazing Grace.

Well, whose voice did I hear joining us? I knew that voice. 'Course I did. Then I saw him, coming over the hill. Worn and grayer than his age. Limping from years of suffering. It was my Jermaine!

I ran to him, and we hugged like you can imagine. Can you believe he found me? Can you believe it? We been having a good time getting to know him again. He's the same for me, always talking about Jesus. Not that I mind anymore, thanks to that Bible you gave me and your example of faith. How grateful I am you did not poison the judge. I am sorry for taking vengeance into my own hands and trying to bring you along with me.

Harriet knows her daddy now. They get along like two birds, singing and pattering on.

If you ever get up here, look us up. We'll have a good supper waiting for you—but not soup!

Angelica

P.S. There's something I never told you. The day I begged you to poison the soup, I went into the judge's room. On the recipe I copied, I wrote, "Five toadstools will kill him," and I put it in Mrs. Graves's purse. In my wretched state, I thought that way she would be accused of killing him instead of you or me. Thank the good Lord and His grace, it never came to that.

Dear Reader,

Writing a book is a journey. At times the journey fulfills, delights, and brings great joy. Other times obstacles such as fear, doubt, and stress get in the way. As I wrote this book, I experienced all those things.

The characters in this book also take a journey. In the historical section, Angelica travels a great distance in harsh conditions to reach the inn's safety. Her outward struggle mirrors her inner battle to overcome destructive bitterness. Prudence's path also takes her to places she never expected.

Tess's journey revolves around finding truth. A customer in the inn's café has been poisoned, and someone dear to Tess is accused. Tess must overcome the twists and turns blocking her path to the truth that will clear her friend. Along the way, she also faces the door to a possible new journey.

Throughout the shifting joys and struggles of writing this book, one thing was constant—for me and for the fictional friends who walk these pages—God's faithfulness. He held my hand when I thought I couldn't take one more step. As Prudence was reminded, when we trust Him with all our hearts, He directs our steps.

Enjoy!
Ocieanna Fleiss

About the Author

Ocieanna Fleiss is the author of several books, including the story of her cardiac arrest that she experienced in 2011. She enjoys speaking at churches, parenting groups, and writers' conferences as well as teaching a Bible class to homeschooled junior high students. Ocieanna makes her home in Seattle, Washington, with her beloved husband and four awesome kids, where they enjoy hiking, swimming, and reading a good book on the many rainy days.

SKATING IN MARIETTA

As I was researching winter in Marietta, Ohio, I came across a black-and-white photograph of locals skating on the Muskingum River dressed in top hats and long dresses. Although I did not use it in the historical section, this photo did inspire my inclusion of the skate-a-thon as an event for the inn's owners to participate in. Although the river does not freeze every year, it does freeze some years. And of course, when it does, locals take advantage of the opportunity for fun on the ice. This is true in both modern and historical times—as the old photo depicted. But, for people in the 1860s, a world dependent on steamboats for travel and to bring supplies, a frozen river could wreak havoc on daily life and even survival. Also, steamboats would sometimes get stuck, and the ice would have to be sawed away. Fortunately, residents of Marietta today do not have to worry about that but can simply enjoy the skating.

Something Delicious from our Wayfarers Inn Friends

Captain Sanderson's Pork and Navy Bean Soup

Ingredients:

1 pound dried navy beans

1 pound pork shoulder or butt

1 onion, diced

1 leek, diced

1 garlic clove, diced

2 tablespoons bacon fat

1 sprig of thyme

1 tablespoon apple cider vinegar

Directions:

Soak beans overnight in cold water. Dice the pork into small chunks and boil in water 1 hour or until tender. Save the stock. In a soup pot, combine the bacon fat and vegetables. Once the liquid from the bacon fat and vegetables is clear, add the thyme and vinegar. Add the soaked navy beans and the pork stock. Simmer for 30 minutes, and then add the pork. Cook for 20 minutes or until the beans are tender. Season with salt and pepper and serve.

Read on for a sneak peek of another exciting book
in the Secrets of Wayfarers Inn series!

Moonlit Shadows
by Becky Melby

July 19, 1863
Near Buffington Island, Ohio

The deck of the steamboat *Katie Isabella* was slick with the blood of wounded men. Blue or gray, they bled and died the same.

Prudence Willard ducked behind a stack of feed sacks and removed her petticoat from beneath her dress. Methodically ripping the muslin into strips gave her a moment of distraction, precious seconds to shut out the chilling chorus of moans that engulfed her.

Stepping over bodies, she walked back to the stern and the man she'd left moments ago with a promise to return with bandages for the arm she knew he would lose.

Too late. All she could do for him now was close his powder-blackened eyelids and pocket the name he'd scribbled with charcoal on a scrap of paper. Lenora Alexander. The girl he'd told her about in weak but urgent words. The blue-eyed girl from Cooperstown, Pennsylvania, who waited for her Robert to return.

If ever she got home to ink and pen and clean paper, Prudence would write the letter.

"Water." The raspy voice came from behind her and became an echoed chant.

It was the one request she could fulfill.

She and seven others had answered the cry—"Nurses. We need nurses"—brought by a bedraggled young man on horseback, after Union gunboats and a thousand Union soldiers rose out of a thick dawn fog and surprised Brigadier General John Hunt Morgan and his band of Confederates. The boy told them about the *Katie Isabella*, now a makeshift hospital. "If you can dress a wound, please come."

Prudence could dress a wound. How many bruised and blistered feet had she bathed and bandaged? Feet that had traveled miles over dirt roads and frozen rivers…feet fleeing to freedom.

But this…This was different.

There weren't enough doctors or bandages or shots of whiskey in all of Ohio to kill the pain. There weren't enough mothers and wives and sisters willing to hold hands, wipe brows, and whisper prayers. There wasn't even enough room on the slippery deck of the *Katie Isabella* to hold more groaning, dying men.

She gave drink to five men, then stood and stretched out the spasm in her back. Fingers reached out and grasped the hem of her blood-stained skirt. "Water."

She looked down at the man in the filthy Confederate uniform. One bloody hand gripped the wide strap of a battered leather satchel. With a deep breath, she dropped back to her knees, slid her hand beneath the man's head, and held the tin cup to his blistered lips. *Love thy enemies.* "God is with thee. His love surrounds thee. He is ever pres—"

The words shriveled in her mouth. Her tongue refused to form the words. Her heart ceased its rapid beating and slammed against her ribs with a force that threatened to collapse her.

That scar. A perfectly straight line above his right brow. A neat scar…thanks to her mother's expert stitches.

Water sloshed from the cup and dropped to the deck. Her hand flew to her mouth to stifle the gasp.

Hatred blazed deep in her chest, spilling like liquid fire into her veins.

Dull eyes stared up at her.

He didn't know her. Didn't recognize her as a grown woman.

She was no longer the little girl whose back he'd flayed with his father's whip.

Janice Eastman set the phone on the polished surface of the front desk. To her credit, she did not slam the phone, nor did she scream at the top of her lungs or fall to the floor sobbing. With dry eyes, and only a teensy bit of panic fraying the edges of her voice, she simply looked up at her two best friends and business partners and said, "The caterer has gone bankrupt. We are ruined."

The expressions on the faces of the two other co-owners of Wayfarers Inn did not reflect any of the dread that was rising in Janice like last year's Ohio River flood.

"We'll find someone else." LuAnn Sherrill, the trio's official list-maker, pulled her phone out of the pocket of her cobbler's apron. "Let's look at our options."

Tess Wallace nodded, spikey auburn curls bobbing along with her optimism. "We still have just over a week to find someone, after all."

Janice looked around the space. The lobby side glowed red from tiny heart lights festooning pots of tall white branches. Red candles in silver holders decorated the fireplace mantel. On the café side, white tablecloths dotted with red hearts covered each table. Small antique bowls, some glass, some china, filled with candy conversation hearts, sat in the middle of each table. And on each table, a tented card advertising the banquet.

They'd decided against a traditional red-themed sweetheart banquet. By a week from Saturday, the trees would sparkle with tiny white lights. The room would be awash in navy blue and white, hopefully giving the illusion of a moonlit night.

"Marietta Moonlight is scheduled for the Saturday after Valentine's Day. Do you know how many other sweetheart banquets, not to mention weddings, are scheduled for this week? How in the world are we going to—"

"We'll do it ourselves." The voice, filled with twice the conviction of the other two, came from the kitchen doorway.

"Winnie. No." Tears stung Janice's eyes as she watched Wayfarers Inn's head cook winding around small café tables to reach them. "You are not going to miss your niece's wedding, and we can't do it without you, and…"

"Nonsense. I can make a whole lot of the food ahead, and you three can cook better than pert near anybody I know. Now where's your faith, Miss Janice?"

Gone. Disappeared. Evaporated. Janice stared out at dark clouds spitting sleet onto the pewter surface of the river. Usually, the view from the front windows of the inn brought calm and an overwhelming sense of gratitude. How was it possible that less than two years since losing her husband and life purpose, she now belonged to what they'd dubbed the Inn Crowd, part owner of a beautiful historic B&B, in business with the two people who had been her closest friends for more than forty years? She took a deep breath. "You're right. We've gotten through worse. We'll figure this out."

Just as she felt the muscles at the corners of her mouth twitch into something resembling a smile, the front door opened, and her son walked in. As always, the sight of her oldest chased the blues away. "Stuart! What are you doing here in the middle of the afternoon?"

Stuart hugged his two honorary aunts, giving them each a peck on the cheek. "Had a break between a hernia and an ear infection. Stacy said I should stop by and see if you need sandbags."

Stacy. Her daughter ran the medical clinic reception desk. Janice's heart warmed at the thought of Stacy looking out for her like this. They'd weathered a few stormy patches in their relationship, but the mother-daughter dance had been much more in sync lately.

Stuart held out a plastic grocery bag. "This was hanging on the door handle."

Janice walked over, took the bag, and pulled out a large heart-shaped candy box wrapped in clear plastic. A square yellow sticky note written in elegant backhand cursive on the top read, "Johnny, meet me at Austyn's at six." A hand-drawn heart dotted the *i* in six.

Tess peered over Janice's shoulder. "Do we have a reservation for a Johnny?"

"No. We have five guests arriving today, and not one of them is a Johnny." Janice looked closer at the box. *Putnam Chocolates.* She pictured the decadent assortment of chocolate-covered deliciousness inside as she set the box on the front desk.

"There's serious talk of flooding?" Tess rubbed her arms as she turned toward the window.

"Depends on how much rain they get upriver." Stuart took off his hat. It was dotted with melting blobs of icy snow. "I'm stocking up on sandbags for the clinic, and the inn is lower than we are."

A bright thought struck Janice, lifting her out of the gloomy mood filling the inn. "We can cancel the banquet because of the flood warnings!" No need to hunt for a caterer. They could simply reschedule the inn's first-ever sweetheart banquet to another time.

Tess didn't appear to share her enthusiasm. "We need the revenue from the event. We've sunk a lot of money into—"

The desk phone rang. LuAnn answered it. She listened for a moment without speaking, silver hair falling across her face as she slowly lowered her head.

Janice held her breath. Whatever it was, it wasn't good.

Finally, LuAnn spoke. "I'm so very sorry, Valerie. No, of course. Don't you worry about us. We'll have no trouble finding a replacement. You just take care of yourself."

"What? She's backing out? A week before Marietta Moonlight, and our keynote speaker is bailing on us?"

"She slipped on the ice and broke her femur."

"But...We can't..." Stuart's arm wrapped around her and she leaned into him. "Couldn't she come in a wheelchair? No. I'm sorry. I know that's selfish, it's just that...First the caterer goes bankrupt, and now this?"

Janice closed her eyes. What would Lawrence have told her to do? Have faith. Trust God to provide a way. How she missed his calming spirit.

"Ma. It'll be okay." Stuart eased her into a café chair.

Her boy. As steady as his father. So confident. It was what made him good at what he did. Doctor. Teacher. Speaker.

Speaker. "Stuart! You can do it!"

"I can do what?"

"You can be our speaker. You'll be perfect. You have such a gift."

"Ma. Nobody wants to listen to a coroner speak at a Valentine banquet. Though maybe I could rework some of my archived talks. I can see it now…" He arced his hand across an imaginary marquis. "'How to Find Love at a Crime Scene Investigation.' Or 'Keeping Romance Alive While Determining Time of Death.'"

Tess, LuAnn, and Winnie giggled. Janice wasn't feeling the humor. "You can talk about young love. Inspire people." *Drop down on one knee and propose to someone.* Okay, maybe that was a bit over the top.

Did her favorite son just roll his eyes at her?

"Seriously, Ma, you know I would, but I've got a deposition on the Monday after the banquet and—"

"Oh! That's right. Forget I asked." Though Stuart hadn't talked about it, other people had. Stuart would be testifying on behalf of a young father who'd been injured on the job. The Moore family desperately needed the compensation due him. Stuart hated these things. So much pressure. She couldn't ask him to do anything that would interfere with his preparation and focus.

The front door opened, ushering in snow-laced February air and a tall man. As he took off hat and gloves, he smiled at each of them in turn. A wide, bright smile on a handsomely chiseled face.

Tess grinned back. "Welcome to Wayfarers Inn. Do you have a reservation?"

"Sure do. RJ Dulak." He set a leather bag on the floor, shrugged out of a backpack, and shed his water-spotted coat.

Janice looked away from the man as Stuart patted her shoulder. "Gotta run. We'll talk." He dropped a quick kiss on top of her head and left.

Back to work. Janice rose to her feet and squared her shoulders. It was her turn to man the front desk. One of her mother's favorite sayings popped into her head. *Do the thing at hand.* She smiled at the man as she stepped behind the desk. "You're with the Love Is conference, right?" She'd looked at the conference schedule online. Geared toward college-age and older singles, the conference name came from 1 Corinthians 13:4-5. "We're so happy you chose Marietta." Though she had no clue why several of the conference organizers had chosen to stay at the inn rather than the Oakshire Hotel, the Love Is venue. She introduced herself and told him a bit about the history of the inn. "Will all of the rooms be on the same card?"

"No. Someday, I hope. This is our fourth year, and we don't have the funds yet. Our people volunteer their time and cover their own expenses."

"Sacrificial serving." Janice hoped he heard the admiration in her voice. She swiped his credit card and got his signature. "Dulak. That's French for 'of the lake,' right? Like Lancelot Dulak in *Camelot*?" She imagined him clunking across the wood floor in full medieval armor.

RJ smiled a slightly strained smile. "Not quite the same spelling. Dulak is Polish. It means 'lives by a quince tree.'"

"Oh." What else could one say?

He tapped the box of chocolates. "Someone's lucky."

"If only we knew who that someone was."

He arched his right brow.

"We don't have a Johnny staying here. The only Johnny I know is a three-year-old boy who comes into the café with his grandma. We've got ourselves a bit of a romantic mystery."

"Interesting."

She held out his room key.

He stared down at the skeleton key with the metal tag dangling from the end. "Quaint."

"Our doors and keys are all original to the inn."

His jaw unhinged, then slowly closed.

"We keep them in a locked drawer."

He nodded slowly. "I design online security systems, but I have connections with people who could offer some on-site suggestions." He pulled a business card from the nicked-up leather bag.

Sekureco. Interesting company name. "Se-*cure*-e-ko. Did I pronounce it right?"

"Almost. Se-cu-*ray*-so. It's Esperanto for 'security.'"

"Very international."

"I thought a Polish name would be cool. Turns out 'security' in Polish is *bezpieczeństwo*."

Janice laughed. "Not so user friendly."

RJ nodded. "Hey, are there safes in the rooms?"

"No, but you have the only key to your room, and I assure you, the locks and the doors are very solid and secure. We have a safe in the office, if you'd like us to lock something up for you."

He considered this. "I'll keep that in mind. Thank you."

The phone rang, and she picked it up, saying to RJ, "Excuse me for a moment, please."

"Wayfarers Inn, this is Janice speaking. How may I help you?"

"This is Maybelline Rector."

A deep inhale shored her up for whatever was to follow. Never could be sure that a call from the director of the Marietta Underground Railroad Museum, the woman who'd once thought the Wayfarers Inn building should be hers, would go smoothly. "What can I do for you, Maybelline?"

"I was just wondering if you'd added anything new to your collection of things you've found at the inn. I'm always referring people to you, and artifacts are always a draw."

Strange little lady. Other than the lantern next to the front door and a few pieces of chipped china, most of the historical treasures they'd uncovered during renovations were on display at the Historical Society or the Campus Martius Museum. "Nothing new, Maybelline."

"Well, then, you'll let me know if you find anything, won't you?"

"Of course." She said goodbye and turned her focus back to their guest. She gave him a quick tour of the main floor and led him to the elevator. Whoever had made the reservations for the Love Is board of directors had specifically requested Woodsmoke and Pine on the third floor for RJ. It was the inn's only blatantly masculine room.

Watching guests' reactions when they first opened the door to their room was one of Janice's favorite parts of owning a B&B. RJ did not disappoint. "Very nice."

The king four-poster bed with its plaid comforter, the old-English hunting scenes framed on the wall, and the low fire in the brick fireplace offered a warm welcome. Janice pointed at a basket of fruit and bottled water, then handed him a list of local restaurants. "I imagine your group already has a plan, but if not, you shouldn't need a reservation tonight."

RJ ran his finger down the list. "Thank you." A wistful smile touched his lips. "I think I know exactly where I'm having dinner tonight."

"Enjoy." She stepped out of the room, closing the door behind her, satisfied that the first of their weekend guests was well taken care of.

Finished with their kitchen cleanup, Tess and LuAnn headed upstairs to relax, and Winnie left for home. Their second guest arrived about five thirty, just as the sun was setting, fingers of orange clawing at the dark clouds as if closing the shades on Marietta. A man wearing a shin-length camel coat stepped in, shaking wet snow from his short blond hair. Like RJ, he appeared to be in his late twenties or early thirties.

Before she had time to greet him, RJ bounded down the steps. "Cam!" Their back-slaps resounded off the pressed-tin ceiling.

Cameron Truman. His name had sounded familiar when the reservation was made, so she'd looked him up online. Their most recent guest was a psychologist with a popular blog.

"Have any trouble?" RJ asked. "Heard there were some flooded roads up by you."

"I came into town last night. Stayed with a friend."

Janice took Cameron's credit card. "We have you in Moonlight and Snowflakes."

"Interesting name." Cameron's broad smile glinted with amusement.

"I'm afraid the room names were created by three women who just weren't thinking of their male guests at the time. We are careful who we put in Lily and Lace, however."

RJ gave him an elbow jab. "Good test of your masculinity. If a guy can handle telling his buddies he's staying in Lily and Lace, he must be secure in his manhood."

The edge of a white gauze bandage showed beneath the cuff of Cameron's coat as he picked up a pen. He tugged his sleeve down before signing the charge slip.

Cameron and RJ wandered over to the coffeepots Janice pointed out.

Moments later, a pale, thin man with bangs nearly covering his eyes held an umbrella and the door for a woman in a short black coat and over-the-knee black boots. Janice checked them in. Without making eye contact, Noah Nichols introduced himself as the person in charge of sound and lighting for Love Is.

Everything about the woman, Natalie Hemmingway, exuded polished perfection, from her runway-straight posture to bright red lacquered nails with fanciful swirls of gold.

RJ stood and strode toward them. "Hey, Noah." He glanced at the woman. "Natalie?"

"RJ?"

"We finally meet in person." RJ extended his hand. They chatted for a moment, and then he told them he was on his way out to dinner, and he'd see them when he got back. "We're still waiting on Franny," he added.

Janice took one of Natalie's bags. "You're on the second floor."

Natalie touched the newel post at the base of the stairs. "I've driven past before but never been inside."

"You're a local?"

"I live in Columbus, but I have family here. They recommended the inn. I thought it would be nice for some of us to stay off-site. Change of scenery, you know."

"I fully understand." Janice pointed toward the stairs. "My two co-owners and I live on the fourth floor."

"Then you do get it. Does one of you have to be here at all times?"

"If not us, then one of our staff. The café opens for breakfast at eight and closes at two after lunch. In the evening, as long as someone is here to answer the phone and take care of anything that might come up, the rest of us are free."

They stopped at Lily and Lace. Natalie turned the key, then gave the expected "Ohhhhh" as she walked ahead of Janice into the room and took in the watercolor of a bouquet of lilies of the valley matted with antique lace hanging above the four-poster bed. Her gaze traveled to the pale green and cream bedspread. "Is there a safe?"

Popular question. "There's one in our office."

Natalie walked to the window and parted the drapes, nodding more to herself than Janice. "This will...be fine." Her voice trailed off to almost a whisper. "Thank you."

Janice went back downstairs and settled into the antique swivel chair in the tiny office behind the front desk. She whispered a short but desperate prayer before beginning an internet search for a local caterer.

She was on the phone to Max's Catering when she heard a floorboard creak outside the office door. After hanging up, she opened the door, looking for an excuse to get out of making the calls. "Tess? Lu?" If one of them had come down in search of ice cream, it would only be polite for her to join them. She walked into the kitchen. No one in sight. Lawrence had always chided her for her overactive imagination. Shaking her head, she went back to the office. Two more calls and two more "I'm sorries" later, the front door opened.

Janice stepped out of the office. Their final guest for the evening stood at the door.

"You must be Franny Simon." Janice rushed to the door to take a heavily dripping umbrella.

"What service." The young woman, who couldn't be far past her teens, slid her hood back, releasing a jumbled mass of auburn curls. "But I'm not Franny." She held out her hand. "Brin McLoughlin. I'm from Boston. I'm just here to look around. I don't need a room." She turned her head slowly from right to left, then up to the ceiling. "Can't believe I'm actually here."

It wasn't unusual for tourists to stop by just to see the inn, though it was a little odd for someone to show up alone, after dark, in such inclement weather. "Have a look around," Janice said. "We have a few empty guest rooms I can show you after you've seen the main floor. Would you like some coffee or hot chocolate while you look?"

"I'd love some hot chocolate. Thank you."

Janice walked over to the coffee bar in the café and added two hot chocolate packets to a cup of hot water, then stirred them in. She carried the cup to Brin, who stood in the corner of the lobby they called the library, looking at a stack of games. Janice handed her the cup. "What brings you to Marietta?"

"I'm going to a conference for singles at the Oakshire Hotel, but to be honest, I came because of this place. And a time capsule."

Janice narrowed her eyes. "A time—" The door chime announced RJ's return. He strode past them, his face a thundercloud. Maybe he had a bad experience at dinner? Janice shrugged and turned back to Brin. "You were saying something about a time capsule?"

Brin gave a nervous laugh. "Oh, I-I just meant in a place like this, surely there's all kinds of old things to look at—you know, antiques, old newspaper articles, that kind—"

She was interrupted by the sound of rapid footsteps coming down the stairs. RJ burst off the bottom step, wild-eyed. "Someone's been in my room, and my bag is missing!"

A NOTE FROM THE EDITORS

We hope you enjoy Secrets of Wayfarers Inn, created by the Books and Inspirational Media Division of Guideposts, a nonprofit organization that touches millions of lives every day through products and services that inspire, encourage, help you grow in your faith, and celebrate God's love in every aspect of your daily life.

Thank you for making a difference with your purchase of this book, which helps fund our many outreach programs to military personnel, prisons, hospitals, nursing homes, and educational institutions. To learn more, visit Guideposts Foundation.org.

We also maintain many useful and uplifting online resources. Visit Guideposts.org to read true stories of hope and inspiration, access OurPrayer network, sign up for free newsletters, download free e-books, join our Facebook community, and follow our stimulating blogs.

To learn about other Guideposts publications, including the best-selling devotional *Daily Guideposts*, go to ShopGuideposts .org, call (800) 932-2145, or write to Guideposts, PO Box 5815, Harlan, Iowa 51593.

Sign up for the
Guideposts Fiction Newsletter
and stay up-to-date on the books you love!

You'll get sneak peeks of new releases, recommendations from other Guideposts readers, and special offers just for you . . .

and it's FREE!

Just go to Guideposts.org/Newsletters today to sign up.

Guideposts.

Visit Guideposts.org/Shop
or call (800) 932-2145

Find more inspiring fiction in these best-loved Guideposts series!

Tearoom Mysteries Series
Mix one stately Victorian home, a charming lakeside town in Maine, and two adventurous cousins with a passion for tea and hospitality. Add a large scoop of intriguing mystery and sprinkle generously with faith, family, and friends, and you have the recipe for *Tearoom Mysteries.*

Sugarcreek Amish Mysteries
Be intrigued by the suspense and joyful "aha" moments in these delightful stories. Each book in the series brings together two women of vastly different backgrounds and traditions, who realize there's much more to the "simple life" than meets the eye.

Mysteries of Martha's Vineyard
What does Priscilla Latham Grant, a Kansas farm girl know about hidden treasure and rising tides, maritime history and local isle lore? Not much—but to save her lighthouse and family reputation, she better learn quickly!

Mysteries of Silver Peak
Escape to the historic mining town of Silver Peak, Colorado, and discover how one woman's love of antiques helps her solve mysteries buried deep in the town's checkered past.

To learn more about these books, visit Guideposts.org/Shop